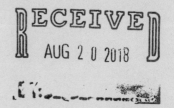

AMULET BOOKS
NEW YORK

Riley Redgate

FINAL DRAFT

Cataloging-in-Publication Data has been applied for and may be obtained from the Library of Congress.

ISBN 978-1-4197-2872-3

Text copyright © 2018 Riley Redgate
Jacket illustrations copyright © 2018 Nathan Burton
Book design by Alyssa Nassner

Printed and bound in U.S.A.
10 9 8 7 6 5 4 3 2 1

Amulet Books are available at special discounts when purchased in quantity for premiums and promotions as well as fundraising or educational use. Special editions can also be created to specification. For details, contact specialsales@abramsbooks.com or the address below.

Amulet Books® is a registered trademark of Harry N. Abrams, Inc.

ABRAMS The Art of Books
195 Broadway, New York, NY 10007
abramsbooks.com

For my kind, brilliant father.
Here's another book that, regrettably, does
not include steam locomotives, linguistics,
wine, Irish clocks, or bird-watching.

Sorry.

EVERY DAY AFTER SCHOOL, SHE LEFT EARTH FOR AN-other galaxy. The launch apparatus was a pine desk in her bedroom that had been loved into ugliness, ringed with water stains and stippled by ballpoint pens. She opened her laptop there, and under the light of the screen, the desk faded, and the apartment, and the corner of Brooklyn through the window. She wrote herself away, into a city of glass tubes that crisscrossed a toxic planet, into the perforations of gently tumbling asteroids, into sunships that breached the surfaces of red giants and emerged crackling with plasma. She watched hordes of aliens catapult through wormholes toward a blue-green paradise braced for war, and she could have sworn she heard the hum of their engines.

Out there, danger wasn't something that erupted purposelessly in parking lots or at traffic intersections; it was *peril*, pure and moral and invigorating. Unifying. Out there, love bridged the space between planets, and betrayal risked the destruction of universes. Life was lived along a spectrum so vibrant it felt ultraviolet. How could the world outside the window seem anything but gray in comparison?

2

A HINDWIND CAUGHT EDEN'S TAIL. THERE WAS A shudder from her ship's flankwake to its nose. In the rearview monitor, three silver ships burst out of the white horizon behind her, heralds for ten thousand more. The entire Ta'adran horde. The admiral's line had broken, and now the world was in her hands.

Eden yanked the accelerator. Her ship could still reach the enemy station, which rose like a mountain from the ice forests. Hideous prongs at its crown were accumulating a gray glow of power. A ghostly beam focused toward their sun: the Ta'adran Stardrainer, poised to harvest every scrap of solar energy.

There was no time for the original plan. She could never break into the Stardrainer and unhook its wiring before it fired. But she had one final weapon: her ship, a fuel cell cutting the air at Mach 4.

Eden slammed an elbow into the rocket prop, and her ship began to scream in overload. The sun would rise tomorrow, and the day after. She realized she'd known for months that she would die defending it.

Mr. Madison set down the pages. "This is my favorite thing you've written," he said.

"Really?" Laila asked.

"Really," he said through a mouthful of soup. Speaking through soup was harder, logistically, than speaking through other foods, so this resulted in a messy splattering situation that Laila pretended not to see, because somebody had to be gentle with him. Mr. Madison was incurably self-conscious and—Laila loved him, so she was allowed to say it—an absolute pushover. To worsen things, he was small and pale and looked about thirteen years old, the human equivalent of a weed that had spent most of its life beneath a boulder. All in all, the type of teacher that kids bullied not because they wanted to do him any particular emotional harm, but because Jesus, it was *right there*.

"Here," said Mr. Madison, with one of those stutter-y, beckoning motions that somehow looked apologetic. He leaned over his desk to return Laila's story. He'd circled so many passages in blue that each paragraph looked like a map of elliptical orbits. Mr. Madison was the type of deeply involved reader who couldn't touch anything without leaving evidence. Laila always emailed him her stories, and he always handed back a copy she could hold. They'd kept this ritual for almost four years.

"Thanks," Laila said, but as she paged through, familiar doubts nudged her. It wasn't that she didn't trust his opinion. When it came to science fiction, Mr. Madison was even more obsessed than she was. They shared a favorite series, *Moondowners*, an epic space opera whose final book was set to release this fall after a five-year wait. He could out-quote her, something hardly anybody could do, even in the *Moondowners* forums. Not that any of this made his opinion more valid, but if she shared taste with somebody, she would've liked to think they had high standards, and if Mr. Madison had high standards, he couldn't consist entirely of checkmarks and exclamation points.

"You're not just saying that, right?" she asked.

He stopped eating, his eyelids aflutter over his watery eyes. The panicked blink.

Laila hurried to diminish the blow. "It's just, *every* story can't be your favorite, right?"

"Oh," he said, mollified. "Hmm. I guess I—" Mr. Madison chuckled. He had a nasal little laugh that obviously embarrassed him. He never laughed during class, just smiled widely and let his narrow shoulders tremble in silence. If you walked down the hall, you could see a half dozen kids mimicking this at any given time.

"I'm not embellishing," he said. "I promise. Have you considered that maybe you're just getting better with every piece?" Mr. Madison had a habit of phrasing even his firmest opinions as questions. Laila could never decide whether this was a pedagogical strategy for engaging students or a depressing inability to show any confidence whatsoever.

Suddenly she felt guilty for second-guessing him. Mr. Madison had read every word she'd written since freshman year, had spent so many thankless lunch periods discussing her stories. Having someone who took her writing so seriously made the whole exercise real in a way that it had never been when she was little, scrawling loopy cursive into the notebook she'd clutched under the gummy light on her bedside table, ten years old and terrified to show her parents even a glimpse.

"I'm curious, Laila," he said, plucking his round glasses from his nose. He wiped them with a microfiber cloth he always kept neatly folded beside his stapler. "Are you proud of this story?"

4

When she realized she couldn't say "yes," she nearly cringed. What did it say if she'd worked for more than a month to write a single twelve-page draft, and she wasn't even proud of it?

Outside, four floors below, car horns blared dissonant chords. Laila glanced through the windows. Thick clouds had trapped the March sun and flattened Manhattan into a lithograph. She caught herself picking at the tips of her black hair—subdividing the broom of split ends—and sat hard on her hands.

"I don't know about proud," she told him. "I mean, it's a first draft. I'm fine with where it is. I can lock myself in this weekend and fix the whole admiral section."

Mr. Madison was usually too nervous about miscommunication to rely on sarcasm, but he surprised her with a wry note: "And are you planning to come up for air at all?"

Laila leaned back in her chair and smiled. These were the moments when she felt like Mr. Madison understood her better than any of her friends did, or even her family. Whenever the world didn't directly demand her attention—between classes, between sentences, on the train—her imagination took over, as reflexive as breath. Laila spent every day yanked taut between this world and another, and he was the only one who knew, because he'd listened patiently to her wandering through brainstorm after bizarre brainstorm; he'd seen her first drafts, fifth drafts, tenth drafts, all ripped down to the phrase and reassembled.

"Actually," she said, "I do have plans. The new season of *The Rest* is dropping tomorrow, so me and Hannah and the guys are going to meet up. Watch a few episodes."

"That sounds like fun. Anything nonfictional planned?"

"Nah," she said. She never planned nonfictional things. At most, she let Hannah and Felix and Leo drag her to dinner every once in a while.

Mr. Madison's nervous chuckle pushed through his nose again. "Laila, you know I'd never criticize your work ethic, but have you ever considered that getting some distance from a piece could be valuable?"

She had to resist a grimace. "Yeah, I see people saying that online. 'Take a break.'" She shook her head. "Maybe distance works for them, but whenever I go a day without working on this stuff, I feel . . . not even lazy, more like . . ."

She took a long moment to arrange her thoughts, knowing he wouldn't push her. Mr. Madison had a type of quiet, reassuring patience that nobody else in this school seemed to understand. In group projects or casual snippets of conversation, other kids always cut her off halfway through a sentence, and the interruption flustered her—and once she'd lost momentum, she could never get her social interaction gears restarted. That left most of the school—Hannah, Leo, and Felix excepted—with the totally misguided idea that "quiet" was her only personality trait.

"I guess I've got this image," she said, "that these stories are already out there, like these perfect little islands floating around, and I keep trying to rope them in, but I keep getting these mediocre versions that only even passingly look like what I want. So I've got to spend all my time out there casting nets, because if I spend too much time away from that universe, I'll go and forget how it feels in there, and I'll get farther and farther from those perfect versions of what I'm trying to do, and—" She smoothed the dog-eared pages in front of her. "This has to feel lived-in, you know? I've got to live in it."

Mr. Madison bobbed his head from side to side, half nod, half consideration. Before he could answer, the bell hammered to signal the end of first lunch, one of three that rotated throughout fifth period. Voices rose into a distant muddle in the hallway.

"Can we pick this back up tomorrow?" Mr. Madison asked. "I'd love to talk more, but if you're late to Ms. Bird's class again, she'll come after me."

"So you're saying I should definitely be late."

"What? No." Mr. Madison went red up to his prematurely receding hairline. "G-go to class." He fussed around with some pencils that didn't need rearranging.

Laila grinned and shook her head. His obvious crush on Ms. Bird might have been gross if it weren't so bewildering. The woman looked more like a member of a biker gang than a calculus teacher. Laila was pretty sure Ms. Bird could have inflicted physical harm on Mr. Madison just by snapping her sharp-nailed fingers at him.

"Laila."

She looked up from loading her books behind the strained zippers of her backpack, tucking a frizzy curl of black hair behind her ear.

"Can you try to do something for me?" he asked.

"Sure. What?"

"Every so often, take a moment—a real-world moment—and let yourself be proud of what you're working on. Okay?"

Mr. Madison's eyes arched into crescents when he smiled. His face was all softness. "You deserve approval from somebody other than me. Nobody could be harder on your writing than you are."

The urgent fires that always seemed to be burning in her chest dimmed. "Yeah," she said. "I'll try."

But the words left a metallic aftertaste. Laila prided herself on her honesty—mostly, she considered herself so vanilla that she had no idea what she would lie about—but she didn't know if she could do what he was asking. "Be proud" sounded too much like, "Go easy on yourself," something her mother always said, and which Laila hated. Her goals were more important than a momentary burst of pleasure that might come from a lapse in self-criticism. She wanted to pierce the furthest frontier of her ability. Satisfaction didn't feature in any step of any plan she'd imagined toward that end.

Laila looked down at her pages, imagined them from anyone else's perspective, and watched them transform into something smaller and shallower. This story would be perfect someday, refined by time and exertion, every facet as lucid as a gemstone's. She had to fit it between her hands and press, press, press until she felt it fuse.

THAT AFTERNOON, LAILA SAT AT HER DESK AND RE-read the crash sequence from early in the story. Eden's glass ship hissed over the ice planet's crust, stirring powder up in its wake. Laila had her steering into the caves and out again, but they felt too secluded from the main body of the battle. Could she redirect the chase over the ocean? No, the frozen waves gave off the wrong atmosphere—too bleak, too remote. She needed something active, something alive. A volcano, maybe, waking after a long dormancy, that would incinerate the alien ship on Eden's tail. Yes. Better. Eden would look down as she passed over the mountain's eye and watch an iris of magma gleam . . .

Then Laila's sister hammered on her door—"Naña, for the millionth time, *dinner*"—and Laila blinked, glanced at the rattling knob, and found herself unpleasantly back on Earth. Also, she was freezing, because their apartment windows had all the insulating power of one-ply toilet paper. Also, whatever their mother was making for dinner smelled like burning fungus.

Laila hit *save* and went for the door. Camille stood barefoot in the hall, teasing a comb through her fragile golden hair, which zigzagged like a cluster of lit filaments in the dry air. Camille had inherited their mother's pale coloring, feline blue gaze, and matchstick physique. Laila, on the other hand, looked unmistakably mestiza, taking after their dad. With her corkscrewing black hair and dark tan, not to mention her general largeness—of height, hips, mouth, eyes—hardly anyone guessed that she and Camille were sisters. Laila's life had been a parade of near strangers squinting at her and Camille and saying, "Oh, yeah, I sort of see it," as if they'd been handed a spot-the-difference puzzle.

"Hey," Laila said awkwardly.

"Hey," Camille mumbled.

They couldn't meet each other's eyes. They were in the middle of one of their biannual fights. Camille was in eighth grade and Laila was in twelfth, which usually left enough distance for Laila to chalk any obnoxious behavior up to her sister's age-related inferiority. But the previous weekend, she'd borrowed Laila's favorite sweater without asking and ruined it with Tabasco sauce, a repeat offense. It was enough of a task for Laila to find clothes that fit her chest and didn't also make her look like she was wearing a circus tent. Now, two sweaters *and* her vintage *The Rest: Season II* shirt were stained beyond wearability, all because Camille had the total inability to keep food inside her incompetent thirteen-year-old teeth.

They padded down the hall. "Writing?" Camille asked.

"Yes."

"Let me guess. I'm not allowed to read this one, either."

"Nope," Laila said, looking down her nose. Camille was growing like bamboo, but for now, Laila would lord the extra height over her for all it was worth.

Camille muttered, "You let *Mr. Madison* read your stuff."

"Yeah, he's my creative writing teacher, Camille."

"So?"

"So, if you were in charge of my transcript, I'd let you read anything you wanted, too."

"Whatever," Camille sniffed, and went back to combing her hair. "You have to show people eventually."

Laila stayed mulishly silent. She hated that Camille had a point. Even Mr. Madison told her on a biweekly basis that she should show other people her writing, and although he never made her feel pressured—Tim Madison probably couldn't pressure a handful of dough if someone gave him a rolling pin—he said enough for her to consider what that exposure would feel like. All evidence so far suggested something along the lines of well-publicized nausea. She'd had multiple nightmares in which Samuel Marquez, an absurdly hot junior who only took creative writing for Mr. Madison's signature automatic A, read out paragraphs from her stories while a full auditorium laughed uproariously.

Mostly she rationalized her privacy by telling herself that other people's opinions weren't the point, but that was a thin excuse. Obviously, writing had private benefits. She wrote to learn who she was. She wrote to make a record of what she'd been. She wrote to see the way her thoughts looked with polish applied. And maybe those inner satisfactions were enough for other people, but to her they didn't seem like the complete set. Someday, she wanted the give and take, the sense of tradition and participation that came from going public with her stories. Ultimately, what was the point of messing around in all this language if she didn't want to communicate something?

"Tell you what," Laila said. "You can read one of my stories if you read the first *Moondowners* book." She worried for an instant about the sex scenes, but then again, she'd read *The Sky Most Gray and Ancient* when she was younger than Camille, and she'd emerged unscathed. Also, there was no chance that Camille hadn't already seen something worse on the internet.

Camille gave her withering side-eye. "That book's like a thousand pages."

"Twelve hundred." Laila chanced another whiff of the air and nearly gagged. "God, what *is* that?"

"Right?" said Camille. For a moment, the fight slipped away, and they made pained eye contact. "I swear it's compost or something."

For the sake of their mother's feelings, Laila forced a neutral expression when they emerged from the hall into the stench of the kitchen. The pair of them longed for the weekends, when their father was in charge of cooking, with the billows of pork-flavored steam, the mountains of rice, the hissing of plump vegetables against cast iron. He'd enlisted them to make llapingachos, potato patties with onions, cheese, and pork tucked into their centers, that weekend. Every time their father cooked something with that much grease involved, he wound up squabbling with their mother, who taught Kundalini yoga to Williamsburg hipsters and genuinely seemed to believe that excess cholesterol could block one's chakras. Apparently chakra blockage tasted like heaven.

Chakras and heart attacks notwithstanding, it would have been impossible to convince her father away from fried foods. He was Ecuadorian, their mother French-Canadian; this earned Laila a lot of, "What an interesting mix," which was an efficient way to make her feel like a sinister genetic experiment.

"Laila's out of her digital prison," her father announced at a decibel level that suggested he was trying to inform the apartments above and below. Her dad was a little too much of everything. Louder than IMAX, taller than a good chunk of the NBA, brawnier than a Greek statue. He even looked too bright, wet streaks of light caught in his black hair, still only half-dry from the shower.

"I'm out," Laila agreed. "Down, Mal. Get off. *Sit*."

The dog blundered into her ankles a few more times before jogging back into his corner, where he slumped onto his side and thwacked his ropy tail against the floor, clearly pleased with everything he had accomplished. Malak was a mutt with the graceful legs of a whippet and the guileless face of a retriever. Counter to both of these traits, their father had named him after *Knights of the Old Republic*'s Darth Malak. Secretly—this had to be secret, because her father was a personal trainer whose reputation was built around being a hardass—Jaime Piedra was the biggest nerd in Brooklyn. He owned the entire *Star Wars* expanded universe novel collection, all read to pieces. At six foot five, he was also probably the largest nerd in Brooklyn.

As Laila settled at the table, she made the mistake of glancing at her phone. With the season release tomorrow, her group text with her best friends had grown so frantic that the vibrate function had started to resemble a metronome more than an alert system. She'd hardly opened Leo's text when her father stopped at her shoulder, a loaf of bread dwarfed in his massive hand, and swiped the warm slip of metal from her grip.

"No phone at the table," he said, a phrase that would surely be inscribed on his gravestone. Laila grabbed for his arm, but he shoved the phone into his pocket and swatted her away. "No. You look at this thing more than you look at your poor old parents." He flourished a hand over the counter. "¡Mira! You're missing your mother's beautiful face."

Laila sighed. "Yes, Dad." Hannah, Felix, and Leo would have to wait. Arguing would only encourage the rest of her father's usual monologue: that he knew she took writing seriously, but it couldn't be healthy spending so much time in front of a computer, especially when she poured hours into all those TV shows, and— *and!*—read books on an e-reader. Couldn't anything just be an object anymore without a glowing backdrop? You never would have seen people ignore one another like this in Quito in 1982. And so on.

Her mother placed a bowl of greenish soup in front of Camille, beside whatever meat substitute she'd decided to prepare. Even Malak, canine vacuum cleaner, couldn't stomach some of these chicken replacements.

"Lolly, would you say grace?" her mother asked. Laila hadn't been able to pronounce her own name until she was six. Her mom had never stopped calling her the bastardized version.

Her father brightened and gave her an expectant look.

Laila drew a deep breath. "Okay." There was nothing to worry about. They'd just gone over this yesterday. She couldn't have forgotten already. "Bendícenos, Señor," she said, "y bendice los alimentos que . . . que vamos a tomar, para . . . nos . . ."

"Mantenernos," her father prompted.

Laila felt prickly with embarrassment and finished the phrase in a rush. "Mantenernos en tu santo servicio. Amen."

"Amen," everyone repeated. Her father gave her an approving nod, but she wished she could rewind. Re-tape her hiccup. If time travel were an option, actually, she would rewind through the last twelve years and tell her child self to take her dad's impromptu language coaching more seriously. She would tell herself to swallow her pride and take Spanish in school like everyone else. Now her Spanish was so fragmented that she could barely talk to Tía Graciela when her father inevitably passed his phone conversations to her (and God help her if she tried to politely decline). She spent half the time saying, "Puedes repetir mas despacio, ¿por favor?" As if the problem were how quickly her aunt was speaking rather than her total lack of vocabulary.

Laila looked to Camille, half expecting a smug expression—her sister could be petty when they were fighting—but Camille was just chipping at her glitter-coated nails. She was going to regret ruining that final layer. Camille had decided last week to sell off her nail polish to her classmates bottle by bottle. She was making shocking amounts of money from this. Someday Camille would be a ruthless businesswoman.

Laila considered again trying to end the fight, but how? Camille had to apologize before Laila could forgive her. This all felt so unnecessary. Because they fought so rarely, neither of them was much good at it. Laila had described it halfheartedly to Mr. Madison the day before as, "Me and Camille are on a break, or something."

"You two are fighting?" Mr. Madison had said mildly. "That's not like you."

"It's more like a stalemate. I already know she's going to ignore me for three weeks and then pretend nothing happened."

Mr. Madison seemed confused. "Did you do something?"

"No, *she* did something, and also doesn't get how the silent treatment works."

Luckily, she and Camille were not required to talk at dinner. It was Thursday, so as usual, there was strife at the yoga studio. Laila's mother never talked about her day job—she couldn't, really, being a psychologist—but the two afternoons a week she taught yoga were invariably followed by descriptions of some conflict between undergraduate volunteers and grown-ass adults.

"Honey," her mother said to her father, with the sly, indulgent tone of gossip, "did I tell you? Justin's threatening to quit over the Amelia problem."

Her father sliced into his fake chicken. "That boy needs to toughen up."

"Well, I'm not so sure. The rest of us can't ignore it anymore, either. Amelia's a sweet girl, really. She gives such clear demos, and students love her classes, and I'm not just saying that . . ."

Laila's mother always assembled a cloud of compliments before letting herself insult anybody. Maybe she thought it negated the blow. All it really did was heighten the suspense.

". . . but how do we *tell* her that she smells like she hasn't showered since 2012?" her mother finished.

Her father snorted. "Say that. Should go over well."

"Emily and her friend—oh, who's her friend? Sally. No, Sarah. They had the idea to plant deodorant in her bag," said her mother.

"Which I don't think is entirely without merit. Mimi, sweetie. Eat your soup."

Camille stared in dread at the bowl. She looked so pathetic that Laila took pity and cut in. "Hey," she said, "I'm still okay to go to Hannah's tomorrow night, right?"

Her parents exchanged a blank look.

"Remember? Season twelve is dropping?" Laila said, trying not to sound impatient. She pulled at the collar of her *The Rest: Season V* shirt, making the screen-printed logo twitch indignantly in her parents' direction. She'd only been waiting for this for nineteen months and twenty-six days.

The Rest wasn't entirely responsible for Laila's "whole sci-fi *thing*," as Camille called it, but the show never failed to keep the fires of obsession burning. Laila had never been so rabid about a show for so long. Concept: with the earth in full-blown environmental collapse, massive motherships transport 0.5 percent of the world's population out of the galaxy, cryogenically frozen until their arrival at a habitable planet. The freezing process is called the Rest, and in order to keep the Resters' vitrified brains at the level of activity necessary to prevent neurological atrophy, a network of nanomachines crawls through their neural pathways, linking them into an intricate virtual-reality system. But this system, meant to simulate the planet they left behind, goes terribly wrong and strands the Resters in a hostile jungle of nightmare imaginings that are trying to kill them off from inside their minds. Meanwhile, back on Earth, the world—the *rest* of the world, *wink nudge*—is spiraling into chaos.

Laila didn't care that the show was about to release its twelfth season, when it had obviously peaked in season five. She didn't care that it had been displaced from HBO to Netflix and now, humiliatingly, to Yahoo. She still hung on every plot twist. Cried at every death. Texted Hannah and Felix and Leo in all caps whenever she rewatched an episode that involved any two characters flirting. They'd introduced gay characters last season. Hannah considered it a victory every time they made it through an episode without dying.

Her father sighed. "Well, you can't come in at some unholy hour of the night again."

"I . . . won't," Laila said uncertainly. "Unholy hour of the night" was a meaningless phrase in the Piedra household. Her parents were asleep every night by 9 P.M., so that they could wake up at 5:30 to run together to Maria Hernandez Park. Sometimes they wore running gear that matched. Laila and Camille remained unconscious for this as often as possible.

"We'll watch three episodes," Laila said. "I'll be home by 11. Promise." Whenever this conversation replayed, she wondered: Was any birthday more useless than an eighteenth birthday? So ridiculous that she was legally an adult when every hour of her life was still somebody else's jurisdiction.

"Can I come?" Camille asked.

"You don't even watch *The Rest*."

"And?" The red tint to Camille's cheeks betrayed her.

"Right. Got it," Laila said. "Don't worry. I'll text you as many pictures of Felix as I can take without him noticing."

"Oh my *God*. That is *not* what I meant," Camille said, with completely unconvincing disgust. Laila wanted to tell her that it was okay, that it had been strange for her, too, and actually for the whole senior class, when Felix had suddenly turned attractive last summer. She knew better than to admit that to Camille, though. Especially not in front of her mother, who'd openly wanted her to date Felix for three years now.

Even if Laila *had* been interested in Felix, she wouldn't have dared make a move for fear of being murdered. Camille was more territorial than a hormonal wolverine.

"Forget it, Mimi," her father said, making a little stabbing gesture with his fork. "I don't want *you* hanging around Hannah, too."

Laila felt a hot jab of irritation. The edge of her spoon dug against the flat of her thumb.

"Jaime," said her mother cautiously.

"What?" He shook his head. "Girl needs an attitude transplant."

Laila couldn't stay quiet. "Yeah, well, you haven't met Hannah's family. You have no idea how well she turned out, considering."

"Hey," her father said. "Don't talk back."

Laila looked to her mother for backup. Of anybody, shouldn't a psychologist be on her side about Hannah's obvious, deep-seated neuroses? Hannah's older sister was the type of person to find joy in walking down a convenience store aisle and snapping all the chocolate bars in half. And her parents? Laila had seen better parenting on National Geographic from species that occasionally ate their young. Hannah was comparatively Mother Teresa.

Her mother tucked a thin ringlet of gold hair behind her ear and avoided Laila's eyes. Her father shook his head, rubbing two square fingers down the block of his cheekbone, and they all ate in silence for a while.

Hannah Park, Laila's best friend, was an acerbic Korean girl who could have collected people's negative opinions about her and created a bountiful scrapbook. From a third-person perspective, Laila knew she and Hannah looked like photographic negatives. Hannah was a perplexing combination of judgmental, stubborn, and extroverted. She liked to pretend she had a core of cold wit where most people had emotions. But she also had the ferocious intelligence that made Laila feel equal parts intimidated and awake. She activated some version of Laila who operated at one-and-a-half times normal speed, somebody who could banter with a quartz sparkle. She looked at Laila with laughing expectancy, with the snare-hit instant recognition of catching your own eye in a momentary reflection.

Now Laila watched her father, wondering if he would actually stop her from going out over something as stupid as his grudge against Hannah. He was glaring into his soup as he ate it, although that could have been an effect of the soup itself, which tasted—unfortunately—exactly the way it smelled.

"11 P.M. sharp," he said.

Laila felt a rush of relief. "Got it. I'll tell them." She held out a hand. "Can I have my phone back? Please?"

He sighed and flipped her phone into her palm like a coin. "Just promise me that when Apple wants to stick a computer chip in your cabeza, you'll say no."

4

THEORETICALLY, THE NEXT DAY SHOULD HAVE BEEN ideal—Friday! New *The Rest* episodes!—but before Laila even arrived at school, she was in a foul mood. She'd told Camille to shut up over breakfast, because the sweater-exposed nerves were still raw, and her father told her sharply that he didn't care who started the fight, it was Laila's job to end it. She descended into a quiet resentment that simmered all the way to the Gates Ave. subway station. The J train showed up so late that when the cars screeched into view, people were packed window to window, and Laila spent the ride crammed against a man who got much too comfortable pressing into her personal space.

From there, the day did not improve. In third-period physics, she and her lab partner ended up with a spectacular 132 percent margin of error. Laila did her best to stuff the assignment into her binder before Leo saw it, but he'd definitely seen her panicked expression, which was maybe worse. As they headed down the hall together, he said, "The lab went well, I'm guessing?"

"Rub it in," she grumbled. "And Dr. Chung gave me that look, like, *you sad little person.*"

"That's how the dude always looks."

"Not when he's fawning over your perfect lab reports."

Leo bobbed his shoulders with an angelic "Who, me?" expression. Leo Major, one-fourth of their *The Rest* obsession group, whose name sounded like a galactic formation and who was exclusively interested in galactic formations, had never made anything below a 95 percent in Dr. Chung's class. Twice as quiet as Laila and just as perfectionistic, Leo was the closest thing to a brother she had. They even looked related: They were both exactly five foot ten and a half, their skin was an identical warm brown, and they both had so many *The Rest*–themed shirts that Hannah kept a running tally of how many times they matched. Today was one of those days.

"Cool shirt," Laila said.

"I got nothing *but* cool shirts," Leo said, drifting toward a classroom door. "See you at lunch?"

"Maybe," she called after him. But when the first lunch bell rang after fourth period, Laila swung by Mr. Madison's room so they could finish yesterday's conversation.

The room was locked and empty. He'd forgotten their lunch plans.

To really round out the day, she slipped on a puddle of some brownish fluid in the cafeteria, and a rainbow of folders cascaded out of her backpack. Before she could stuff them all back in, Hannah reached under the table and snatched one up—the hazard-orange folder where Laila kept Mr. Madison's hard copies.

Laila's heart stumbled horribly. "Hannah."

Across the table, Felix and Leo exchanged a glance. Hannah was already unfolding the pages. "Yes?"

"I'm warning you . . ."

Hannah gave a feral smile and let her dark eyes bore into Laila's. This was one of several reasons people were terrified of her: the Hannah Park stare. If it weren't enough that Hannah was beautiful, in the same way an ice storm or a forest fire was beautiful, she also had the habit of making more unbroken, intense eye contact than was comfortable for anybody.

Hannah started reading aloud. "The day they called it war, Eden knew she had to fix the impulse generator on her back left wing."

"Hannah!" Laila snatched for the papers. "Freaking—*stop* that—"

"'Freaking,'" Hannah repeated. "You're so cute."

Laila caught the story and yanked it away. "Stop it, cojuda."

Felix choked on his soda. Leo clapped him on the back.

"Fine, fine, good Lord." Hannah slouched back into their half of the booth as Laila scraped the rest of her papers into order. "What's a 'cojuda'?"

"It's like, 'moron'."

"Don't shoot the translator," said Felix, "but it's also what you call a dog that didn't get fixed."

"Awesome," Hannah said. "I love thinking about dog penis right before eating."

"You asked for it, story thief," Laila muttered. As she slid into the booth beside Hannah, she remembered Mr. Madison's words. "You know nobody could be harder on your writing than you are." But Mr. Madison had never met Hannah. Laila doubted any of her stories were good enough to show her, or worse, smart enough. Hannah loved *The Rest*, but she considered the show a guilty pleasure and never read genre fiction—no fantasy, no thrillers, no sci-fi. No fun. Hannah consumed a steady diet of Dostoyevsky, Fitzgerald, and anything the *New Yorker* described as "elegiac."

Laila wondered if she could build up to Hannah. Start with somebody less brutal. What about Leo or Felix?

"I know I'm beautiful," Felix said, "but didn't your mom ever tell you it's rude to stare?"

Laila looked away. "I'm not staring."

"It's only because she's desperately in love with you, Felix," Hannah said, "and wishes you to ask her hand in marriage."

"Nah," said Felix, with a brilliant smile. "I know the way that looks on a girl."

Hannah lifted one eyebrow. "Really? Which girl? I'll send her a condolence card."

Laila and Leo exchanged an idle look. Over the years, they had set up an intricate look-exchange system, able to convey any possible emotion about Felix and Hannah's back-and-forth: exasperated, amused, knowing. This was a necessary coping mechanism. Hannah and Felix's entire friendship was a comeback contest in which nobody would ever get the last word. That had been obvious from the early days, when the four of them had been stuck together by alphabetical fate at a table in their freshman English class—Major, Martinez, Park, Piedra. Within a week, they'd realized they were all *The Rest* superfans. Within two weeks, Hannah and Felix had begun ferocious debates as to whether the captain of the USR *Washington* was secretly evil, the most hotly contested theory among fans.

"Who's ready for season twelve?" Laila asked. "You're coming, right, Felix?"

Felix frowned. "What? Yeah, of course I'm coming."

"Hey. I wasn't sure. You did that thing where you didn't answer my text, but then you Snapped me like nine straight pictures of you eating sorbet, so I know you had your phone."

"Typical," Hannah said. "What is it, bulking season?"

"Wrestlers don't bulk," Felix said sourly, and he bit down with a grotesque crunch on a forkful of salad.

"Also, who bulks on sorbet?" Laila muttered to Hannah.

"I don't know. Middle-aged moms. Also Felix."

They traded grins. Felix was a collection of ridiculous habits glossed over by a thin veil of machismo. These days, he didn't have any problems finding girls to date, but until sophomore year, he'd been so short and scrawny that people had still asked him what elementary school he went to. He remained hypersensitive to anything that might nudge a girl's needle away from thinking of him as datable. Being a fan of *The Rest* fell on the losing side of this scale, as did his love for mid-nineties grunge rock, as did his possession of a life-size poster of Sputnik, as did the truly obscene amount of time he spent on his hair. Sometimes Laila wondered if the girls Felix dated knew anything about him at all, besides the fact that he was muscular and had great bone structure.

"I'm wondering if the new season's actually going to be good," Leo said. His eyes were obsidian dark and unfocused, chin perched on the heel of his hand. He tended to drift off like this. Sometimes Laila thought Leo was the most normal of the four of them, even-keeled enough to temper her obsessions, warm enough to balance out Hannah's sharp edges, reliable enough to force Felix to be halfway punctual. Then again, he also seemed to spend most of his time mentally distant from the earth, as if loosely tethered by an astronaut's cable.

"No," Hannah said. "Come on, Leo. Like, fuck no. The trailers are total manure. Watching this show is like Stockholm syndrome at this point."

Laila and Leo traded another look. Hannah had been saying this sort of thing with the same unflappable authority since freshman year. She took years to admit she liked anything. This also went for people. They'd all been watching *The Rest* together for a year and a half before Hannah begrudgingly referred to Felix as "acceptable."

"Yo, wait," said Felix. "I didn't show you guys, did I?" He tugged his wallet from his backpack and flashed an ID at them.

Hannah snatched the slip of plastic and tilted it toward the fluorescent light, letting the holograms lift off its surface. "Not bad. Not as good as Leo's, though." She clicked its edge against the lunch table. "Does this mean I don't have to ask my sister to get all the liquor for your birthday party?"

"You're off the hook," Felix said.

"God, that's a fucking revelation, then. Your dad's or your mom's place?"

"Mom's," Felix grunted. Mr. Martinez was an advertising agent who lived on the Upper East Side with his second wife. They mostly pretended that Felix and his mother didn't exist, but occasionally his father was struck by guilt and overcompensated for his absence by letting Felix throw parties at his apartment. Felix, for his part, talked about his father roughly once every three months, with the tone of voice he might have used to talk about filling a cavity.

"It's going to be great." Hannah tilted her thermos and slurped her noodles pointedly at Laila, who sighed. Felix's eighteenth birthday party was a week away, and Hannah had been trying to badger Laila into coming for weeks, but Hannah's descriptions had made the process sound about as appealing as getting her appendix removed without anesthetic.

"I won't have fun when I'm the only sober person there," Laila said.

"Au contraire," said Hannah. "You can be like a drunk-person anthropologist. Like the David Attenborough of drinking culture."

Laila tried not to smile. Sometimes—not that she would ever admit this—she wished she drank. Never to *be* drunk, which seemed equal parts boring and embarrassing, and definitely not for the hideous, unholy taste of alcohol. But when her friends came back with stories of sloppy nights drenched in regret, the enthusiasm of their conversation made Laila wonder if she was missing something by staying sober. Some deeper truth about the human condition. Although she wasn't sure how the secret to enlightenment could hide inside the pounding migraines that made Hannah sleep through first-period physics on Monday mornings.

Her curiosity wasn't enough to overcome the worry, though. What if she was one of those drunk people who blabbered gibberish in languages they only half spoke or, worse, made out with everybody within a fifteen-foot radius? Laila's entire experience with kissing was an awkward, garlic-flavored incident in the aftermath of junior prom last spring. It wasn't as if she required a shower of rainbows and birdsong when it happened the next time, but not being hammered would be a good baseline requirement.

"You guys have fun," she said. "Send me embarrassing texts at midnight or something."

Hannah sighed. "I swear, someday you're going to look back at senior year and wonder what it would've been like if you weren't such a recluse, and you're going to be all, 'Hannah! Alas! Why did I allow the ephemeral pleasures of life to slip past me?' And—"

"I don't talk like that."

"—*and* I'm going to resist saying 'I told you so,' because I'm not an asshole."

"No percent of what you just said is a fact."

Now her friends were the ones trading looks. Even Leo looked amused, which Laila thought was pretty rich, since he only ever went out when his girlfriend, Angela, pleaded for several weeks in a row. Angela went to some fancy private school on the Upper East Side. She and Leo had been dating since seventh grade, and sometimes they were the only thing that made Laila believe that love was real.

"All right," said Felix. "Don't relax or have fun, ever. Stay home and write about aliens."

"I will. Thanks for the advice . . ." Laila picked up Felix's fake ID. ". . . Quincy Chase Wellington from Wyoming?"

When Felix shrugged, it was more of a shoulder spasm. He moved like a wet cat. "Apparently I'm adopted."

Hannah let out a shout of laughter. "*Quincy Chase Wellington?* Oh my God, that sounds like a BBC extra."

"Or a law firm," Laila said.

"Or some clown in the Financial District yelling into an earpiece about '*buy solar!*'"

"Or—"

"You two." Felix shook his head. Waves of oil-black hair shuddered down to his shoulders. "Always ganging up on me."

Laila and Hannah bobbed an identical insouciant shrug. He wasn't wrong.

"You're just so easy to gang up on," Hannah said, but Laila kept an eye on his expression to make sure they hadn't injured his feelings, which could be delicate. Felix liked to pretend he was the hardest guy in school, especially around his boys on the wrestling team, but Laila had stopped falling for that when he'd cried for a straight half hour after *The Rest* killed off the dog in season ten. Since Felix's wrestling friends were cooler than any of them—a bunch of wiry, good-looking Puerto Rican guys—Felix also liked to pretend he was being charitable by hanging out with the three of them, and that everything they did or said to him was a minor persecution. Laila figured he wouldn't have kept inviting them to his apartment to watch movies if either of these things was true.

Felix had adopted his favorite long-suffering facial expression. "You're lucky I'm even coming tonight. You know I had this date lined up with Imani Morgan?"

Hannah looked insulted. "What? She's way too pretty for you."

"Yeah, well, *your* last girlfriend was twice as hot as you."

Laila cut in. "Let's maybe keep Virginia out of this?"

Hannah made a grumbling sound of assent. She was on good terms with most of her exes, but Virginia was the exception. They'd broken up three months ago, but Hannah still received weekly texts that alternately 1) begged Hannah to Just Talk About

Things One More Time or 2) told Hannah she was a heartless bitch who would die alone.

Everybody wound up looking at Leo, who was reading something on his phone. After a long moment, he realized he was being watched. He flashed his phone screen. "Lunar eclipse in May," he said, cheerfully.

Hannah grinned as she stretched a licorice ladder between her teeth. "I don't know how you put up with us, Leo."

Laila looked between the three of them and felt a wave of fondness followed by sharp, sudden restlessness. They'd received the last of their college admissions letters the previous week: Hannah was bound for Caltech, Leo was going to Northwestern (with Angela), and Felix was deciding between Brooklyn College and Syracuse. If, God willing, Laila got off the wait list for Bowdoin College—perched on the coast of Maine—none of them would be under six hours apart.

The prospect of this final downhill stretch, their last months together, wouldn't have been so terrifying if the others had seemed anywhere near as dependent on her as she felt dependent on them. Lately, Laila had started to picture their friendship as something alive, something she was clutching in a vise grip so that it couldn't escape, but holding on that tightly only gave her a close-up view as it choked out its last moments right there in her hands. She kept remembering how Hannah's older sister had told them, in a frighteningly casual way, how the friendships she'd thought meant everything in high school had withered in college, turned into pencil-sketch outlines of the paintings they'd once been, and all the participants had sat back, watched it happen, and declined to file any protest.

Creative writing was Laila's sixth-period class. She arrived to find a substitute, a long-haired Indian lady, poring over a piece of paper on Mr. Madison's desk. He hadn't forgotten Laila after all, then. A small relief. Exhausted, Laila sank into her seat, glad for the mind-numbing assignment she knew the sub would pass out. Nobody in the history of civilization had ever *learned* something from completing a worksheet in response to a movie, but the exercise was a well-loved substitute-teacher tradition, like the ritual mangling of Avi Srichandanray's name during roll.

But when the bell hit and the woman looked up from the desk, Laila frowned. That wasn't a sub. That was Ms. Vaswani, who taught honors biology. Without her, who would explain humiliating diagrams of the reproductive system to a room full of grimacing sophomores?

"Good afternoon," Ms. Vaswani said. She closed the door. "Actually, if you could all just . . . yes, please put away your things?"

Laila felt something unsettle in the center of her body. Teachers at this school didn't make polite requests; it was an invitation for demolition. Now even Samuel Marquez, who as a rule never paid attention to anything that happened within the confines of room 431, had gone still-faced, his dark eyes affixed on Ms. Vaswani.

"Everyone," she said, "I'm afraid we have a tough situation on our hands. For the foreseeable future, Mr. Madison will be on medical leave. He was hit by a car yesterday evening."

Laila's hand slackened around her pen. Her mind slipped into defensive kickback. Logically that couldn't be true, because she would have known, she would have heard. With the world's instant information systems, how could she have gone the entire school day without knowing? But the question had hardly surfaced before the answer yanked it back under: Mr. Madison was part-time, only taught afternoons, so his first class was fourth period Intro, all freshmen, so word might not have gotten back to Laila within a two hour window, so all this was possible after all, so she stared at Ms. Vaswani and realized she'd missed a stream of words, long seconds in which the woman's lips had seemingly been rolling against each other and releasing strange, muted tones. Now the sound sharpened. An SUV had made a turn into him when he'd been halfway up a crosswalk. His injuries were extensive— nerve damage, broken ribs, severe concussion—but after surgery, he was stable.

He was stable. That was what mattered. Relief dissolved Laila's attention span, and words about substitutes and assignments seeped through with groggy slowness.

She felt dazed, as if she'd been slapped half a dozen times. Not even thirty seconds ago, all the day's irritations had felt so involving. Now her anxiety about her story seemed petty, and the wait for the train, and the physics lab corrections that would only take an hour, anyway. During every one of those distractions, Mr. Madison had been unconscious beneath a scalpel.

Laila couldn't remember the last thing she'd said to him. It suddenly seemed important to remember, but no matter the angle she used to think about yesterday's lunch period—thinking herself back through the door, into this seat—nothing came.

The rest of the day elapsed in static fuzz. Her seventh period teacher didn't address the accident, seemed mostly normal, but now that Laila knew to look, she caught hints of expressions that teachers normally had no business wearing. Laila found herself staring at her French teacher, Ms. Benson, who was famous throughout the school for having exactly one facial expression—the impatient, hyperalert look of a rat terrier. But now her eyes were glazed, her voice subdued. She watched Ms. Benson's throat turn into columns of tendons and wrinkles between French phrases as the tiny woman swallowed hard, pulling at her braided necklace the way Camille did to her jewelry when she was nervous. Who was this person? What alternate planet was this? The only real thing was her phone, alive and moving in her pocket, where her friends' reassurances built up. Every so often she looked down at it, the corner of a glowing screen peeking out of her pocket, and felt herself slipping inside that digital place they had together, where the world was made out of words and everything was safe.

LEO HAD INSISTED THEY POSTPONE THE WATCH PARTY so Laila could have a little time to herself, but now, with time to herself, she wished she had a distraction instead. Dinner had gone as expected. When she'd given the news, her mother had gasped like a 1950s movie star and gone on to unleash a barrage of questions, most of which Laila couldn't answer. Her father, on the other hand, had shaken his head and said, "Good teacher. That's a shame." Camille didn't say anything at all and suddenly seemed very young.

For once, none of them gave Laila any grief about hiding away in her room for the evening. She considered starting the new season of *The Rest*, but Hannah would have considered that an unforgivable betrayal, so she wound up at her desk instead, laptop open. But something weighed her down, keeping her from liftoff. The laptop looked alien: the font serifs were harsh, unfamiliar little spikes, and the word processor's background looked too bright, and as she reread her story, Eden's conflict seemed overblown and melodramatic. At the same time, the sentences themselves seemed simplistic. Flavorless. As if, instead of coming from her brain alone, they'd been cobbled together from a thousand other people's voices.

She'd just begun to delete swaths of paragraphs when a knock rattled her door.

She should have known her mother wouldn't let her hide the whole night. Laila's mother's clients paid good money to talk to her about their problems, but Laila sometimes felt like the psychology degree put an unbridgeable gap between them. Every time they talked about a problem that actually mattered, Laila felt as if her mother was flicking a switch, transforming from family into a doctor figure, remote and empty, made out of training and diagnoses.

"Come in," Laila said, but when the door swung open, it wasn't her mother in the threshold.

"I swear to God," Hannah said, shutting the door behind her, "if your dad's going to make fun of my hair every time I come over, maybe he should work on his bald spot."

Laila just looked at her, and for the first time since the news, the world felt recognizable. Here was Hannah, with her stupidly messy crimson pixie cut and her mismatched earrings and her giant white-and-gray T-shirt that dangled off one tan shoulder. Here was Hannah with her crotchety remarks, holding some book as thick as a fist and smothered with award stickers, index finger stuck between the pages like a bookmark, built out of known quantities.

For a moment, neither of them spoke. Laila knew Hannah's silence was an offer: either to talk about the accident or around it. In that moment, she could have hugged Hannah just for giving her the choice. Laila had relived the announcement for five hours, remembered it every several minutes with the dizzy cold shock of closing her eyes too tightly during a fever. She didn't want to translate any of that into conversation.

"Sorry," Laila said. "He hates short hair on girls. And hair dye. So."

Hannah's expression resolved. Onward, then. No difficult conversation. Laila knew Hannah was secretly glad, even if she would never admit it.

"You're chewing again," Hannah said.

Laila stopped chewing on her hair. Out of all the nervous tics, she wished she'd landed with one that didn't make her look like a maladjusted goat.

Hannah flopped onto her bed. "Are you writing?"

"Yep."

"Sorry about lunch, by the way. I wasn't actually going to read past the first line," Hannah said in the perfunctory way she always offered apologies. Hannah appeared to dispel guilt as easily as somebody might wave away a gnat, which didn't seem fair. Laila felt guilt and embarrassment and regret in metric tons, carried over years too long. That was residual Catholicism for you.

Laila closed her laptop. "Sure you weren't."

"Hypothesis," Hannah said, stacking Laila's pillows behind her head. "Is one of your characters based on me? Is that why I can't read it?"

"No," Laila said, too quickly.

Hannah's face filled with glee. "Holy shit, I'm right. You wrote me into something. Did you give me an epic battle? Please tell me I have amazing sex with a hot alien."

Laila's cheeks burned. "Shut up, I didn't write you in," she said.

In actuality, she kept writing Hannah into her stories by accident. These adaptations of her became a little more ruthless every time. In a story from sophomore year, Hannah had been an ace sniper. In the latest, she made a cameo as a mercenary. Laila couldn't help it. Hannah's particular mixture of *I-don't-give-a-shit* and *I-care-so-intensely-that-the-sheer-force-of-it-could-shatter-glass* bled onto the page whether Laila wanted it to or not.

Otherwise, Laila kept the contents of her life strictly partitioned from the contents of her stories. She didn't want her innermost thoughts about the people in her life publicized. In some nightmare parallel universe, she'd probably written a thinly veiled Samuel Marquez into a makeout scene, and he'd inevitably found it in some dramatic revelation. Even the concept made her cringe.

Her bedroom filled up with quiet, wall to wall, from the Ecuadorian flag strung up on one side to the massive *The Rest* mural tacked opposite. Hannah looked disinterested, the way she always did when she was deeply invested in something. She was icing over. Laila felt it happen, like the distant cold breath of an air conditioner.

She wished she didn't *care*. She imagined shoving that orange folder into Hannah's hands and telling her, go ahead, read it, and if you don't like it, I can always change it. But of course she couldn't.

"Mr. Madison's on your side," Laila said without thinking. "He always tells me I should show more people my stories."

After a pause, Hannah said, "You think you'll visit him?"

"I bet he's got family coming in already," Laila said, but the second the words were out, she questioned them. She knew Mr. Madison's parents had passed away, and he'd mentioned once that he was an only child. "I don't even know if I'm allowed to visit him," she added. "He's probably still passed out, right?"

"Maybe. Still, though. Did I ever tell you about Virginia's cousin?"

Laila tried not to look too interested. Hannah had five ex-girlfriends, none of whom she'd dated for longer than four months, and she never volunteered information about any of those relationships. At this point, Laila, Leo, and Felix didn't bother asking Hannah about her exes, or about anything personal, really, because they knew any question would get instantly redirected. Crushes and relationships were part of the undercurrent—vast pockets of context Hannah refused to address, which also included her entire pre-high-school life, as well as information about her family. The three of them hadn't met Hannah's parents until halfway through sophomore year, which had probably been strategic, since Mr. and Mrs. Park had been awful to Laila and worse to the guys. They hadn't known she had an older sister until last July, when Molly had come home from her senior year of college and started plying Hannah with watery beer. Hannah never even talked about her other friends, a white-and-East-Asian friend group that was so proportionally white and East Asian that they looked like an advertisement for an exchange program. In general, it was like being friends with a CIA agent.

"What cousin?" Laila said.

Hannah lay back on Laila's bed, staring at the diagram of the *Moondowners* planet that hung above. "She had this cousin on life support. Every few weeks, she went up to his room and read books to him, and news, and fucking—I don't know, like, recaps of this show he used to watch."

A hard knot had beaded up in Laila's throat. "Is he all right?"

"No idea. Weirdly, she doesn't put information about her co-matose cousin in her angry-ass drunk texts." Hannah sighed. "But she used to talk about how she'd hold his wrist and feel the blood going and that was, I don't know, like this stabilizing thing for her. So maybe seeing Mr. Madison will help even if he's not awake."

"Would you go with me?"

Hannah paused. For once, she wasn't making eye contact. "When?" she asked, offhand. Laila had grown sensitive to those hints of caution beneath the monotone.

"I don't know." Laila hadn't even meant to ask the question. The idea of Hannah in a hospital seemed inappropriate somehow, wearing her uniform of ratty jeans and distressed jacket, emitting the waves of hostility that always came along with her discomfort.

Before Laila could retract the question, though, Hannah had said, so quietly Laila wondered if she'd hoped the words into existence, "Obviously I'll go."

Laila wasn't sure she trusted this hospital to promote human health, given the downright venomous lifelessness of its waiting room. The average coffin looked more geared toward human comfort. And why were all waiting rooms equally, identically depressing? She'd seen this room fifty times if she'd seen it once: muted greens and teals were stirred into the color scheme, which otherwise consisted of a flood of beige, white, and fluorescent glare. The quiet music was the string-instrument equivalent of somebody humming tunelessly under their breath. The lines of chairs snaked around the waiting area in vaguely intestinal formations. And the room's most colorful elements weren't the indecisive Kandinsky-knockoff canvasses, but the grid of thick plastic cubbies that offered pamphlets with titles like *YOUR LIFE WITH HIP DYSPLASIA*.

"This place looks like disappointment feels," Hannah muttered.

"At least you're not waiting for a syphilis test," Laila said, flicking a pamphlet into Hannah's lap that read *SYPHILIS: THE FACTS*.

Hannah swatted the glossy paper back. "Yeah, thank God. Pass me the herpes one?"

Laila had called ahead to make sure Mr. Madison was in visiting condition. Still, they waited for twenty minutes before a nurse admitted them through the swinging door behind the receptionist. Walking into the ward was like drawing a deep breath. There was something relaxing about finally seeing motion in a place that demanded urgency, doctors walking with purpose, paging through reports, nurses adjusting IVs that swayed at the top of slender poles. Laila caught glimpses through the occasional window into brightly lit rooms. The glow reminded her of the neon coolant bulbs that emerged from the submersion tanks in *The Rest*, lights that seemed to melt against the white background of the Resting Room. A holding chamber full of unbreathing, motionless people.

At room 613, Hannah took a seat, and the nurse allowed Laila into Mr. Madison's room. The room was small, and—once the heavy door clicked shut—quiet. The air smelled of talcum powder and disinfectant. A band of windows was mostly curtained, darkening the room, but an open sliver offered a view of a nearby apartment building's brick face. The overhead lights were heavily dimmed, making the white blankets on his cot look tan.

She'd expected his body to be hidden by a trapeze of suspension cords, slings tucked into elevated casts and bandages wrapped over every joint, but whatever apparatus they'd used on him was invisible beneath his bedcovers. By appearances, nothing had happened but a hard punch to the face. Bluish bruises had trickled into his left eye socket, purple sinking into a dark well beneath. She'd never seen him without his glasses. His face looked too small and too empty.

"Hi, Mr. Madison," Laila said.

"Laila," he said, with a painful-looking smile. "Great to see you, as much as I can see you without glasses." He was speaking slowly, but the clarity was reassuring.

"How are you feeling?" she asked.

"A little woozy. Sorry it's so dark. Concussion light."

"No, of course, that makes sense. I don't mind." She moved a chair to his bedside and sat. "How long do they want to keep you here?"

He blinked. This happened in slow motion, too, eyelids drifting down as if he'd fallen asleep a moment, twitching up reluctantly as if his muscles were too tired even to do that much. "Not long. The doctors just want to make sure there's no intracranial swelling, and then they'll transfer me to a physical rehab center. I'll start therapy over there."

"Right," Laila said. She'd thought of a list of questions to ask on the way over, reassuring questions—why couldn't she remember a single one? Suddenly she felt as if she shouldn't have visited. In a way, she felt as if she'd never seen him before, not like this, as somebody who could be affected by the world's random incidents.

Teachers were supposed to be insulated from that. Even seeing them walking to the train was enough of a disruption to the routine.

She felt distant, suddenly, looking down at this friendship that she'd thought was a contiguous part of her life and realizing it was an island. She'd thought of their friendship as personal, like what she had with Hannah, Felix, and Leo. Maybe even more personal, because Mr. Madison knew so much about her private thoughts and ambitions. But what did she have of him? Laila could have written an essay on Felix's relationship with his father, who treated every interaction with Felix like a transaction. Laila could have described for hours the way Leo seemed hammered into quietness by his gregarious father and his worrying mother, the way he seemed to take refuge in other galaxies because space was the only thing as quiet and distant as he was. God knew Laila could have written books about any aspect of Hannah's personality. But Mr. Madison? When had she ever known a part of *his* life that way? He was too professional to let her see past the curtain. She suddenly felt like she was shrinking with embarrassment, that she'd never seen how much their relationship revolved exclusively around her.

"What was the accident like?" she asked out of nowhere, before she even realized she'd been wondering. Then she felt a cold shock of humiliation. How inconsiderate could she possibly be? "Wow," she said. "I'm so sorry. Forget I just asked that."

"Doing research?" he said and tittered. Only the right half of his face could commit to the laugh. "No, I'm joking. Honestly, the parts I remember aren't very impressive. The impact was . . . well,

I think the adrenaline dulled the pain. Mostly I was disoriented because I really *flew*. A few rotations. My head hit the curb. That was the first thing to hurt. The rest didn't set in until the ambulance."

Laila nodded. She looked for an answer that didn't involve the words *me* or *I*. "You seem okay."

"Good. I feel okay, I'm just tired. And I hate to miss your last quarter. Your class is such a good group of kids."

Laila was horrified to feel her eyes burning. If she cried, he would try to console her. This wasn't about her. She blinked hard.

"Have you met the substitute?" he asked.

"I don't think they've found one yet."

"They have. I got a call." When he smiled again, the painful creases made her imagine his face cracking like porcelain. "This might be for the best, even."

"What?" Her voice rose. "No, it isn't."

"Oh. I . . . well . . ."

He sounded so small and pathetic. She hated that she'd raised her voice. Of course he couldn't argue like this. Now her eyes were watering again. She couldn't shake the horrible suspicion that she was the only visitor he'd had. She wouldn't be able to visit him in rehab, would she? That wasn't for her. Too private, too personal.

"Do you think I can send you emails at the rehab center?" she asked.

"Oh, the doctor says I'm not allowed to look at computer screens. Any screens." He lifted his eyes to the television across from him, which was turned off. Laila remembered when a kid from some SoHo school had slammed Felix's head into the wrestling mat their sophomore year, giving him a concussion so serious that his mother had hidden his phone for a month, doctor's orders.

"But," he went on. "I'm sure I can ask somebody to print out your emails. I'd love to read whatever you write next, or hear how things are going with the new teacher. Maybe I can even write a short reply for them to type up."

"Okay," she said. "That sounds great. I'll do that." The room had one other screen, angled away from Mr. Madison. Laila watched the graph of his heart rate that spiked there, the numbers that charted his blood pressure in sans serif. She followed white wires to the plastic clamps over his fingertips and thought of the medical nanotechnology that *The Rest*'s crew had aboard the USR *Washington*. This seemed insufficient in comparison. She didn't trust these cheap, plasticky-looking wires to fix him. His bed blurred into a fuzzy pill as her tears brimmed over. She forced herself not to sniffle. "I'm really sorry this happened," she said.

"Not ideal," he said, "but thank you for visiting me, really." And she realized he couldn't see her crying, because he wasn't wearing his glasses.

When she was back in the hall, she realized Hannah was already holding a box of tissues. She laughed, running her knuckles over her eyes. "I'm that predictable?"

"Yeah, well, you cried at the end of that episode with the bugs," Hannah said, plucking three tissues from the soft plastic X with three quick hushes. "It's a low bar."

Laila arrived home to a quiet apartment. A wrapped package sat on her bed, a collage of tape and loose ribbon. Laila tugged it open. Soft wool, red and white, sagged out. A clean version of the sweater Camille had ruined. She lifted it, hesitant, to her nose. The wool smelled like the light, nonspecific perfume of a department store, the spritz of a dozen different scents.

Laila turned to call back into the hall, to ask, but Camille was already at her door. "Are you going to stop being mad at me now?" she asked, with a somewhat half-assed attempt at her usual imperious tone.

"How did you buy this?" Laila asked. The original had been a gift from Tía Graciela, who had expensive taste.

"I told you I was selling my nail polish."

"That was for—? You didn't have to."

Camille screwed up half her face in the *yeah right* expression that her friends had transmitted to her like a disease. "Do you want it or not?"

Laila hugged the sweater to her chest.

"Yeah," Camille said. "That's what I thought."

"Did Mom tell you to do this?"

"You think I can't do anything nice if Mom doesn't come up with the idea first?"

"That's not what I meant. Thank you, seriously." Laila climbed onto her bed, sweater still hugged close. "Also, I'm not mad at you."

"Sure."

"I'm serious. I've had bigger things to worry about the last couple days."

The belligerence leaked out of Camille's voice. "I know," she said uncertainly. "You just seem angry, ñañita."

Don't get into the details, Laila told herself. It wasn't fair to expect her thirteen-year-old sister to prop her up emotionally. "I am angry, I guess," she said. "Not at anybody, though. Except that idiot driver who didn't look where he was going."

"Yeah. What a *dumbass.*"

"Language," Laila said wearily. Camille got an obvious adrenaline rush from cussing; unfortunately, as a rule, this made cussing about thirty times less cool. Laila wondered if Camille had picked up the habit from Hannah. God only knew how, but Hannah made curse words sound at once effortlessly natural, slyly ironic, and brutally edgy, the ideal every stoner kid with a skateboard seemed determined to achieve.

"Fine, fine." Camille sank into Laila's beanbag, her bony behind punching her deep into the hush of beans. She thumbed the worn spines of the *Moondowners* series on Laila's bookshelf, flanked by the older classics, C. J. Cherryh on the left, Andre Norton on the right. "What are these even about?" Camille asked, pulling out *The Sky Most Gray and Ancient.*

"How have I not told you yet?"

"You tried once. I left the room."

"Cool. Right. Well, last chance to leave."

Camille didn't move.

Laila sank into an explanation she knew like a monologue, having already given it to Leo, Felix, and Hannah. There was a lot of ground to cover. *Moondowners* was set on a planet with a single Pangaea-like continent divided into nine regions, eight of which were struggling to take power from the ninth, which had maintained control for two hundred years. Crisscrossing the planet's mostly oceanic surface were the orbits of seventeen moons. Each moon's core secreted an elixir called Na-Thira, whose composition differed on each moon. One small, corn-yellow moon contained a well of poison; another generated a radioactive gel that, smeared on any organic substance, caused invisibility. The ruling region, the Darsinnian Isles, had control of the most valuable moon of all, whose caverns were full of a serum of eternal life. An injection of the serum had the side effect of sterility, though, so the inhabitants of the Isles had lived for half a thousand years and never had children.

"What?" Camille said, overflowing with scorn. "How does it take immortal people seven books to win?"

"Immortal, but not invulnerable," Laila said. "The Darsinnians can get killed like anybody else. Also, I don't think they're going to win. The seventh book is actually—a lot of people think the Darsinnians are going to end up on top, but I'm like, come on. They're all terrified of dying, because when someone immortal dies, it's this permanent impact on the Isles' population. I bet in the final battle, they'll end up running."

"Okay, so what's the point?" Camille asked.

"What?"

"What's the point of the series?"

"Debatable," Laila said, bouncing on her starry bedspread. Camille was probably just humoring her, but even talking about the series was easing a weight from Laila's shoulders. "The main throughline is about war," she said. "Like, trying to keep your humanity in horrible circumstances, even though some of the characters are so enhanced that they're not really human. But there's this whole framing device . . . basically, there's this secret colony of people inside one of the moons, and they're called the Watchers, and they're these self-appointed historians who are actually relating this whole chronicle to foreign solar systems. So their job is to be impartial and stay distant, but—" She cut herself off. "I don't want to spoil anything, or you'll never read it."

"I'm not going to read it."

"Come on. Please? I read the first one when I was your age."

"'*When I was your age . . .*'" Camille croaked, hobbling out of Laila's beanbag. "Fine. But only because Dad keeps trying to get me to start the *Star Wars* books, and I'm running out of excuses not to."

Laila felt her lips tug. "Be careful with it. Robin Jensen signed that copy. To me. I *met* him."

"How?"

"He lives in Brooklyn."

Camille considered the book's immaculate binding. "I'm going to dunk this in ketchup."

"Don't even joke, tonta."

Camille's smile was a streaky apparatus of yellow rubber bands strung between her braces. As she tugged *The Sky Most Gray and Ancient* from its lineup and collapsed back into the beanbag, Laila took her laptop from her backpack, and the last of the stiffness between them evaporated.

The fight had been stupid. They'd always known how to negotiate their push and pull: Camille pushed, and Laila didn't push back. Laila sometimes wished that she could be something else with Camille than the one who capitulated, but that was how the dynamic had to be if this was going to work, at least until Camille grew up a bit. Laila could be other things to other people, and for now, she couldn't push anybody in any direction. She felt like an object to be moved. Maybe that was why her friendship with Mr. Madison was perfect. Neither of them was ever allowed to be the assertive one with anybody else.

Laila opened her laptop and picked over her half-deleted story, but the heavy thing that weighed upon her hadn't let go. She felt the heaviness skewing her trajectory, sending her toward a different galaxy. She let the computer's blue light burn into her eyes for so long that they began to ache, but words wouldn't come. She couldn't imagine the war this time, couldn't make herself picture the threat toward a planet. All she could think about was the way a threat to a single person could feel like a threat to a universe.

6

MONDAY, SIXTH PERIOD. THE REPLACEMENT WAS AL-most late returning from lunch. Laila was already judging them, whoever they were. Mr. Madison's classroom was preset every day before any of them set foot through the door, lectures and related videos loaded on the projector, readings waiting on the desks. He had a punctuality obsession. The only time Laila had seen him genuinely irritated was when someone slunk in forty-one minutes late to their fifty-five-minute class period, and nobody blamed him. At that point, it was more respectable to skip.

Thirty seconds before the bell, Laila heard the clunk of boots. Mr. Madison and his dad sneakers wouldn't have made a sound, and they wouldn't be walking through the door right at the strike of 2:15.

The replacement appeared, nineteen pairs of eyes began their analytic scan, and Laila's resentment stilled like simmering water removed suddenly from heat. She was tall, golden-skinned, and square-shouldered, her thin mouth affixed into a flat line. Some-where in that age range where Laila couldn't distinguish how old grown-ups were, exactly—thirtyish to forty-fiveish. She had gunmetal-gray eyes, kept her hands behind her back like con-cealed weaponry, and wore an expensive felt coat buttoned to her neck over black skinny jeans. A leather satchel hung over her shoulder. Somehow this all looked formal.

She wasn't what Laila had expected. Laila didn't know what she'd expected, actually, but it wasn't someone who looked *cool.*

Their principal, Dr. Albert Greene, a reedy, balding man with a mustache reminiscent of a particularly bushy centipede, loped in behind the substitute. "Everybody," Dr. Greene said, breathless. He always sounded a little breathless. It didn't help that he spoke almost exclusively in sentence fragments, which stuttered out of his mouth as if a manufacturing mechanism in his throat were catching on something repeatedly. "Good afternoon," he said. "A few announcements about what to expect for the rest of the semester. *So* pleased to introduce—oh! Yes, of course, let me take that—"

He cradled the substitute's satchel as if it were a priceless artifact and placed it on Mr. Madison's desk. Dislike ignited in Laila's chest, and she took an extinguishing breath. Obviously the woman had to use Mr. Madison's desk. Obviously. It was just that Laila couldn't look in that direction without expecting to see him looking back. It was just that all this felt like an attempt to erase the fact that Mr. Madison was their *actual* teacher, especially since Ms. Vaswani had removed all of Mr. Madison's decorations, including his *The Rest: Season IV* poster, which had triggered Laila's first real conversation with him. Freshman year, Intro to Creative Writing had been her lunchtime elective. One week into the school year, she'd started talking about the show to Mr. Madison, and she hadn't been able to stop. God, Laila wondered, how had he put up with her? She'd been so annoying then. He'd been so patient.

She kept seeing the pattern of bruises over his eye. She fixed her eyes on Dr. Greene's mustache instead.

"*So* pleased," Dr. Greene began again, "to introduce Nadiya Nazarenko."

Laila looked at the woman again. She knew that name. Why?

She scanned the class. Everyone else seemed unfazed.

No. Not everyone. In the front row, Peter Goldman's back had gone ramrod-straight, and his protuberant blue eyes looked ready to emerge from their sockets. At the beginning of the year, Peter Goldman had told everyone that his favorite book was "*The Fountainhead*, I've read it four times, or God, maybe *Lolita*?"; also, he'd once referred to Laila's second-favorite sci-fi series, *In the After Path*, as "escapist trash." Laila had debated writing him into a story as some sort of ill-fated hyena.

"Ms. Nazarenko," Dr. Greene said grandly, "is a literary giant. The author of seven books that have, as the *New Yorker* put it, been foundational to the landscape of the modern novel. The winner of last year's Pulitzer Prize for her most recent book, *A Flight of Roses*. An international bestseller, with more than twenty million copies of her books circulating worldwide."

Now the whole class was Peter. Unblinking. Cartoonishly bug-eyed. Laila could hear the thin breeze whispering past the windows outside.

"She's also a dear friend, and as a personal favor, for which I am just *so* grateful," Dr. Greene shot her a look, mustache quivering with emotion, "she's agreed to teach the remainder of your class this year."

Nazarenko had perched on a stool beside the whiteboard and

was watching Dr. Greene with removed curiosity, as if she'd never met him before.

Dr. Greene went on. "Difficult circumstances, I know. We all wish Mr. Madison the quickest of recoveries. But this is a tremendous opportunity for you as young writers. A true privilege, really, to learn from her. She's one of the finest authors of her generation, and—well, enough from me. I'll let you take it from here, Nadiya. Thank you again, really."

His wheezing voice left a vacuum of silence behind.

The door closed. Nadiya Nazarenko made no move to stand.

"Is anyone absent today?" she asked. Her voice was flavored with half a dozen accents. Her vowels were little adventures. She sounded like she was from nowhere at all.

Heads shook. "No," murmured Peter Goldman, sounding reverent.

"Good. Names." From her vantage point on the stool, Nazarenko pointed down the rows of desks, and the students introduced themselves. The basketball players at the back, who comprised five-eighths of the class's male population and were here for the GPA boost, sounded wary as they gave their names, as if they were reconsidering the contents of their birth certificates.

When Laila said her name, Nazarenko's eyes brushed hers. The skin on Laila's forearms prickled hotly. Odd tendrils of thought frayed out. She'd seen *A Flight of Roses* every time she walked into a bookstore for the last year, columns of amber covers in tall vertical displays. She'd been determined to maintain her animosity to Mr. Madison's substitute out of loyalty, so that if she visited him again, she could honestly tell him she wished he could come back, but the goal suddenly seemed childish. Twenty million books? The *Pulitzer*? How had Dr. Greene convinced this woman to spend one day here, let alone the rest of the year?

Nadiya Nazarenko stood, and stood. She moved slowly, gracefully, as if underwater. "Explain to me how you used to do this," she said, scanning the class. Her voice was smooth and impassive and utterly without volume. She must have known she didn't need it.

Along with a few other kids, Laila half-lifted her hand. The movement wasn't wholly voluntary. She felt like a cobra lifting her head before a charmer.

"Harden," Nazarenko said with a casual glance to Gigi Harden. This had to be faked, Laila thought, feeling almost indignant. Nazarenko couldn't memorize everybody's names and faces instantly. She was wearing an earpiece. Somebody was feeding her information. None of this was real.

Gigi Harden, who had so many piercings that her ears drooped in surrender, said in her usual anxious rush, "Um, usually we get in and we free write from prompts on the board, or sometimes we had outside readings, but he only gave us a couple reading quizzes. If people wanted to share their stuff, then we workshopped, but not like a serious seminar or anything."

"I see." Nazarenko removed her coat and folded it over Mr. Madison's desk. She returned to the stool. "I've never believed in writing classes," she said. "I consider them useless. A poison of the market economy, which has taught us that everything can be commodified. Every writing class I've seen has been a mercenary blend of subjective criticism and thinly veiled envy."

Laila watched in a stupor. Nazarenko's gestures were purposeful and rotational, as if she were folding dough. Who talked like that? Last year, in French, they'd learned that every place on earth had its own filler sounds, the *uhs*, *ers*, and *ums* that signified thought or delay. *Like* in English. *Alors* in French. *Pues* in Spanish. Clutter and redirection and hesitation. Everywhere except, apparently, wherever the hell this woman was from.

"Naturally," Nazarenko went on, "when Albert asked me if I'd like to try instructing a class myself, I accepted. I wanted to see what the excitement was about." She folded her hands in her lap. She wore three silver rings: neat, unadorned bands. "First, let me clarify an important point. I don't consider fiction a precious concoction of emotion that deserves coddling. I won't instill in any of you a false sensation of success. The antidote to progress is complacency."

Laila didn't dare look to the back of the room, but she could imagine the stricken expressions on Samuel Marquez and his friends. In her fingertips, though, a strange new pulse began to beat. Suddenly, as if a password had been entered, she had access to the memory of her final pre-accident conversation with Mr. Madison. She remembered his soft request, "Be proud," and how she'd agreed to try—but all the while, the fierce little voice that guided her every action had whispered those words: *The antidote to progress is complacency.*

Nazarenko bent her lips in a motion that imitated the essential shape of a smile, and the classroom seemed to bend a degree toward her, drawn in. "Please turn in in your most recent submission," she said. "I'd like a sense of your status."

Frantic fumbling ensued. Papers sluiced up the aisle between busy hands and landed in stacks on the front desks. Laila pulled the copy of Eden's story from its orange folder and watched Mr. Madison's blue circles disappear ahead.

Laila spent the rest of the day imagining the procession of her class's stapled pages from Nadiya Nazarenko's leather bag into her silver-ringed hands, and from there, onto a gleaming walnut surface where Nazarenko would peel her story out of a stack of everyone else's work. She imagined a heavy-barreled pen between Nazarenko's fingers and margin notes left in sharp script. By lunch the next day, she felt sick with nerves.

Thanks to the hair, Hannah was a difficult person to miss at any given time, but she never stood out more than when she was alone. Isolated in their usual corner booth beside one of the allergen-friendly refrigerators, looking like a single matchstick, red on tan on a wash of white linoleum, she drew Laila's eyes instantly.

Laila slid into the booth across from her. "Where are the guys?"

"Leo's doing some extra-credit thing with Dr. Chung."

"Is he not satisfied with his 103 average?"

"Only a 104 will do. And Felix—" Hannah nodded across the cafeteria to a booth where Felix faced a girl in a suede jacket. "Went on that date with Imani on Friday, apparently."

"Wow. She *is* pretty," Laila said. Her voice stuttered across the last word. The original thought had been, *Wow, she* is *hot,* and the sentence had transformed on the way out. Laila couldn't talk about anybody like that. Not even her celebrity crushes, not even avatar of perfection Samuel Marquez. A barrier of shame as impermeable as plexiglas walled her off from everything sexual, every thought, every action, even something as small as the difference in connotation between saying "pretty" and "hot." Hannah had teased her about this once and had stopped when Laila didn't come close to smiling. Her inexperience didn't feel charming or virtuous, like she was some good-girl persona from a movie. It felt furious and heated, humiliating and childish, as if physicality were a language she was supposed to have learned, and here she was in senior year, surrounded by a horde of native speakers, unable to translate the most basic concepts.

Mostly, she blamed her reluctance to touch the topic on her own awkwardness, but she did wonder sometimes if her ex-Catholicism was the actual source. After all, she still couldn't even say "Oh my God" without a basal section of her brain wondering if the syllables were a disgrace to the chamber in her heart filled with Jesus's grace, even though she hadn't been to church since sophomore year. In eighth grade, she'd picked up a confirmation name—Mary, sort of a starter confirmation name for the people who were thirteen and already checked out—and her religious journey had been a gentle decline into nothingness since then.

Her parents had been disappointed, especially her father, but she hadn't been able to resist. She had too many questions about the Bible's stern prescriptions, and when they weren't the Bible's, they were the community's. Maybe she could have overlooked the questions if she hadn't stopped believing, but she had. She hadn't wanted it badly enough, so it had left. Religion was needy that way. Religion also wouldn't have wanted Laila to look at Imani Morgan this long, to imagine the feeling of her hair or her skin or her mouth. Needy *and* jealous. No wonder she'd cut the cord.

Hannah cleared her throat. Laila looked away from Imani quickly.

"So," Hannah said. "I've been hearing some tales about the new lady. She's famous or something, right?"

"Or something. She won the Pulitzer last year."

Rare shock flashed across Hannah's face. "She—*Nadiya Nazarenko* is your teacher? I've read her shit! It's quality."

"Stop, I'm already terrified she's going to hate my story."

"Well, yeah." Hannah had already regained her composure. "But I mean, if she does, fuck it. She doesn't write sci-fi. And she still only gets one opinion."

"Her opinion isn't a normal opinion, though. I mean, she *knows* people. I bet she could get my story published if she wanted."

Hannah made an indecisive sound. They were both on their phones now. Felix had texted them about rescheduling.

Felix (12:14 a.m.): I caved. I watched the first 5min of the season......if we dont meet up tonight ill watch the whole ep. Hannah is ur house open?"

"Felix, our savior." Hannah looked at Laila triumphantly. "Perfect distraction. *The Rest* tonight?"

Laila nodded, but even the promise of the new season seemed pale. Someone besides Mr. Madison had read her story. She'd wanted to refine that piece into perfection before she showed anyone else, let alone a real author.

In sixth period, she arrived in Mr. Madison's classroom feeling as if Nazarenko had been perched on that stool in front of the white-board for weeks, waiting to pass down her verdict.

"Grades," Nazarenko told the class. "You'll receive only one test score for the remainder of the semester, a mark out of one hundred. I'll revise that score every week according to the progress of these pieces. You're welcome to start from scratch as many times as you'd like." She paused and concluded, "I'm mostly saying that there's no need to panic."

The class laughed without humor. It didn't actually sound like a joke.

"You'll find your current grades on the final page," Nazarenko said with a wave to the papers gridded across Mr. Madison's desk. "Help yourself."

Laila slammed her thigh into her desk in her haste to stand and jockeyed Peter Goldman out of the way. Her story was easy to find, pages longer than anybody else's. She returned to her desk and rifled the packet open to its last page.

32/100.

Laila let out a noiseless breath as her packet flapped shut. Her face stung, as if in a strong sea wind.

Once she could move her fingers again, she thumbed through the chapter, expecting Nazarenko's notes to spiral across her pages, a zigzagged field of strike-throughs where Mr. Madison had scribbled his circles, some sort of explanation. But as the chaos of grade-collection subsided to her left, she found two lonely annotations over a dozen pages. Page two, first line:

Eden's heart beat hard ~~in her chest~~.

I would hope it isn't located anywhere else.

And page six, halfway down:

Eden's fingers tightened on the trigger of her ~~phaser~~.

Take me to your leader.

She reread the notes. "Take me to your"—what did that even mean? Laila felt the urge to laugh that sometimes blossoms out of other, contradictory emotions, like hysterical sadness, or—as in this case—cold horror. She wasn't even comforted by the equally horrified expressions around her. A queue of thoughts formed that she immediately tried to kick away, because they were obnoxious and arrogant, and she knew it. Thoughts like, *Who cares if they all got Fs? None of them are* supposed *to be good at writing.* But why was she supposed to be good? Because she'd assigned that to herself? Because she'd trusted the word of one person?

I wouldn't lie about your writing, she heard, muted, as if from an adjacent room. She knew Mr. Madison wouldn't lie, but what did honesty matter? Someone didn't have to be a liar to be wrong.

Panic welled up in her like a geyser. The Bowdoin wait list. She had to resubmit an updated list of academics and extracurriculars by May, and next quarter didn't start for another week. If this was supposed to be their only grade for the entire quarter—if Bowdoin saw an F for her final quarterly grade, even if the year wasn't over yet—

She looked up at Nadiya Nazarenko, who wore a measured look of study, like a scientist watching a labyrinth of rats. Laila's clouded thoughts stilled and cleared. Hadn't she known? Hadn't she looked at this story on Friday night and felt something like revulsion? Hadn't she felt this paranoia for four years, been unwilling to accept

Mr. Madison's praise because at her core she'd known she could do better?

Now that her fears were confirmed, she was free to move forward, upward, and there sat the person with the answers. Laila felt a pang in her palm. Her fists were clenched so tightly in her lap that her story's staple had cut into her lifeline. Maybe Nazarenko's guidance would puncture her, but something would grow back over the injury, not scar tissue but armor, gleaming and valuable. She remembered losing her teeth in elementary school and prodding her tender gums with the point of her tongue as they'd healed, each probe a shock of pain to the root that became addictive. Cariña, her father had said, don't play with those spots, you want an infection? But she'd never been able to stop. She kept testing, kept pushing, kept exploring those sensitive spaces until the protrusion of the tooth bit her back.

After seventh period, Laila forced her way back into Mr. Madison's classroom before the last few sophomores trailed out, looking stunned and bloodless. Despite the final bell, Nazarenko hadn't risen from her stool. She'd taken a notebook from the breast pocket of her felt coat and split it open in her lap. She wore that coat like a military uniform, lapels creased at rigid angles, black steel buttons gleaming as if she waxed them on the hour, dark scarf cinched at her golden throat.

Nazarenko considered the notebook but didn't write. Laila knew that the woman was aware of her presence, like a spider feels vibrations radiating out from foreign matter stuck in its web.

When Nazarenko lifted her eyes, Laila lost courage and found herself looking down at her phone, which had appeared in her palm.

"Yes?" Nazarenko said.

Laila slipped her phone back into her pocket. "This comment you left on my—"

"Shut the door."

Laila shut the door.

"Sit." Nazarenko pointed to a desk in the front row. Laila nearly tripped in her haste to get up the aisle.

Nazarenko tucked her notebook into her breast pocket as Laila took the desk. "Go on," she said.

"'Take me to your leader,'" Laila read on the sixth page. "What does that mean?"

"It's something of a joke. Shorthand for 'I've read this before.' Derivative material is especially glaring in a genre that prides itself on its capacity for innovation."

"Oh."

Nazarenko had a painter's way of examining faces, calculating slopes and depths in a way that felt both mathematical and intimate. "Do you disagree?"

"No! No, this isn't—I actually wanted to ask what else you thought. I mean, with the grade, I thought you must have other, you know, critiques."

"Who left the circles on that copy, Piedra?"

"Mr. Madison."

"What were his thoughts?"

Laila was embarrassed. Not for herself, but for him, so easily impressed. "He said to be proud," she mumbled.

"Speak up."

"He told me I should be proud of this. I mean, he always does that. He says I'm my own worst critic."

Nazarenko unleashed a laugh, a raw, throaty noise, as if a wolf were trying out amusement. "If you're your own worst critic, you haven't met the right critic."

Now I have, Laila wanted to say, but she couldn't muster the courage. "Yeah," she said instead, and she hated how bland the word sounded, hated how sentences wouldn't flow to her tongue as immaculately formed as they apparently did to Nadiya Nazarenko's, because now she was searching, and searching, and this wasn't the patient silence Mr. Madison always offered. Everything about the woman on the stool exuded expectancy, a deeply ingrained disapproval that had to be counteracted instantly if there was to be any hope of dislodging it, but what could impress her? What sort of writing did she want to see? They didn't even talk about writing in class. Today Nazarenko had given a lecture comparing Afrikaans sentence structure to French sentence structure, which seemed like an excuse to show off her fluency in both. The day before, she'd given them a lecture on geode formation. The lessons weren't uninteresting, but how was any of this relevant? At all?

"S-so," Laila said, flush with heat from cheeks to palms. "Did you . . . maybe . . ."

"What I wrote is what I think," said Nazarenko. "I'll see you in class tomorrow."

Laila stammered something along the lines of a thank-you or an apology, and when she was back in the hallway, she couldn't remember having stood, retreated, or made eye contact. She had to splay her palms against the slick cinder blocks for a moment and look up into the gridded lights, breathing like her mother always told her—in for seven, out for six—because her heart was beating like a pulsing thumb hit with a bludgeoning object.

THE METHOD AUTHOR
by Eliot Sandberg,
senior correspondent

for *Letters*

When I meet Nadiya Nazarenko, author of Catalina's Mothers *and* A Flight of Roses, *my first task is not to measure the person before me against the reputation that precedes her. The eccentric novelist has a brand of notoriety that authors rarely attain, the type that transcends accolades and enters personal fascination. Even a decade and a half later, I vividly remember the rash of eager, hushed conversations that followed her 2002 New York Times profile, which ran prior to the release of* Catalina's Mothers. *The piece confirmed the rumors about the ambitious debut novel: Nazarenko cloistered herself in a nunnery in the Alps, population seven, and lived in complete silence for more than four years in order to plumb the psyche of the eponymous character. In the novel, Catalina is the second coming* of Jesus Christ, born to an Italian nun—a virgin, of course—and kept in isolation for the first thirty-one years of her life for fear that she, too, might be killed.

The stunt, as many consider it, wasn't an isolated incident. Nazarenko's second novel, The Taste of Less, a polarizing 190-page paragraph written in the first person, focuses on starvation. The author lost a rumored forty pounds over the eight-month course of its writing, not a small percentage of the five-foot, six-inch woman's body mass. Photographs show a skeletal figure in dark glasses walking the streets of Cape Town, where the novel is set. Hospital records also show that Nazarenko admitted herself to a psychiatric ward after writing her next book, Never Sweeter, which centers on the intertwined lives of five serial killers.

Although I arrive at our scheduled lunch with the intent to ease into discussions of these topics, Nazarenko does not. The first sen-

tence she says to me is, "Nadiya,"
and after an agonizing handshake,
the second is, "To preempt the fore-
play, I didn't murder anybody for
Never Sweeter." Somehow, she makes
this sound charming.

(Continued on page 6)

From: Laila Piedra <lpiedra2000@gmail.com>

To: Tim Madison <timothy.j.madison87@gmail.com>

Subject: stuff   5:03 PM

Hi Mr. Madison,

I get why you were talking up the substitute now. I can't believe Dr. Greene got somebody famous to substitute at good old Impact Future Leaders Charter School. Actually, I can't believe Dr. Greene knows somebody famous.

I still wish you were back, though. She's failing everybody. Some people shouldn't be trusted with power. Hannah sent me this article, and apparently, Nazarenko's also a murderer. Here's a link, hopefully they can print it out. Hi, printing-out person!

http://lettersmagazine.com/2017/method-author.html

I asked Felix about what he did when he had his concussion, and he said he listened to podcasts. If you want to listen to something, the audiobooks for *In the After Path* are awesome. The narrator sounds like the voice of God. Also, Hannah, Leo, Felix, and I are going to start watching the new *The Rest* season tonight! Finally. I can write you recaps of it since you can't watch TV, if you want.

I guess that's it. Camille and I aren't fighting anymore, thank God.

I hope you're feeling better and I hope you'll be able to write back.

Laila

7

"FINALLY," HANNAH SAID. "COME IN."

"I still beat Felix, right?" Laila stepped in from the cold light of the streetlamps.

Hannah closed the door and shut out the dark. "Obviously you still beat Felix. You could get incinerated by a comet and get reincarnated and make an odyssey across three continents and still beat Felix."

In the mudroom, crusts of slush were drooling off Leo's sneakers amid half a dozen pairs of Hannah's shoes. As Laila pulled off her boots, Hannah asked, "Did you read the article?"

"Yeah."

"It's wild, right? Did she like your story?"

Laila shook her head and tried not to remember the precise red loops of the number 32. All she wanted was to sit in a dark room with her friends, not talk, and watch beautiful people struggle in glorious high-definition. "Is the TV set up?" she asked.

"Yep." Hannah let the change of subject go without protest. "My parents use that thing so little, it's still set up from season eleven."

"Despite hiatus?"

"Despite our sadist-ass showrunners and their Chinese-water-torture release schedules, yeah. Come on."

Laila followed her into the foyer, where chevrons of hardwood zigzagged away toward the kitchen. Overhead, a light fixture trembled like an extravagant mobile, discs of glass suspended by delicate fibers from gold-brushed rods. She'd never quite grown numb to this place. Laila, Felix, and Leo hadn't known that Hannah came from obscene wealth until late freshman year, when they'd shown up for a *The Rest* watch party here, in Brooklyn Heights, to discover that her family owned a six-story townhouse. The place could have passed for a small museum, each floor a confection of heavy brocades, lines of antique Korean pottery, and gilt-framed oil art. Laila still remembered the knot of nervous laughter that had yanked tight in the middle of her throat the first time she'd crossed this threshold, and the way she'd met Leo's eyes, then Felix's, knowing they were restraining the same shout of disbelief.

"My parents say I've got to be home by 10," Laila said. "School night."

"Okay. We can still fit three episodes in if you take a cab home."

"I don't have—"

"I'll get it," Hannah said, and Laila didn't argue. Hannah had funded so many late-night cab rides for the others that Laila had begun to suspect she was trying to irritate her parents by spending as much money as possible, as if they would ever notice. Hannah's parents hardly ever even seemed to come down from their fourth-floor quarters.

"Correction," Hannah said, glancing at her phone, "we can still fit three episodes in if Felix gets his ass here in the next ten minutes, which he'd better, or I'm going to kill him."

"You should probably sharpen your weapon of choice," Laila said.

Hannah took a running jump onto the living room sofa. Leo bounced with her impact. He was scrolling through something on his phone, a snow-dusted beanie pulled low over his locked hair.

"Speaking of which," Hannah said, putting her feet up on a wine-colored ottoman the size of a bed, "when you write me into your next story, can you give me a space halberd?"

"Ignore her, Leo," Laila said.

"You know I am," Leo said. He tucked his phone away. "But if she gets a space halberd, I get a sword that opens passages in the fabric of space-time."

"Fine."

When Felix arrived bundled in a parka, Hannah was sprawled at the base of the massive television, remote balanced on her stomach. "Finally," she announced, pressing the power button, "His Highness deigns to join us peasants." The screen flickered from dead black to live black, slightly indigo-tinted. Hannah rose to her feet with a pointed stretch and yawn at Felix, her red hair bobbing ostentatiously against her grandparents' sea of faded art. "Anybody want something to drink?"

"Gee, thanks, honey," said Felix. "And when I get home tomorrow, there better be dinner on the table."

"Honestly, go to hell," Hannah said. "Leo? Drink?"

"I'm all good," Leo said. Laila must have blinked, because his hand was now overflowing with chocolate-covered raisins that he was siphoning into his mouth. His pocket rattled, chocolate shell against thin cardboard. God knew how Leo ate exclusively trash and maintained a waistline that was approximately the circumference of Laila's left thigh.

Hannah fetched a pair of beers for her and Felix. "Don't spill any of that on the upholstery," she told him, and then she closed her eyes. "Oh my God, that was the most mom thing I've ever said. You have to forget that happened."

"Too late," Leo said.

"*It is written, never to be unmade*," Felix rasped in the voice of the child prophet from *The Rest*. Laila grinned. Felix's impressions of the cast members were unparalleled, but he refused to put them on the Internet no matter how much Laila and Hannah urged him.

As Hannah settled beside her, Laila hit the light, turning the living room into a black cavern. Hannah pressed her thumb deep into the gummy resistance of the *play* button. The screen lit up and swallowed the rest of the world.

A beautiful bullet of a spaceship arced through an asteroid belt, past stones mottled purple and gray, withered as peach pits. The mute rush of space evolved into a tinny whine, then a roar as the camera rushed between platinum hullplates into the spaceship's interior. A smooth shot tracked through kilometers of white-tiled hall, over neon filigree laced into steel walkways. Then, at last, appeared rows of murky human forms suspended in their tanks, cryogenic fluid shifting through the clouds of their hair. The drone of spaceship operation tapered. A slow shot passed through the glass into a tank, focused on a woman's face. This was Grayson, one of Laila's biggest *The Rest* crushes. Grayson was earnest and optimistic, brave and unyielding, one of those characters who got landed with a new romance every season because the showrunners killed off her love interests with sadistic regularity.

Darkness followed a tremor of the camera. A bulbous blue eye flashed, and beneath it glinted a greenish tooth the size of a forearm. They went under with Grayson, into the nightmarish chasm where her mind would fight for its life, along with every other surviving member of the ship, against monsters of incomprehensible quantity and ferocity.

They watched three episodes without speaking. *The Rest* was sacred and could not be interrupted. Against all odds—the Yahoo! hosting, the *twelfth* season—Laila's mind crept outside the borders of her body, transplanted into this imagined space like the first time she'd watched this story. She lost herself to the point that she jerked whenever someone dodged a scything claw. She hardly breathed during the rapture scene back on the dying Earth when the nine-year-old prophet boy removed his oxygen mask.

In the brief gap between episodes two and three, she came back to herself enough to recognize her own exhilaration. Someday Laila was going to reproduce this in somebody. This was all she wanted to do with her time alive: make something, anything, that would grip someone—anyone—like she was being gripped. Make someone feel seen, as she felt seen, and transported, as she felt utterly elsewhere. Make someone feel as free and light as dust.

After episode three hit the credits, Hannah killed the TV and cracked her knuckles, a horrible rippling pulse of sound. "Thoughts?"

Laila couldn't answer. There were too many sentences percolating, all punctuated with frothing excitement and capital letters, none fully formed.

"The dude who wrote the books tweeted that he thinks this is the best season since five," Felix said, his phone illuminating the scruff along his jawline. "But he's got that hard-on for Lilly Whatever, so who knows if that's his actual opinion or if he's talking through his dick."

"Again with the unwanted penis imagery," said Hannah, but Felix didn't reply. His heavy brows had pushed together, and now he was typing so violently he could have been trying to punch holes in his Android.

"What's up?" Laila asked.

After a silent moment, Leo said, knowingly, "Is it your dad?"

"Nah," Felix said. "Sebastian. He says Samuel Marquez is trying to come to my birthday party and fight."

"Like, fight *you*?" Laila said. Then she realized Leo and Hannah were both looking at her. They did this whenever Samuel Marquez passed their lunch table, too. Her temperature rose a half-dozen degrees. "Don't look at me," she squeaked.

"Sorry, cabrón, you're not getting through the door," Felix muttered, thumbs darting across his screen. A cheerful bloop announced the arrival of another message from Sebastian, and Felix sat forward, making Hannah's sofa creak. "All right, that's bullshit." Felix looked around at them. "She dumped him like a month ago, and he's telling me to back off, can you believe this guy?"

"Ah," Hannah said, taking a long swig of beer. "Imani."

"Just don't escalate, Felix," Laila said tiredly.

Hannah snorted. "You'd have a better shot telling a literal escalator not to escalate."

"I'm not starting anything. It's Marquez," Felix said. "He's acting like I'm making Imani go out with me. She's going out with me because she wants to." He smoothed back his dark curls to punctuate how ridiculous it was that he would have to make any girl go out with him.

"Well," Leo said, "good thing somebody here is dying to talk some sense into him."

They were all looking at her again. "What are you talking about?" Laila said. "I've never even spoken to the guy."

"Might I remind you," Hannah drawled, "of sophomore year in April, when he, I don't know, asked you for a pencil or something, and I had to listen to you talking about how making eye contact with him felt like getting set on fire?"

"Hannah!"

Felix cackled. Laila shoved Hannah, who let the momentum throw her back against the sofa arm. "God, why do I tell you anything?"

"Why do you tell me *everything*," Hannah corrected, with a wicked smile. Whenever she talked about Samuel, she used a tone of blistering irony that made everything twice as humiliating. She lay down on the sofa, her knees hooked up over the arm now, crown of her head nudging Laila's thigh. "Whatever. We're entitled to tease you after watching you do nothing for three years. Right, Felix? Leo?"

"Hmm?" Leo said, face obscured by his phone. "I mean, yeah. Yeah. For sure." Laila snuck a look at his screen. Angela had texted him a photo of herself with an Australian Shepherd puppy, whose pink tongue was lapping her dimpled cheek. Sometimes the pair of them were so sickeningly cute that Laila wondered if the whole thing was staged.

"Drop it, okay?" Laila pleaded. "Just hire a bouncer or something, Felix. You're not going to brainwash me into making an idiot out of myself in front of him."

"Did you say 'brainwash'?" Felix turned toward her, making the oaken sofa whine. "Hang on," he murmured. Felix had long eyelashes that made his deep-set eyes look absurdly dramatic whenever he showed the slightest hint of worry. "Wait."

"What?" Laila said.

"They've . . . *they've deleted the files.*" He broke into the voice of the quartermaster aboard the USR *Washington*, nasal and high-pitched. *"Her brain, it's washed. Her memories! They're gone!"*

"Dude," Hannah said.

Leo dropped his phone for once, leapt up from his pouf, and donned the pilot's thick Southern accent. *"And all that's left is . . . good God and damnation! Switch to live view. The Raveners—they've got her!"* He staggered toward the sofa with his hands forming claws.

"Leo," Hannah warned him. "Leo, d—"

"Aaaaagh!" Leo clamped a hand to his chest and toppled onto the sofa. His back impacted directly into Hannah's stomach. Her breath thumped out, her mouth popping open so wide that Laila could see the dark aperture of her throat, the rosebuds of her tonsils.

"Dammit fuck," Hannah wheezed. "Oh my *God*, I think you cracked my ribs."

A helpless, high-pitched giggle. Laila clapped her hand to her mouth to strangle the sound, but Hannah was already staring up at her in comical betrayal, and Felix started hooting, too, sliding down his side of the sofa until his back went flat against the seat cushion. Laila's laughter began to tug down at her stomach, to steal her breath, and she keeled over until Leo's wrist slid across her back, Hannah's head shifting in her lap, her own legs buried densely in the soft velveteen, bare ankle against somebody's denim. "Y'all are so fucking weird," Felix said, muffled, from somewhere in the mass of them locked together. "You know that, right?"

"*The mind collective has fearsome patterns*," Hannah croaked. She couldn't even hold the boy prophet's accent until the end of the sentence. They dissolved again. Laughter formed coils around them, thick rings between their bodies and the world. The galaxy drew in and in until its entire contents were this room, hardwood to crown molding, this light, gold splashes from low iron cages, and the feeling of this proximity, heat, and security. The timeline had broken like a seal and let loose something weightless. For a crystal instant, Laila was borne up on its back and was invulnerable and immortal, and she was never going to let them go.

"HEY. LAILA. *LAILA.*"

Her nose had been buried so deeply between the pages of *In the After Path*, volume XIV, that a muscle in her neck pulled when she looked up. Peter Goldman had materialized six inches away, angled toward her in a way that forced his feet to shuffle sideways in a crab walk. He palmed his phone into his jacket and then snaked one freckled forearm into his backpack to sort through a clutter of chewed pens, all while keeping pace and watching her intently, because Peter Goldman never did only one thing at one time. There was a weird grace to the kid's simultaneous movements. For somebody with the bodily structure of a Pez dispenser, he operated with shocking confidence.

Rubber soles whined behind them. Now Laila did stop walking. The quintet of basketball guys from their class trailed behind Peter, expectant, much like a school of scavengers might trail a shark. This felt off to Laila. The basketball team was known to be cool, and Peter Goldman was known to have the popularity of gonorrhea, but spatially speaking, Peter Goldman was clearly the ringleader of whatever was happening here. A semicircular one-foot margin separated him from his—what, cronies? They looked like cronies.

"Hi, Peter," she said, not looking at Samuel Marquez. Leo's voice nagged at the back of her mind, telling her to do it, bite the bullet, swallow the cyanide, talk to him. She was convinced that if she ever spoke words to him, a chemical reaction would catalyze somewhere in her lower torso and she would burst into flame. She kept picturing Hannah's scornful expression. Clearly Hannah thought there was no chance.

"Hey, what are you up to," Peter told her. That was the thing about Peter. His questions sounded like suggestions. His suggestions sounded like declarations of superiority.

"I'm going to the cafeteria," Laila said. "Because, you know, it's lunch."

"No, hang on," Peter said. "I want to talk about Nazarenko."

Her face must have let involuntary interest show, because, looking satisfied, Peter opened the nearest classroom door. The room was dark and vacant. Peter flicked the lights, and the basketball guys slouched in behind him. Laila considered running, but curiosity overpowered her sense of reason, and she followed.

"Okay." Peter shut the door. "What'd you get on that paper she gave back yesterday?"

"Wow. That is so far from your business."

"Look, I don't care. It doesn't matter to me. Actually, none of this matters to me, I got into my school early decision." (Dartmouth. Everyone knew he was going to Dartmouth.) "But everyone got an F on what we turned in, and it's going to mess with people's class ranks and GPAs, so for people who aren't accepted yet, it's a problem, so I'm just looking out for everybody, and obviously she doesn't know how to teach. Right? It's obvious, right?"

The basketball guys' heads bobbed, except Samuel Marquez's, because he was checking his phone. A safe window to look at him. Laila took advantage for a blissful instant. He was tall and crooked, hip angled, head tilted perpetually, one hand always twisted into a pocket of his jeans, so secure in his ungainly composite parts that he seemed older than everybody else in his grade. Hannah was the same way.

Laila looked back at Peter. She didn't want to agree with any of what he'd just said, especially the implication that he was investigating this for anybody but himself, but the fact remained that she'd had a dream last night about a faceless Bowdoin admissions officer transforming into Nadiya Nazarenko and blowing up her application with a nuclear weapon, so maybe there was something worthwhile in hearing him out.

"I got an F, too," she said.

Triumph drew him upward. "I *knew* it," he said, and shuffled out his assignment. "Like, look at this! Madison gave this a 99." He flipped it to the back page. "And she—" *22/100*. Laila shouldn't have been so satisfied that she'd beaten Peter's score. That wasn't an achievement.

"What are you planning on doing?" Laila asked.

"Getting us a new teacher, obviously."

She stiffened. *No*—he couldn't get Nazarenko fired. Laila hadn't proven herself yet. "Greene won't replace her," she said. "There's no way."

"You don't know that," Peter said. "If everyone tells their parents, they'll *make* Greene get rid of her."

The basketball guys traded looks. Clearly Peter hadn't pitched the parent section of the plan to them yet. Laila hated the idea of asking her parents to fix her school problems, as if she were some red-faced seven-year-old running off a playground to tattle. Some furious coalition of parents going over a teacher's head to the administration would be even worse. It seemed so entitled, like complaining to a hand-wringing store manager that an employee charged you an extra dollar.

Of course, telling their parents raised other problems. One of the basketball guys echoed her thoughts. "Bro," he said, "if my mom sees this thing, she's not making any calls for me. She's locking me in my room until I'm twenty-five."

"At least you got a two-digit number," said one of his friends.

"Also," Laila said, "first you'd have to make sure it *is* everybody who got an F."

"It is," Peter said. "We left you for last."

Laila frowned.

"We thought she might've given you something else," explained a second voice behind Peter. Laila scanned and experienced an imploding sensation. Samuel Marquez was looking at her. He'd had a previous thought about her. She comprised a fragment of his consciousness. That was ridiculous. Laila choked a little bit on her saliva.

"But now that we know it's everyone," Peter said, "we have ironclad proof that she's just an atrocious grader, so." He gave her a mocking salute. "Thanks for failing, too."

"No, hold up. She hasn't even been here a week. You have to wait."

"Oh, *do* I?"

"You were excited when she got here."

Peter looked half betrayed and half taken aback. "I mean, yeah, hello, because that was before she was a sadist."

"But this grade is going to change," Laila said. "She told us it would, so there's not a case yet."

"What is this? What's your point? Do you want her to stay?"

Laila was a terrible liar, so she asked with as much scorn as she could manage, "Do you *think* I want to keep getting Fs?"

Nobody answered. Good.

She looked around at the others. "I'm just saying, if we wait and she doesn't give out better grades after a couple weeks, then she doesn't have the easy excuse anymore. You know she's going to say she's training us to edit if parents make calls. We're all going to look oversensitive, and it won't change anything."

The mood of the basketball hivemind was shifting her way, nod by traded glance. *Of course* they were seduced by the idea of hiding these grades from their parents.

"Okay," Peter said. "Fine. Two weeks. But I don't see why she would change our grades when she isn't giving anybody notes. She's supposed to, you know, *teach*, being a *teacher*, but she hasn't put a single *word* on anyone's stuff."

"What?"

"Yeah. Nobody else got any comments, either. I asked everyone." Peter was filled with unstoppable momentum now, his weight shifting from neon sneaker to neon sneaker, one hand fanning the air wildly as he flipped through his assignment. "Look at this. Look! This is eight pages. It's like she didn't read it. Nothing."

Laila watched Peter's work flash by in grayscale animation,

but the shuffling flip of it, the piercing crack of his indignant voice, faded until a fast-growing whine of excitement drowned everything else. Those few red words she'd received. The space they occupied in her mind expanded and pulsed and hissed for her attention. Not a mark on anybody's pages, except hers.

As the others trailed toward the door, she felt fearless. "Hey," she said, before she could stop herself. "Samuel."

Samuel turned back to her, and she was pinned like a butterfly to corkboard. Then they were alone.

"What's up?" Samuel asked.

Oh, this was a mistake. She watched his lips curve around the words, and a kaleidoscopic burst of possibilities clouded around that tiny, boring phrase. She imagined him looking at her with the same casual consideration and asking other questions, quandaries about the meaning of life, unending what-ifs, ones she'd dreamed up for the both of them to ask and answer, the sorts of private, ridiculous questions she and Hannah traded at 3 A.M. during sleepovers. The idea that he could look at her for more than an instant and remain unaware of her fascination was mind-boggling.

"You, um," she said, and flooded back into her body, and realized she had nothing coherent to say. "I heard you told Sebastian—I'm friends with Felix, is the, yeah."

Samuel's mouth formed a stubborn line. "What about him?"

"Don't fight him. Please. He's an idiot. You can figure this out without hitting each other."

"If he's an idiot, why are you friends with him?"

"What, none of your friends ever act like idiots?"

Samuel considered her for a long moment. Then a smile broke his surly expression. She felt like she'd grown three inches taller, but she had to look away. How could somebody have teeth that white and skin that smooth without digital enhancement? Did he even have pores?

"Look," he said, more calmly. "I got no problem with you. I don't want to fight, but tell Martinez to leave Imani alone. If he doesn't, I can't make any promises, I'm happy to get into it, you know what I'm saying?"

Laila nodded. She didn't actually know what he was saying. Most of that had seemed contradictory. But she'd had fifteen functional seconds of conversation with Samuel Marquez, and that deserved some sort of affirmative gesture.

"Sorry about Goldman, by the way," he said. "Dude said he had a *plan*, he didn't say he meant telling our parents. My dad would kill me."

"God, same," Laila said, and unspoken understanding passed between them. God bless Latin parents, bringing people together. "Hopefully Nazarenko's trying to help us."

"Maybe." Samuel put his shoulders back so he seemed a little taller, a little broader. "You know," he said, "she wrote something on *my* paper. I didn't want to say anything 'cause all the guys were so mad she didn't even underline anything on theirs."

"Wait." Laila yanked her story out. "Me, too. What'd she put on yours?"

He showed her. From what she skimmed, Samuel's story was about a guy trying to sleep with his best friend's sister. Nazarenko had circled a description reading, "The way she touched him made him feel on fire down there," and had written, "Sounds as if he may need medical attention." Laila tried so hard not to laugh that she wound up blinking tears out of her eyes. God, and now all she could imagine was Samuel Marquez feeling "on fire down there." She didn't know where to look. His face was definitely off limits. All she could think was how hysterically Hannah would laugh when she heard about this.

"You think she's trying to say something?" Samuel asked. "Like maybe we didn't actually fail?"

Laila took a slow breath to deflate the bubble of hysteria. She considered the possibility that these were throwaway comments, but this was Nadiya Nazarenko. The way she walked, the way she spoke, the way she turned her head—every fraction of every movement was dangerously precise. She pictured this woman who met a reporter having calculated his thoughts so extensively that she could address his biggest question before he'd even said a word. She didn't think Nazarenko could do something careless if she tried.

"I hope that's what she means," said Samuel. She could tell from his inflection that he was surprised to find himself saying any of this aloud. "The guys talked me into taking the intro class, but I actually like this. I don't know. I thought I was okay at writing." He shrugged his big shoulders, looking self-conscious.

Laila knew she was taking too long to reply, but over years of keeping subconscious tabs on Samuel Marquez's behavior, she'd never once suspected he might be in Mr. Madison's class because he *wanted* to be there. Did that assumption make her judgmental? Unobservant? Also, if she'd thought he was just some basketball player who didn't care about writing, or reading, or school, why had she been fascinated by him?

No, she knew why. Because he was a pipe dream, and they'd seemed to have nothing in common, and he was beautiful and distant and she wanted to strive for the beautiful distant things her entire life. She had no idea what to do now that there was something between them, some tiny fragment he'd seen fit to share with her. Her thoughts were accelerating dangerously. If he'd shown her a pensive side of himself he never let slip in class, soon enough, they could both be sharing vulnerabilities. She would learn a hundred thousand things she could never have guessed about him. Maybe he had an athletic older brother in whose footsteps he'd unwillingly followed, but secretly he longed to be the next Junot Díaz. Maybe he had a childhood memory he'd never revealed to anyone—the huge, terrifying feeling of looking up into the white-painted strut ceilings of a Home Depot and realizing he had no idea where his parents were, and he'd squatted by the 3/8-inch zinc-plated hex nuts waiting for them to call his name over the intercom—the sort of microscopic fiber in the fabric of his life that Laila ached to know, that she was sure nobody else would ever have sought from him. Maybe Samuel Marquez, the blank slate of her imagination, was actually as kind as Leo, as loyal as Felix, as brilliant as Hannah, and maybe he would decide the same things of her, and then as graduation approached, a sudden, unplanned first kiss would turn into a first date would turn into first everything, and it would all feel like a stream of high-octane adventure rather than reality. Some heightened version of the truth. They would brush hands, and it would feel like the end of the world.

Before Laila could let her frenetic mental calculations slow down, before she could allow logic or fear back in, she said, "I think every word means something."

He looked at her from the frizzy part zigzagged into her thick hair to the soft sweater Camille had replaced to the rhinestone watch at her wrist to the knotted and re-knotted neon laces of her sneakers. "Hey," he said, "what if we kept comparing notes? I bet we can figure her out."

She nodded, they locked eyes, and Laila saw the same thirst she felt. Not for each other, but for the idea that they could each be something great.

She abandoned the hall to the cafeteria, strode for the stairwell, and ran up four flights. Pits of her lungs aching, she came into the elective hall and through the door to find Nazarenko still at her stool, chewing, something splayed in her lap that she was reading with a frown. Her jaw moved with a left bent when she bit down. To see the woman eat felt invasive. Bodily functions didn't fit her aesthetic.

Laila fussed with the zipper on her jacket, grasping for extra seconds of preparation. By the time she faced Nazarenko properly, she had caught her breath and felt, if not ready, on the verge of it.

"Yes?" Nazarenko said.

Laila strode up the aisle, her fists tight at the outer curves of her thighs, holding her body fast under the probable onslaught. "You only left notes for me and Samuel," she said. "You wanted us to ask."

Nazarenko flicked an apple core into the trash. "Ask?" she said, not looking at Laila. She wasn't grading papers, Laila realized, or reading a Hannah-style tome. She was paging through a catalog of cooking utensils.

"Ask for advice," Laila said. "For—I don't know, for an explanation."

"And . . . that's why you're here," said Nazarenko, surveying a page full of stainless-steel nonstick pans. "To relay this epiphany."

"Yes. I mean, no. I want to know what you thought about my story. What you *really* thought."

Nazarenko flicked to the next page of her magazine. Whisks and butcher knives. "What do you do outside school?"

"What?"

"What do you do, Piedra. Outside school."

"I . . . I basically just write."

"What else?"

Laila balked. "I don't know, I—"

"You don't know."

"Reading. I read a lot."

"That was assumed," Nazarenko said. "Do you have friends?"

"Yeah, of course I have—"

"What do you do together?"

"We, um . . . we watch this show we all like." It sounded as small and miserable in the open as she'd worried it might.

Nazarenko let the magazine slap onto Mr. Madison's desk. She extracted her notebook from her coat and paged through with excruciating deliberateness. At last she stopped, looked up at Laila, and tapped the page three times with her index finger. "You have two choices," she said. "I can read this to you, or you can leave now."

Laila held still, staring at the window of jagged red lines beneath Nazarenko's nail.

"Very well." Nazarenko lifted the notebook. Laila had the sensation of sitting on the subway tracks as the J train roared toward her.

"This student can write a coherent narrative and turn a distinct phrase. Unfortunately, her piece's strengths end well within those confines. The plot contains nothing original, nothing even passingly surprising, and I can only assume that the student has tried to substitute pulp science-fiction narratives for her own life, given that there are no echoes of reality's chaos or contradictions here. Rather than lacing a predictable otherworld setting with incomprehensible jargon, the student would do well to refocus her efforts on building a world through the creation of a character with a detailed history. Unfortunately, she seems disinterested in character altogether."

Nazarenko licked the tip of her thumb and turned the page, a process that seemed to last several months.

"This piece," Nazarenko went on, still with perfect neutrality, "is a portrait of war and risk drawn by a person who has clearly never seen the face of either. The student doesn't seem to grasp that the enormity of loss stems from the fundamental assumption that human life is interesting and valuable. This is a story about the supposed destruction of humanity populated with not a single recognizable human being."

Laila tried to swallow, but something against the back walls of her mouth was dry and refused to grip, and she thought, for a second, that she might choke. When *had* she risked anything, really? She looked back through her life and saw a procession of school-day routines, chores, conversational chatter. She felt like a witness to the massacre of all her time. For a horrible moment, she wondered if she'd only ever written science fiction to build an escape chute from her life's insistent monotone.

Nazarenko placed the notebook back into her pocket. "Revisions are due Monday morning."

Laila nodded, but she couldn't leave and couldn't reply. In the thick silence, she heard an echo of a second, more familiar voice. "Have you ever considered that getting some distance from a piece could be valuable?" Mr. Madison, she realized, had been giving her the same advice.

A reservoir of energy loomed suddenly behind a dam Laila hadn't known was there, walled up between her ribs and skin. She had to surface from her virtual reality, rip the intubation from her throat, and let the world pour in. She had to mine real life for raw material until her product came out of the furnace alive and breathing, sternum heaving, blood raging. She was going to make something that even this watching figure, wordless and elegant, perched on a pedestal before her, couldn't ignore.

Still her words were quiet and halting. "So what do I do?"

Nazarenko gave her a thin, unpleasant smile. "You never ask that question again."

Laila (3:47 p.m.): Felix, what time is your party tomorrow?

Laila (3:47 p.m.): Hannah, shut up

Hannah (3:48 p.m.): ? I didn't say anything?

Laila (3:48 p.m.): You were typing something obnoxious

Laila (3:49 p.m.): I could smell it in the air

Laila (3:49 p.m.): like sewage

Laila (3:50 p.m.): "omg are you actually going to LEAVE your HOUSE"

Hannah (3:51 p.m.): fair.

Felix (6:27 p.m.): lol its at 9.

Hannah (6:30 p.m.): SEE YOU THEN, HERMIT

She was pulling at bits of her torso, brown pinches of flesh that didn't seem to sit in the right place. The shirt had fit last year and was one of the only pieces of clothing she owned that felt presentational. The neckline drew a diagonal from the left side of her neck to her right armpit, preempting a sleeve. For Laila, a one-shouldered shirt was the outer boundary of edgy fashion. Mostly she owned landscape clothing: heathery T-shirts, dark denim jeans, and black pants so nondescript that they could disappear into any backdrop. She'd had experience with being physically noticed in elementary school and would gladly have lived the rest of her life without repeating any of that.

Nobody had given her serious trouble about her weight for years, but being the fat kid in elementary school was so much visibility so early, it created an impact that never really smoothed away. Every identity felt final and fateful back then—being the smart kid or the quiet kid or the short kid—even if the traits didn't stick, even if they weren't actually accurate. In Laila's memory of fifth grade, a boy named Jeremy Bowman had the freakish shape of a stick insect, impossibly tall and knobbed at every joint. She'd looked at a yearbook last fall and the discrepancy had stunned her. In those photos, he was normal. Sure, on the tall side for a ten-year-old: maybe five foot one, with a more triangular jawline than the other kids. But Laila remembered a caricature. So she suspected that in everybody else's caricatured memories, she wasn't the chubby little girl from the photos, either, but something exaggerated to the point of distortion, and that was the old version of herself she carried around, too: mostly invented, impactful anyway.

"Lolly, I love that shirt," said her mother, who had appeared in the door.

Laila met her eyes in the mirror. "Really?"

"Yes, really, absolutely," said her mother, who never used just one affirmative when she could use eight. "I haven't seen you wear it since last year. You know, I thought about giving it away."

Her mother had hardly entered the room before she started straightening up. Laila's grandparents owned a bed-and-breakfast in Quebec, and her mother still had habits left over from working there when she was young. Instinctive cleaning, stacking the family's plates whenever they ate at a restaurant, using a towel to smooth stray water off the edges of a sink after she washed her hands.

"Are you going somewhere?" she asked.

"Yeah," Laila said. "Felix's eighteenth birthday party."

"Oh, wonderful. Getting out and about will be good for you, I think. What a tough couple of weeks, huh?"

"I've had better," said Laila, wondering if her mother was trying to coax out some secret anguish about Mr. Madison's accident. She wasn't wearing the Deep Sympathy facial expression, so that was a good sign.

"Well, wish him happy birthday from me," her mother said. "Felix is so nice. So handsome." She raised her eyebrows, which, unlike the rest of her hair, were the dark color of burnt caramel.

"Stop. He's dating someone, Mom."

"That's a shame."

"No, it's not." Laila laughed. "I don't know why you're so set on me dating him."

"Because he's a good friend," said her mother. "Your father was my best friend for years before we started seeing each other." She stopped behind Laila, arranging Laila's volumes of hair. Laila loved seeing herself beside her mother. At five foot ten and a half, Laila hardly ever felt small, but her mother still had half a head's height on her. Anything less would have made her father look like somebody who'd married a gnome.

"And," her mother added, "Felix is so *nice*."

"Okay," Laila said, bemused. "Are you worried I'm going to date somebody who isn't nice?"

Her mother's hands rested on her shoulders, her nails ten beads of uneven blue that Camille had lacquered with a gummed-up brush. "Well, Hannah is your best friend."

The hesitance in her mother's voice was the only thing that gave Laila the restraint not to shrug her grip off. Even then, her voice came out more snappish than she intended. "I'm not dating Hannah."

The sentence felt strange to say. She pictured Hannah then, suddenly and vividly, the way her lips pulled to the side when she was thinking hard, the pair of dark freckles seeded into her brown irises. Even in her imagination, Hannah looked unimpressed. Laila's face grew warm, and she couldn't meet her mother's eyes anymore. "I should go," she said. "I'm going to be late."

"So, we're obscenely early," Hannah said, thumbing Felix's buzzer.

"What? We're on time. Didn't he say nine? He definitely said nine."

"Like I said: obscenely early."

During the walk up to Felix's fourth-floor apartment in Crown Heights, Hannah gave a summary of every person invited, divided into two tiers: those Felix wanted to come, half of whom wouldn't show up, and those Felix didn't actually want in his place, but whom he'd invited anyway to fill space. "Anyway," Hannah said, "we're going to beat everybody there, so we can introduce you to whatever other weird people come an hour and a half early. God, I hope Samuel doesn't show up." Hannah glanced over at Laila. "Did you end up . . . I don't know, talking to him, or whatever?"

Laila didn't know why she hadn't told Hannah yet. After meeting with Nazarenko yesterday, she'd retreated to the cafeteria and sat quietly while the others dreamed up ideas for Leo and Angela's fifth-anniversary celebration. Laila had said nothing about Samuel, about his secret interest in writing, about the pact they'd made to play Nazarenko's game together, and she felt even more reluctant now.

She wasn't afraid Hannah would tease her. They teased each other about absolutely everything, with contractual regularity. Mentioning those ten minutes in the classroom felt wrong in a different way. She didn't know how Hannah would react. How could this be the thing that was too personal to share?

"No," Laila said. "I, um, I thought about saying something, but I got scared."

Hannah's expression cleared. "Yep. Obsession is the root of all fear."

"I'm not *obsessed* with him. He's just a perfect physical specimen."

Hannah laughed. "So romantic. When somebody talks about me like I'm a science fair experiment, I'll know I've found The One."

"Oh, Hannah," Laila said in a dreamy voice. "Your hair is redder than an algae bloom that would cause massive coastal die-offs."

"Perfect. Where's my engagement ring?"

"Hidden in the Champagne we can't legally buy yet."

Grinning, they passed an apartment door that leaked a cloud of weed scent down the hall and another decorated with a bedraggled wreath.

"So," Hannah said, "why'd you change your mind, hermit?"

Laila wanted to tell Hannah what Nazarenko had said, the accusation that Laila hadn't lived enough for her writing to come alive, but her voice failed again. Hearing the criticism had been humiliating, but telling Hannah would be worse. Maybe Hannah even agreed with Nazarenko. Hadn't she told Laila again and again that someday she'd look back and have regrets?

"I wanted to make sure Felix didn't get his nose broken," she said, finally.

"For real," Hannah said. "It would ruin the celebratory atmosphere." She banged on Felix's door. "FBI, open up."

In the tense moment before Felix answered, Laila dipped her fingers into her coat to pull at her neckline. Hannah had reassured her that nobody cared what anybody else wore to house parties. Apparently somebody had worn a fluorescent blue Morphsuit to Isabella Bianchi's start-of-school party last August. But, planning for the temperature of Felix's apartment when it was twenty people beyond fire-code capacity, Laila had changed her one-sleeved shirt for the only tank top she owned. This was beginning to feel like a dangerous move. She hadn't worn this since the summer before junior year, and now her boobs bubbled up toward the scoop neck as if they were trying to make an escape. The rest of the tank top, of course, sagged around her ribcage like a sock stretched out by thirty years of wear, but hugged her stomach in a death grip. So many plus-size clothes fit like they'd been modeled on a thin person's body and expanded outward, so they weren't appropriate for an actual fat girl so much as a thin person digitally magnified to computer-glitch dimensions.

"Hey," Hannah said.

"What?"

"You'll be fine, L."

Before Laila could accuse her of secretly being a nice person, Felix answered the door visibly drunk and waved them in. "Laila! You made it? For real?"

"Yeah, try not to choke." She hugged him. "Happy birthday, old man."

"Where's your mom?" Hannah asked. "Did you lock her in there?" She nodded to the corner. Felix had moved the sofa against his mom's bedroom door and rotated the bookcase toward the wall, hiding the glass knickknacks on the shelves.

"She's at the restaurant," Felix said. His mother was a manager and bartender at a steakhouse in Fort Greene whose prices made even Hannah cringe. Her schedule rendered Felix's curfew basically nonexistent, although it didn't stop his mom from trying.

Felix's wrestling friends stormed him. Laila mumbled a greeting to them and followed Hannah to a cooler on the kitchen counter.

Hannah slapped an icy beer into Laila's hand. The can's weight felt stupidly significant, like the key to a gateway beyond which lay her second life. She wondered if Camille would think differently about her if she knew Laila was drinking. Laila wouldn't have been surprised if Camille were drinking already. Her friends were the type, the early-blooming even-featured girls who acted invincible, looked invincible, were for all intents and purposes invincible. Laila didn't even know how to pretend to be anything other than perpetually vulnerable.

"Need some help?" Hannah said, taking Laila's can, popping the tab, and handing it back.

"Thanks, so helpful, I've never opened a can before."

Hannah grinned. "You looked nervous. Have some."

Laila steeled herself and took a long drink. She resisted the temptation to gag. The sticky fizz itched down her throat like contaminated water and left a rancid aftertaste.

"Awful, right?" Hannah said. "Don't worry, after three of those, you won't care about the taste."

"Three? Veto." Laila knew how that story went. After three beers, she would be staggering drunk. Then she would spot Samuel Marquez across Felix's living room and think it was a great idea to try and talk to him. She would hesitate; Hannah would cajole her, possibly drag her over. After she sufficiently humiliated herself, she would leave the party crying and swearing to herself that she'd never do this again.

"One beer," she said. "One."

"Your body processes a drink an hour," Hannah said. "Drinking one beer at a five-hour party is like drinking one coffee to get through the week. Oh, look, the whole gang's here."

Leo grabbed Hannah into a hug with a swish of his windbreaker. "Hey, tiny," he said.

"Where's your girl?" she said, still suspended in the air. "Do I need to hide?"

"Angela's still on the train and still doesn't hate you," Leo said. His high, mild voice was nearly swallowed in the bopping bass. He put Hannah down and shucked off his windbreaker. "Back me up, Laila."

"Uh," Laila said. Angela had once asked Laila if they were all friends with Hannah out of pity.

The door flew open, rescuing Laila. A communal "HEY" of recognition roared from corner to corner as a dozen people streamed in. Felix flicked off the living room light, leaving only a diffuse fluorescent glow seeping westward from the kitchen counter, and the tall windows punctured with the distant Manhattan skyline, the gray wash of cloud that netted eight million lights. The fourth-floor walkup had the uninterrupted view going for it. With that tiny alteration, the awkward scattering of people lost in too much empty space transformed into a dim, intimate event. Laila would have been able to pretend it was classy if she hadn't been holding something that tasted like chilled extract of plastic bag.

The room broke into subdivisions. Around the bookshelf huddled a squad of phone-checking loners. The bright U-bend of the kitchen tiles rang with conversation. Music from a Bluetooth speaker clotted up in one corner, although a song couldn't finish before somebody hijacked the mix, creating a bizarre montage of moody electronica and bubblegum pop and Kendrick Lamar. The couch, inevitably, looked like a rough draft for a harem.

"I'm going to get another drink," said Hannah, who had already drained her first.

"Wait," Laila said, but Hannah ducked behind a guy wearing a superhero T-shirt. Then Laila was alone, surrounded by backs and arms and profile views of strangers' faces. She wasn't sure how her phone found her hand so quickly, as if a magnet in her palm had yanked it from her pocket, or bag, or wherever it had been. As she tapped from app to app, scrolling through previously read messages and an email inbox with no new emails, the jitters stayed at bay. Phones were magic. Now she was disguised as a girl who had some other calling in the world, which was of such pressing importance that surely she had no time to talk to *these* plebeians.

A pleasing blue icon alerted her to a new email. She opened it, triumphant. She wasn't even pretending anymore.

From: Tim Madison <timothy.j.madison87@gmail.com>
To: Laila Piedra <lpiedra2000@gmail.com>
Subject: stuff   9:12 PM

Hi Laila,

Thank you for the recommendations! I asked my nurse if she could hunt down those audiobooks, and she returned with a Walkman disc player and a stack of CDs. Between that and the yellow notepad I'm using to write this reply, I feel like a time traveler. I'll have to ask you not to reveal season twelve's secrets to me—unfortunately, I'm allergic to spoilers!—but it's kind of you to offer. I'll be able to use a screen myself in a week or two.

Ms. Nazarenko sounds like an interesting woman to meet in person! I hope the class isn't being too hard on her,

Laila snorted.

but I'm sure you'll all learn a great deal. She is truly a world-class author, one of my personal favorites! When I was a freshman in college, I loved telling people that *Catalina's Mothers* was my favorite novel, and I made good friends from doing so. Some books are made for conversation. If you haven't read that one, I would highly recommend it—a dynamic and mesmerizing story, not that she needs me to sing her praises!

Rest assured that I am in good hands, and doing well. I've begun physical therapy, which is hard work, but the team here are great people and to feel myself making progress is very satisfying.

Please do send your revised story when you get a chance!

Sincerely,

Mr. Madison

"Figures Felix would buy the worst beer ever," Hannah said, reappearing with another silver can. "I asked him where he was hiding the good shit, and he was like, that is the good shit, and I was like, you're hopeless."

"Hey! Hannah!" Two members of Hannah's other friend group pushed through the phone loners, dressed in boxy felt coats and wispy scarves. Laila knew the boy, Ethan Xu, but the other must have been Bridget Whitman, the new girl who had transferred last month, because Laila didn't think she'd ever seen her before. Impact Future Leaders Charter School wasn't small—fifteen hundred kids—but Laila knew the seniors' faces by now, especially the distinctive ones, and Bridget was distinctive. Wire-framed glasses encircled her spoon-round eyes. A silky chestnut bob clung to the middle of her neck, spiked earrings protruding from the curtains of hair like miniature flails.

"Hey, you two," Hannah said. "Bridget, this is Laila."

Laila stowed her phone into her pocket but left her fingers loosely curled around it. "Nice to meet you," she said.

"Yeah, absolutely. Nice to find out you're real," Bridget said. "Sorry. That sounded rude. We've got this joke that since Hannah's always talking about you and I've never seen you, you must be her imaginary girlfriend in Canada."

"Dude," Hannah muttered into the lip of her beer, "shut up."

Laila felt a sting of hurt. Felix teased Hannah about dating virtually any girl within eyeshot, and Hannah never sounded like that when she replied—so curt, so embarrassed. Was Hannah that humiliated at the idea of caring about her? Laila knew Hannah wanted people to think she was above earthly relationships, but Laila was also used to being the exception to all Hannah's rules.

Maybe Hannah regretted that Laila had come to this party at all, that she had to be associated with Laila. Laila turned her phone over and over in her pocket, wondering if she could leverage it to escape.

"Better than Ethan's fake boyfriend in Minnesota," Hannah added.

"*He's not fake, we met on the internet,*" Ethan said.

"And you two are adorable," Bridget said, with a knowing tone of placation that, for some reason, irritated Laila. Based on Hannah's stories, Laila had assigned Bridget a voice, height, and facial features that didn't at all pair with reality. The mismatch disconcerted her, as did the realization that she'd created some out-of-character fanfictional version of an actual human being. Real-life Bridget had, first of all, a lofty English accent. Hannah hadn't mentioned she was apparently a transfer from London. The voice itself emerged in a high, ethereal tone that reminded Laila of the dream-runner's voice in the *Moondowners* audiobook. With this girl's crinkled silver dress and widely spaced eyes, it was easy to picture her kidnapping dreams through a digital siphon and smuggling them over the bridge above Tan-Wua Chasm.

Also, why hadn't Hannah mentioned that Bridget was gorgeous? Hannah always mentioned when a girl was gorgeous. Laila glanced over at her, but Hannah was scrolling through Twitter.

"Oh, Hannah," Bridget said, "did you get a chance to send in my order?"

"Yeah, on it."

"Order for what?" Ethan said.

"I need a fake ID," Bridget said. "I get here two months after turning eighteen, and suddenly I'm not allowed to drink anymore. It's rubbish."

The beer sweated against Laila's palm. The novelty of this—the setting, the alcohol, the premeditated future lawbreaking—compounded, each element making the others exponentially more stressful. "How, um, how does it work?" she asked, trying to sound casual.

"There's this guy in Williamsburg," Hannah said. "He makes these new ones that scan and everything. You just send him, like, identity-theft amounts of information, and voilà."

"How much is it?" Laila asked.

Now Hannah was frowning. "Wait. Are you actually considering this? After two years of me badgering you?"

"Maybe," Laila replied. Now Hannah's eyes were fixed on hers, critical, probing. Laila had the sudden fear that Hannah could pull her conversation with Samuel Marquez from the recesses of her memory, that she would predict that Laila was only here because a teacher had told her to be here, and wasn't that pathetic? Laila's hand tightened on her phone. She checked her home screen just to break eye contact, but she knew the feeling of Hannah's scrutiny, and she knew Hannah hadn't stopped studying her.

"Oh my God," Ethan complained. Somebody at their back had hoisted the Bluetooth speaker onto his shoulder and was propelling it like a battering ram through the kitchen. He shoved at their circle, squeezing them out of the linoleum alley, and they spilled into the living room as the volume rose.

Most of the room had started dancing. Laila staggered into someone's shoulder. A quarter-size drop of beer leapt from her can, hit her thigh, and soaked a dark spot into the denim. A hand caught her shoulder, steadying her. "You okay?" said a girl with glitter trails painted down her face. The sound barely poked through the sampled guitar. Laila nodded. The crowd tumbled and rearranged her toward the sofa, where two couples (three? unclear) were entangled in practically Cubist strains of body parts. Her calves bumped a solid surface. She climbed up and backward to retreat, drained the last of her beer, and warmth sparked behind her cheeks, wrists, fingernails. She drew a hot breath of air recycled out of fifty throats. She wondered if this was the shard of the night she would remember in ten years, run up on a microfiber storage ottoman in the corner of Felix's living room, fingertips brushing his ceiling, looking out over a dark meadow of bobbing heads and bodies that jerked with the insistent buildup of the repeating electronic phrase. In the corner hovered a dozen illuminated rectangles clasped in dark hands. Outside, across the river, were buildings built out of stippled lights, high offices whose inhabitants were working too late, broadcasting their presence with lamps in the windows. Laila realized that she was tipsy, her mind skipping seconds, slipping vacantly across moments, and she lifted her phone and took a ten-second video to preserve the time more clearly, and the software made it loop, performing the same sweep of the room again and again from door to skyline, and up here, separated from all these people by a screen and two feet's height, she waited for a sudden hit of loneliness that didn't arrive.

10

Eden had been to the trading post every week for twelve years and had never seen the place so busy. The ceramic floor disappeared under herds of feet wrapped in brightly colored reinforced cloth. She ordered breakfast not to eat but to listen. She slid into one of the vertical booths that hovered in a corner and listened to the table of Southstar Defectors below, who were talking like Southstar Defectors did. Loudly. There were Ta'adrans in the back room, they said, who were selling their old tech.

Eden drank her cattail soup slowly. Her mother hated Ta'adrans. The would-be colonists had stayed on the coasts after the war, as if they hadn't arrived with the intent to replace every person here. Eden wasn't sure how she felt. The surviving Ta'adrans were families, not soldiers. Their fighting forces had been ruined. And she needed to fix the impulse generator on her back left wing. If the Ta'adrans were selling the tech stripped from their old ships, some of the fastest in the galaxy, could she really turn her back on the chance? . . .

From: Laila Piedra <lpiedra2000@gmail.com>
To: Tim Madison <timothy.j.madison87@gmail.com>
Subject: stuff   6:23 PM

Hi Mr. Madison,

I had a conversation with Ms. Nazarenko since I sent my last email, and she inspired me to rewrite the whole piece. I just turned the new version in this afternoon—it's attached to this email.

Do you ever make something and get nervous right away that nobody will remember it? I was going through old emails and found this story I sent you in early freshman year, and I didn't even remember writing it. It's about this kid who's a space patrolman even though he's twelve, so he's this obnoxious prodigy. Reading it, I sort of wondered whether I was trying to make myself that kid, and now I don't remember, and that's so weird, because I feel like the old me has disappeared forever and this might be the only record of the way I was then, if that makes sense.

Maybe you should write a story while you can't look at screens and send it to me, if you have time to kill! We could trade.

Anyway, I'm glad physical therapy is going well. Get ready for that bit with the bomb in the second *In the After Path* audiobook, because they add an actual bomb sound effect, and whoever did the sound mixing wasn't that good, so the explosion is incredibly loud. Just be ready.

Laila

From: Tim Madison <timothy.j.madison87@gmail.com>
To: Laila Piedra <lpiedra2000@gmail.com>
Subject: stuff   8:45 PM

Dear Laila,

As wonderful as ever—bravo! Something this small-scale is quite a divergence from your usual stories. I'm glad you're breaking out of your shell.

I hate to say this, but I haven't written anything of my own in years. I simply prefer reading. There are so many good books in the world, and I already feel as if I don't have enough time to get through everything I want to read. That said, I'm flattered that you would want to read any story I might have to tell!

As for the story about the space patroller: do you mean the one about the boy who lives on the dormant volcano slopes? Call my lenses rose-tinted, but I remember loving that story, and I thought its protagonist was a hoot, too.

Sincerely,

Mr. Madison

Laila was rereading the story on her phone on the way to sixth period, which was useless, since she couldn't change anything now. They'd turned in their first revisions yesterday, and the anticipation of getting them back had made her jittery all day. At lunch, Leo had asked her if she needed to listen to some of the eight hours of meditative music he had on his phone. She'd agreed. As the ethereal taps of a vibraphone floated through the earbuds, she'd pictured him stargazing to this soundtrack upstate and felt a single, fleeting moment of relaxation.

Not anymore. As Laila took her desk, she shielded her phone screen with her hand so she could keep reading. Scanning her own writing in public felt arrogant, a feedback loop pushing her own voice back into her mind, but she needed reassurance that she hadn't vomited something totally incoherent onto the page. *This one is different*, insisted a voice she couldn't quell. *She could like this one.* Even Mr. Madison had admitted the story was unusual for Laila.

She closed the document. She needed to keep her hope under her heel.

She glanced over her shoulder. In most classes, the time immediately before the bell was occupied by students frantically compressing conversations into two-minute increments, sitting on desks or the backs of chairs or anything else they could get away with, trying to capitalize on their own time before the bell handed the power to the teacher. Not this class. Everyone had already settled, watching Nazarenko, who was scribbling in her notebook again. She looked strangely small today, folded up on her pine stool, hair neat like a newsboy cap. Samuel Marquez's eyes were fixed on the stack of papers face down on Mr. Madison's desk, and Laila wondered if he'd spent the weekend the way she had, shut away in her room in a fever of productivity.

At the bell, Nazarenko swept the papers up and walked the aisles to distribute them. They flapped like doves into waiting hands. "Most of you have kept all but a paragraph or two of your original assignments," she said with faint disgust. "I promise you, two dozen words were not the difference between mediocrity and excellence. Make a habit of burning something to ash before expecting a rebirth."

That reassured Laila. Not only had she scrapped the entirety of her original story, she'd also emerged with a piece eight pages longer. Nazarenko couldn't say she hadn't put in the work.

The woman passed Laila's desk. The rush of air she left in her wake smelled cold and clean, like water. She dropped Laila's story without making eye contact. Laila bent the back page open so quickly that the edge of the paper sliced deep into her index finger.
37/100.

Nazarenko had left her one sentence:

Length and quality are uncorrelated.

The criticism impacted again on a soft, unprepared surface. Laila watched the wave of grimaces ripple through the rest of the class, paper by returned paper. She watched Peter Goldman's fist crumple the corner of his story, watched Samuel Marquez press his eyes tightly shut so that his dark eyelashes formed a comb against the top of his cheek.

Laila's teeth sought purchase on the slick wall of her cheek for the rest of the class. By the time she stood, she'd tasted blood for half an hour. Something was calcifying at her center. A hard knot of resolve tying into place. The new quarter started tomorrow. She had four more weeks before Bowdoin's deadline to update her transcript, four more chances to get this right.

After school, she returned to Nazarenko's classroom, closed the door, and approached the stool. Nazarenko was reading a novel today, a slim paperback volume with pages so dark with age they reminded Laila of skin.

"I got rid of the war," Laila said. "And the saving the world."

"That you did."

"I—I went to—I got out of the house this weekend, I based the story on that."

"You left your house to buy illegally smuggled spaceship parts?"

"No, I just—"

"Why did you leave your house?"

"I went to my friend's birthday party."

"And what did you do there?"

Laila foundered. She couldn't say she'd drunk her first beer. Could she? Was that the sort of thing Nazarenko was searching for, the type of risk she'd identified as missing from Laila's first draft?

"I met this new girl," she offered instead. "Bridget. My best friend Hannah introduced us."

"I see. What did you think of her?"

"She was intimidating, I guess. She's really pretty, and she's from London, so she's got this cool accent."

"Did you like her?"

"I—I don't know, we barely talked."

"Did you feel insecure because she's pretty?"

"What?"

"Did you feel attracted to her?"

Suddenly Laila's face was a wash of heat. "Excuse me?"

Nazarenko waited. The creases around her eyes, the low auburn strokes of her brows, seemed to focus her gray irises. Laila couldn't make herself respond. She remembered the little peaks of Bridget's ears breaching from her thick hair, and the view of her collarbones above the scoop-neck of her shirt, and even the way she'd held her drink, fingers poised in an elegant fan against the cold-dulled aluminum.

Laila had tried not to think about these things, had tried not to notice. She always tried, and failed, not to notice. Hannah liking girls seemed so certain, so natural, but in Laila's head the concept was a mess of guilt and confusion. The twins in her fourth-grade Sunday School class had whispered about *lesbians, gross* whenever one girl, April with the overalls, walked by, and in the time between second and sixth grade when Laila had acquired knowledge of every swear word in the world—not that she would ever, she'd promised herself, use them—she'd heard so many different angry words for *gay* that she couldn't help but associate it with bullshit, hell, and damnation.

So hadn't she been mentally snapping a rubber band against her wrist whenever she looked at a girl too hard since then? Pursuit was impossible. Even boys, whom she was supposed to like, she was disallowed to want. Her parents had explained since she could remember that all kinds of love were equally beautiful, but "show, don't tell" had been Laila's operative adage since elementary school, and the world had shown her something else. So now, on the other side of this stew of contradictions, where was she? She guessed she was pansexual, a word acquired from the internet, from people who seemed more confident in it than she was: *Yes*, she still couldn't say, *I could want anyone, any gender, any type.* Any person in the universe. Past layer and layer of self-consciousness, she knew it was true. But admitting the want was excruciating. The idea that somebody could look at her and just *see* it made her want to cry.

Nazarenko leaned idly forward. "You and your story alike seem averse to the idea that human beings might affect each other. From your first page to the last, all we know of your main character is that she needs some part for some spaceship: a flavorless, transactional goal. We have no sense of how other people impact her. Why? Because human impulses would distract from the goal?"

"No, I . . . I don't know."

"Then find out. Interrogate your instincts. Insecurity isn't shameful. Attraction isn't an embarrassment. Interpersonal affection isn't a side note to be glossed over. Whatever the nature of the material that forms between two people, it's the backbone of literature."

"But attraction *is* embarrassing," Laila blurted.

That fleeting, unpleasant smile tugged at Nazarenko's thin mouth again. Nazarenko slipped a playing card into her book as a marker, a crumpled Bicycle, and folded the book shut. The back cover was a colorless photograph of a marsh. "Not to everyone," Nazarenko said. "If all your narrators share your anxieties, try autobiography."

For an instant, Laila hated the woman in front of her, hated her cold gray eyes and her felt-coat uniform and her international success. She hated Dr. Greene for bringing Nazarenko here, and she even hated Mr. Madison for being impressed with her books. But Laila couldn't stop looking at her. Couldn't stop holding her breath between Nazarenko's sentences, as if the woman's words were oxygen.

Laila didn't want to write about herself. She wanted to leave herself, slip out of the cocoon of her life and unfurl oddly colored wings. If Nazarenko could diagnose Laila's neuroses from reading one of her stories, she hadn't gone anywhere at all. She was still wrapped up in herself, in the dark.

"Think of engaging with other people as an expansion of vocabulary," Nazarenko said. She stood. She was several inches shorter than Laila. That seemed wrong. "Reach out. Touch. Fear people, want people, feel whatever you will feel, but be there with them, be right up next to them."

"I—" Laila said, meaning to protest, explain that she *did* engage with other people, but a thin overlay of memory lay across her vision. The corner where she'd stood and watched everybody else dance.

Nazarenko tucked her book into her bag, shouldered it, and strode past Laila for the door. "I don't want to read your walls," she said, voice smooth and even as glass. "I don't want to read your hang-ups. I don't want to read skeletal concepts of people who operate without the influence of a limbic system. You are not an archaeologist excavating and presenting old bones. Your work is in the connective tissue. Give me some DNA, or don't bother."

The classroom door closed with a *click*.

—

Laila (4:40 p.m.): Hi, it's Laila, is this Samuel?

Samuel (4:43 p.m.): Yeah hey, what did you get yesterday?

Laila (4:45 p.m.): 37.

Samuel (4:45 p.m.): 28 over here

Samuel (4:46 p.m.): This is fucked haha

Laila (4:47 p.m.): Have you been talking to her?

Samuel (4:52 p.m.): Yeah she basically told me to make friends with a stranger

Laila (4:52 p.m.): Oh, that's not too different from what she told me! Did she say why?

Samuel (4:55 p.m.): not really... i do hang out with the same five dudes all the time, maybe shes trying to get me out of my comfort zone I guess? or maybe she really does want my parnets to hate me

Samuel (4:55 p.m.): *parents

Laila (4:55 p.m.): *parrots

Samuel (4:56 p.m.): *peanuts

Samuel (4:56 p.m.): lol anyway, what did she tell you?

Laila (4:58 p.m.): She wants me to connect with people more.

Samuel (5:02 p.m.): Well you could meet some of my friends

Samuel (5:04 p.m.): Me and Sebastian are going out Friday, im going to meet some random person to make our weirdass teacher happy, want to come?

Laila (5:04 p.m.): So

Hannah (5:04 p.m.): Yes?

Laila (5:04 p.m.): about that fake ID

UNDER FORTY-EIGHT HOURS LATER, HANNAH SLID A pair of fake IDs across the lunch table, courtesy of an anonymous mega-felon in Williamsburg.

"I get two?" Laila said.

"Yeah," Hannah said, "so if a bouncer looks at you funny, you can run and still have a copy."

Leo blinked owlishly. "Laila. You let her wear you down?"

"No, no, I needed them. You're a lifesaver," Laila added to Hannah, burying the cards in her backpack's deepest pocket.

"God, I know. What would you do without me?" Hannah gave a toothy smile. The fakes, indistinguishable from the real thing, had been embarrassingly easy to order. The process operated through a website, Fake-Wizard.it, that looked like a sixth grader had assembled it in 2008 for a social studies project. Submit a request through the bare-bones HTML of the Fake Wizard's secure form, include a photo and vital statistics—only as accurate as you wanted them to be—and pick up within forty-eight hours at a random drop location. This time, the Wizard had planted the contraband inside the lining of a filthy hoodie, which he'd left under a crate in a Bushwick alleyway between a decaying laundromat and an artisanal tea shop. This process had been relayed last night to Laila through Hannah, who had gushed for upward of a half hour about "this James Bond type shit." Hannah never cared about practicality when dramatics were available.

For two hours, Laila had drafted, deleted, redrafted, and agonized over the text she'd sent to Hannah with her information. She'd had to pick and choose which pieces of her identity to preserve: Keep her birthday as February 3, or change it? Keep her name, or choose a new one? Eventually, she'd picked May 2, a freshly minted Taurus, and changed her last name to Zambrano, her grandmother's maiden name. Part of her had expected the police to hammer at her door the instant she'd hit send. (This had to be traceable, right?) Hannah had reassured her, though, that half the seniors had these, and the only person who'd been caught was Sara Hurst, who apparently had handed a bouncer her real driver's license, apologized, swapped it out, and said, "Wait, I meant this one."

"What are they for?" Leo asked absently. Sometimes Laila wondered whether Leo was actually interested in half their conversations, or whether they were just an agreeable distraction between physics lessons.

"Yeah. Spill," Hannah said. "You owe me."

Laila looked over Leo's shoulder to the lunch line. Felix was picking at his fries while waiting for the register. A girl with cornrows was examining her strawberry milk carton with suspicion. Behind her, two blond boys were listening to an earbud each. Laila stopped chewing on her hair. This was an accomplishment. She shouldn't feel conflicted about telling her best friends.

"I ended up talking to Samuel Marquez," she said. She paused, expecting Hannah to laugh, or splutter, or crow some snarky comment that sounded as if she'd prepared it months in advance, but suddenly Hannah was very still, and Laila rushed on. "I—I started out asking him to leave Felix alone, but we ended up talking, and he seems cool, and we're going out tonight."

"Laila," said Leo. "That's huge."

Hannah made a distant noise of agreement. *Mm.*

"Can y'all not tell Felix?" Laila asked, tracking his progress toward their table. "I'm scared he'll be weird about it."

"Lips, sealed, et cetera," Leo said, but as he started texting, Laila knew Angela would know within thirty seconds.

Hannah finally spoke. "You're *going out* going out?"

"No," Laila said quickly. "Sort of. Felix's friend Sebastian is also coming. There's this bar—it's not a date. We're not, I mean, it's just . . ."

"Okay," Hannah said.

Laila glanced her way, but Hannah wasn't looking at her. Before she could say anything else, Felix sat down. They didn't speak about it again until Hannah texted her that evening.

Hannah (6:45 p.m.): hey would you want me to come tonight?
Hannah (6:45 p.m.): not trying to cockblock you, just so you don't feel outnumbered, especially since you don't know those guys
Hannah (6:45 p.m.): also since it's your first time out. Idk. Just let me know

Some set of muscles seemed to loosen across the span of Laila's back, and she let out a deep breath. She realized she'd been worried that Hannah was angry.

'*Interrogate your instincts*,' reminded a glass-smooth voice in the back of her head, but Laila didn't want to think about why Hannah might have been angry. She was too relieved. She was already typing a response.

Laila (6:46 p.m.): Yeah sure, I'll tell them!

Her heart buzzed quietly throughout the duration of dinner. She rubbed Malak's soft paw with a bare foot, listening to the family reports. This was a rare week during which everybody had wound up in a buzz of a mood: Camille had been picked to lead one of the trios in her spring ballet recital, her mother had been given a class in the 6 P.M. slot on Wednesdays—yoga prime time—and her father had found a copy of one of the only *Star Wars* expanded universe novels he didn't already own (*Lando Calrissian and the Starcave of ThonBoka*, hardcover, 1983). He'd dug it out of a rummage sale in the East Village. Her father attended a good rummage sale with the determination of a miner approaching a vein of emerald. The sheer amount of junk Laila had watched him sort through when she was a kid and unable to opt out of these journeys. Statistically, he had to find something worthwhile at least once.

"So," Laila said, "I have a semi-date tonight."

"You do not," said Camille.

"Thanks for the vote of confidence."

"Lolly, that is so *exciting*," said her mother.

"Don't get excited yet," said her father. "I need some details before you're going anywhere."

"I'm going to see a movie with this guy Samuel Marquez. Hannah and one of his friends are going, too, so it's only sort of a date."

"Samuel Marquez, like the guy you're always stalking online?" Camille said.

"*Camille*," Laila said through gritted teeth.

"What movie?" asked her father.

Laila took a generous bite of fritada, trying to remember what movies were in theaters. "Uh. I think it's called *Days Without Sun*? He already got the tickets. We're going to an eleven o'clock showing. I know that's kind of late, I hope it's okay."

Her father sipped his beer, thinking, but Laila's mother put a hand on his wrist. "I think that's just fine, sweetheart." She glanced at him. "We had a few late-night dates too."

"Gross," Camille muttered.

Seizing the opportunity to disgust Camille further, their father launched into a reminiscence of one of these "late-night dates," and Laila felt the pressure ease from around her chest. She almost couldn't believe her parents had believed her. Maybe they hadn't and were only humoring her because, in eighteen years, she'd never missed a curfew they'd set, done any drugs, or even *had* a date before this. Laila knew her father had been a rebel at her age. Sometimes she wondered if he wished she were a little edgier. Not enough to worry, but enough to recognize himself.

Hannah arrived at her door at 10:30, and by the time they reached the bar in Williamsburg, which was somewhat blasphemously named the Ave Maria, Laila's nerves had made her insides queasy and her outsides damp.

"Just don't projectile vomit," said Hannah, helpfully.

A square-jawed man in a bomber jacket occupied the majority of the threshold, glancing over IDs. As they approached him, Laila had the sense of facing a mid-level video game boss, the type you could only defeat by dying repeatedly so you could figure out which of its appendages were the most susceptible to poisoned blades. Except that if he caught her, she wouldn't respawn. She would—Hannah hadn't explained this. Go to prison? Run? Beg for mercy? Procure a poisoned blade? Why hadn't she been prepped for this step?

The bouncer handed back Hannah's ID and gave Laila a two-finger beckoning motion. She surrendered the card, toes pressing into the indentations in her boots. He traced a penlight over the holographic stamps and looked at her face. She looked back, her facial muscles in pain from the forced stillness, and imagined what the Bowdoin admissions board would think when a criminal charge appeared on her record in her updated transcript, and what the inside of the courthouse would look like at her summons as she sat flanked by thirty-five-year-olds with speeding tickets and/or backgrounds in petty thievery.

He waved her through.

"Thanks," she choked, stumbling on her way over the threshold.

The walls of the Ave Maria were reclaimed wood, the type of rough, hideous plank that someone might untangle from a clot of seaweed on the beach, rinse off, and resell at a boutique in the West Village for $380. The lanterns above the bar offered just enough light to make the place feel like dusk rather than midnight. In the comedown from the brightness of the streetlamps, the people at the bar didn't seem to have faces. As if being here wasn't disorienting enough.

"Are they here yet?" Hannah asked.

"No, still on their way."

Laila and Hannah slid into a booth. Everyone around them was old. Mid-twenties old, not *old* old, but enough to make her feel misplaced.

"So, your first bar," Hannah said. "Is your mind expanding?"

"Not really. This is less . . . everything than I pictured."

"What did you think?"

Laila could only dredge up fragments now. She'd pictured light, color, and motion. A night painted on in unusual makeup, constant flirtation with a carousel of strangers, throats exposed as heads tilted back in endless rounds of shots. "I guess you said 'going out,' and I pictured not sitting still at a booth in a relatively quiet room."

"It's early. Patience."

"Hey," said a voice. Laila looked up, and all the nerves she thought she'd left at the threshold writhed back into life. The warm half-light made Samuel and Sebastian look carved out of amber.

"Hi," she said, her voice half an octave higher than usual. "Um, this is my friend Hannah."

"Yeah, I think we had Spanish together last year," Samuel said. "What's up?"

"Not much. I'm gonna get a drink," Hannah said. "Laila, want me to grab you something?"

"Whatever's fine," Laila said. As Hannah backed into the shadows, Sebastian took her spot across from Laila, and Samuel slid into the seat beside her. His knee brushed hers. The contact made something jump in her stomach. She tried to ignore that she could smell him (too-strong body spray), and that his forearm was right there on the table within touching distance, and that they were here in a bar together, and that whenever she pictured college, this was her exact mental image. A man who called himself DJ Saint Lightning had started up the massive speakers stacked at the back of the bar and accumulated a small, shuffling crowd.

Laila flicked through a mental card deck of small talk, but the guys were finishing a conversation. "Sorry—really quick?" said Sebastian, giving her a glance.

"No, sure," Laila said and folded her hands to restrain the urge to look at her phone and free them of her attention. *Be present*, she told herself.

Sebastian was one of Felix's good-looking Puerto Rican friends on the wrestling team. He looked hardly anything like Felix, though, dark-skinned with loose curly hair that hung in a cloud around his protuberant ears. He and Samuel were both visibly cooler than Felix, and so, by Laila's estimate, about seven degrees cooler than her. They wore several different textures of black and their conversation was packed with proper nouns. That must have been what it was like to have too many friends. It sounded stressful and overinvolved.

Still, a tiny part of Laila wondered if she would have been part of this crowd if she were Boricua, too. It was hard not to be, if not envious, hyperaware of how many Puerto Rican kids there were at school. An actual community. Laila knew of exactly two other

Ecuadorians at Impact. She'd never had the sensation of blending into something larger, the way Felix did so comfortably.

"So, basically," Sebastian said to Samuel, "Stacia takes me to that concert at Turntable. It was E.Sides and some terrible opener I can't remember, but get this: We go with David and Robson and the boys, and Robson's ticket doesn't scan, so Natasha says—yeah, she was there, too, the hot one?"

"Blonde?" Samuel said.

"Uh-huh. She's like, wait, allá, I saw this hand truck around the corner. So we stack this cart off the street with cardboard boxes and Robson wheels it through the loading bay and nobody says shit, man, not a *word*. He just walks in. So that's what you do."

"Nice."

"It was blue as fuck."

"Blue?" Laila asked.

"You know," Samuel said. "Blue."

"I don't," she said. The proximity made looking at him difficult. The booth was so minuscule that making eye contact felt inherently romantic.

Hannah returned, slurping at something neon green and packed with ice. She passed a drink across the table to Hannah that, in the light, could have been a warm golden-brown or blood red. "Mai Tai," she said, sliding in beside Sebastian.

Laila took a drink, the ice kissed her upper lip, and at the first nip of liquid, she flattened her tongue against the roof of her mouth. Apparently Mai Tais were assembled by dissolving a pint of sugar into a nickel-thick layer of bleach.

"Is it good?" Samuel said.

"Yes," Laila said.

"Okay, so blue means—it's like . . . like *cool*." Sebastian spoke with the slow frustration of somebody translating a sentence into a language they'd half-forgotten. "But not cool like, 'oh, chill.' More, weird cool. Hype cool. I can't believe this happened cool. Like, 'I did a backflip off the bleachers and didn't die—it was so blue.'"

"Jesus," Hannah said, "this memelord in my bio class keeps saying that. Is it from something?"

"Oh, yeah, you've got to watch it," Sebastian said. "There's a video of this dude tripping balls on a roof in Missouri. Maybe not tripping, I don't know, but definitely on some bad shit. So his friend takes this eight-minute video where he asks all these questions, you know, 'What's your favorite sex position? Hey Tyler! Say what you did this weekend,' and this poor asshole is staring up at the sky, so he just keeps answering with descriptions of the word blue." He let his eyelids droop and put on a feeble wheeze. "*'Dude . . . it was so . . . blue.'*"

"Huh," Hannah said. "Guess I'd better start saying it before Twitter kills it. And old people. And late-night hosts trying to sound hip with America's youth."

Samuel laughed. He had a gentle, chuckling laugh that seemed too small for his body. Laila laughed, too, almost proud, because she'd brought Hannah here, and Hannah was successfully interacting with people, and she could still remember Hannah in freshman year, who could hardly manage five minutes' conversation without saying something so insensitive that the people around her exchanged incredulous glances. Not anymore. She'd changed. They'd both changed.

Laila had forced down half the Mai Tai and was feeling friendlier than usual, stomach hot and uneasy. This was okay. *She* was okay, staying upright. Hannah was a good set of training wheels. The drink tasted less disgusting now, her eyes had adjusted, and all the mid-twenties-old people who had felt threatening an hour ago had remained blessedly disinterested in her.

Hannah was studying Samuel with her chin perched on the heel of her hand. "So, Laila told me you're a writer," she said.

"I didn't tell her that," Laila said. "I mean. Not that you're not. I just."

"It's cool," Samuel said with a smile. Laila buried her nose back in her drink, and Samuel went on, "Yeah, I like doing it, but I wouldn't call myself 'a writer,' though."

"What do you write?" Hannah asked.

"The story I'm working on now is about a guy who's been in love with this girl forever, so he ends up cheating on his girlfriend, even though this other girl doesn't love him."

"Wow," Hannah said. "Sounds like a role model."

Heat cramped into Laila's cheeks. "Hannah."

Angry cries from the back of the bar interrupted, alerting them to DJ Saint Lightning's sudden abandonment of the tiny stage. Laila craned her neck to watch the crowd shuffle through several chants of protest before settling on the somewhat lackluster "WE WANT MUSIC. WE WANT MUSIC."

The door at the back reopened to cheering, but instead of DJ Saint Lightning, two figures emerged. One scurried to the equipment. The other, holding a microphone, had the type of tension built into his impossibly tall body that keeps skyscrapers upright. The cheering faltered, switched registers.

"Oh, shit," Sebastian said. He was half out of the booth. "Is that Knight Gard?"

It was. Laila knew this because the crowd had mutated into a thirty-armed monster, every arm Snapping or photographing or recording the stage, and the remaining cheers had dissolved into voices yelling over one another. Knight Gard was a twenty-three-year-old rapper, actual name unknown. After his two-part mixtape had become popular enough to be inescapable, he'd started a series of renegade pop-up shows in Brooklyn. So far, this had seemed like an exercise in how strange a place he could draw interest. A playground in Park Slope at midnight. The frozen foods aisle of a Crown Heights deli/grocery. The least successful show so far had taken place in the Jay Street–Metrotech subway station. Several thousand people had drifted past, assuming he was a louder-than-average busker with better-than-average production. Social commentators gleefully noted in the following weeks that if anybody had stopped to look at his face—if anybody had just looked up from their phones, counter to the trends of this heartlessly disconnected society, and afforded some attention to the human beings around them—they might have realized that they were in the presence of a Grammy nominee. Then again, that day, some people had been dashing down the platform to squeeze through the closing doors of the A train so they wouldn't be late to work for the third day that week, and others were discussing Swiss politics with friends they hadn't seen in four months, and others were in fact on their phones: They were commenting "so pretty!!" on an aunt's profile picture, or responding to a panicked email from their intern, or texting an ex-girlfriend a painful message about which possessions went to which person, so that day their participation in the universe had been elsewhere, geographically.

"Go," Hannah said, leaping out of the booth. "*Go.* We have to get up front before this explodes."

They made it up to the speakers with assistance from Hannah's elbows. Knight Gard started his set with the screech of car tires. A jagged beat thumped down over sly, persistent bass, and then came his distinctive shout.

The mostly white crowd—they were in that part of Williamsburg—didn't seem to know what to do with the track, which was unfriendly for dancing in everything from subject matter to the clattering, arrhythmic bass. They knew the words, because over the last year, most of America had internalized the lyrics to "Up and Downers," but the crowd couldn't say the vast majority of them, due to 1) the charged history of reclaimed language and 2) being terrible at rapping. Instead they stood in place, nodding as if in agreement, holding up their phones. Laila wondered whether to record the performance herself, but she was close enough to be mesmerized by the silver grid of the mic head pressed to Knight Gard's lips, and someone else would put a better-quality version on YouTube, anyway, and she remembered Nazarenko telling her, "be there with them," and she let herself stand, swaying, hands folded beneath her biceps, watching. The pressure and noise built until Laila felt a hot stone on her chest and had to escape down a long set of stairs toward the bathroom. She collected herself in the stairwell.

Over the course of a quarter hour, she waved a half dozen girls past her toward the bathroom. The seventh person she waved past slowed at the motion instead. She looked up. Sebastian had stopped on the step beneath her.

"Hey," he said. "Samuel wants to know if you're doing okay."

"Oh, I'm fine, it's just loud."

"Okay. I told him to come down here himself, but that's Samuel," Sebastian said. "Such a guy's guy. You know? He's not into the asking everybody about their feelings." He leaned against the wall. "Me, I'm more sensitive."

Laila wanted to laugh, but she settled for a smile with too much motion around the edges. She loved people who were blatantly self-descriptive. "I'm easygoing." "I'm so high-energy." "I'm the biggest introvert." "I always hunt down what I want." Like they were sketching out a cheat-sheet in case others forgot their personalities.

Courtesy of the alcohol, a break in conversation didn't feel like an urgent problem anymore, but Laila decided to speak. "The whole world's up there. It's so hot. I needed some room."

"Having room is great," Sebastian said, and to demonstrate the freeing properties of having room, he stretched out his arms. He moved onto her step. His sudden tallness startled her out of her examination. She wasn't removed anymore, was aware of her own body again in a way that reminded her of looking in a mirror. He pressed his hand to the red-painted cinder block beside her head, a gentle punch that stuck. The beer bottle looked thick in the vise of his knuckles, and its neck brushed her ear. The glass was warm, as if he had just breathed onto its surface. The light spread over his forearm like margarine and caught on the moles dotted up to his elbow.

For a moment she wondered why this was happening, and then she remembered Felix mentioning after a sloppy night out that Sebastian tried to kiss anything with a mouth after half a dozen beers. She had a mouth, and apparently the beer in his hand was the half-dozenth. Clockwork.

"You're not with Felix, are you?" he asked.

"What? *Felix?*"

"All right, just asking." At a foot's distance, Sebastian's features were exaggerated, large nose like a scythe, round eyes like new moons, full mouth like a child's pout. She wouldn't have been able to pick his face out of a crowd ninety minutes ago.

But wasn't there something relaxing in that? She'd arrived hoping that something would develop out of a conversation with Samuel, but kissing Samuel would come with four years' expectation. Kissing Samuel came with the possibility of making Felix furious, and—Laila was certain of this, somehow—Hannah, too. Sebastian was hot, actually, and more importantly, he was *there*, and this was an isolated unit, just a kiss, nothing else. For a second she wondered if she was only considering this because she was drunk, but so what if she was? Wasn't she going to have hundreds more kisses in her lifetime, wasn't it an inexhaustible resource, why did she need to be precious about it when there was somebody cute right here who wanted her?

When she considered all the variables—the first bar, the underground show, the company of her friends, the nice clothes she'd bothered to wear, the otherworldly orange light that made her feel like she'd walked into a Darsinnian transfer point—she identified this as being a story she wouldn't mind telling and retelling when people asked her, in college, forever into the future, how her first real night out had gone. A wild night in neon orange and electric blue, utterly temporary.

"I like smart girls," Sebastian told her, and he clearly had more to say, but she just said, "Good," and pressed her mouth up against his until she could taste everything he'd had.

12

THE VENEER OF TIPSINESS HAD DULLED BY THE TIME Laila crept back into her room, but a bed of heat still lay low in her torso. As she tried to sleep, it hummed. She remembered the tang of beer hovering over her lips, the gentle but eager way Sebastian had touched her breast. How he'd reached up under her T-shirt and explored with clumsy, grasping motions. The air had suddenly been warmer than the air trapped in the crowd upstairs. Beneath her stomach had grown a sensation like strangulation, but without the easy fix of releasing the force and breathing in. Tension had gathered in the backs of her thighs and in the divots of her collarbones and at the arches of her feet and between her legs, and none of it had dissipated on the way home. She was still built out of frustration.

Laila drew a corner of her comforter between her legs to press away the palpable pulse. She tried not to think too hard, pushing away the words as they arrived—*turned on*—but guilt awoke at the back of her mind like an itch. She forced it all back—the sensation, the awareness, everything. She'd learned to ignore her body. She did what she'd been told, and she still felt ashamed.

The next day, as she ground through a stack of homework, her thoughts came back and back again to the night before. Not to the kiss, the bitterness of liquor, or the discomfort of her spine pressed against the cinder block, but to the ache between her thighs, the way a hard touch at her neck had shot heat down past her navel.

Finally, she reached the bottom of the stack, and the only assignment that mattered. She opened her laptop, summoned up the notes she'd jotted from her last meeting with Nazarenko, and created a new document.

"'We have no sense of how other people impact her,'" read her notes. "'Why? Because human impulses would distract from the goal?'"

The blank page seemed dangerous today. The surge of want from last night still had dark spots dancing in her eyes. This desire for something more than superficial touching, something next, a need squirming through her memory that made her feel excited and wrong. "*Attraction isn't an embarrassment*," she told herself, and yet the idea of putting any of this into words wasn't just embarrassing but frightening. If she wrote a character's physical attraction, wasn't that laying her own sensations bare? Admitting all this to anyone who came across the page?

She shifted in her chair, heat budding again in her cheeks and legs. She placed two fingers between her legs, pressing against her jeans, but the tension multiplied instead of dissipating. She pulled her hand away and closed her eyes, breathing in for seven, out for six. *Your hang-ups*, she thought. *Your walls*. And suddenly the embarrassment wasn't with her lingering arousal anymore, but with her reluctance to acknowledge it. When she couldn't touch herself, could hardly think about her own body as something sexual, of course she couldn't imagine someone else touching her without a sense of airlessness, of asphyxiation.

Laila found herself chewing on her hair, and that was, for some reason, the tipping point, the bit of anxiety that made her so impatient with herself that she made up her mind. She went to the door and locked it. Even if the lock came loose, which happened occasionally, the delay would give her enough time to grab the towel stationed on her bedside table, and she would stammer out some excuse about showering. Genius. Foolproof.

She lay back on her bed and stared at the moisture mark on the ceiling where she'd once sticky-tacked a poster of a favorite character from *The Rest*, before the showrunners had massacred his personality in season eight. She lifted herself back onto her shoulder blades and maneuvered her underwear around her thighs, off her legs. She left her T-shirt on, because she already felt weirdly exposed. Blinds were shut, right? Yes. She'd shut them. And already checked twice. Why was she *nervous*? There was literally nobody to impress. God, how could Felix do this all the time without a sheer boner-killing terror of somebody walking in on him? She hated that she knew anything about Felix's "habits," but he discussed them so freely.

Laila was almost impressed by the tectonic shift that had occurred from middle school to freshman year when it came to talking about anything sexual. In sixth grade, her class had watched a mortifying series of sex-ed videos that they all instantly vowed to strike from memory. But maybe the teachers had actually timed that pretty well, because not long afterward, rumors floated up behind hands about the couple who had "visited the kitchen," a euphemism confined to the halls of William Henry Harrison Middle School that meant they'd kissed, *with tongue.*

In seventh and eighth grades, it became normal to hear about other kids kissing, and kissing with tongue, and even *second base* (!). At the same time, a slow collective awareness grew around the fact that masturbating was a thing that existed. Nobody knew what to do with that—was it normal to try it? To like it? To talk about it? So the activity inherited all the shame that had been shed from kissing, and kissing with tongue, and *second base* (!), which was why Laila felt so blindsided when jokes about jacking off became widespread. For boys. Laila was sure that the phrase "jacking off" was the thing that gave them leeway on this. Purely on a phonetic level, *masturbate* sounded like some hideous medieval practice that had to be confined to deep night with the lights off, possibly while incense burned to purify the air. The word sounded like a cross between *masticate* and *disturb*, for Christ's sake. If a less-appealing conglomeration of syllables existed, Laila couldn't name it.

But "jacking off" was another action entirely. So cavalier! So silly! Everyone had a story about somebody almost walking in on them while they were in the act. Except, said an uncertain countercurrent, only losers who couldn't get laid jacked off, right? Except, no—"Of course I do it, all guys do it." Also: "Ms. Wallace called me up to the board the other day and I had the hugest boner and I can't believe everybody didn't see." Also: "That guy's such a dickhead, a ballsack, a dick." The terminology circulated and percolated until it had no impact, meant nothing, might as well have been a recorded announcement about delayed subway service on the 1-2-3 lines. But Laila hadn't ever heard a girl joke about masturbating. Even Hannah was unlikely to joke about vaginas in general.

When Laila imagined somebody saying the word *dick*, it was a male voice, but strangely, when she imagined somebody saying the word *pussy*, it was a male voice, too. Maybe she'd never touched herself because she'd never felt like that territory was hers to claim. Or maybe it was because for fourteen years, she'd felt to her core that guilt was the correct response to desire, and that self-deprivation of every kind had some inherent goodness.

Laila placed a hand on her thigh. Her fingers were cold. Did this require music? She took a breath that made her chest shake and lifted her fingers between her legs, brushed them into a thatch of hair with an unfamiliar, wiry texture. She couldn't look down at herself, just stared at the stain overhead and wished this didn't feel somehow clinical and dirty at the same time. How was she supposed to feel? She had no reference point. From curiosity, she'd read her share of online smut. Mostly fanfiction smut, which was just stupidly easy to find and came with the benefit of a preexisting attachment to the characters. That was the problem with porn, which she'd tried watching once for about two minutes. Personality was absent from the equation, substituted out with interchangeable body parts. Although, to be fair, nobody was watching a four-minute video called "Best Friend's Wife Home Alone ! ! !" for the character development.

Anyway, the smut she'd read was mostly incidental, embedded in a larger romance, so the sex scenes were filled with narrators' passionate realizations about their partners' emotional baggage.

Laila appreciated the authors' attention to interior life but also didn't know how to reconcile swoony devotion and/or furious emotional heat with descriptions of the actual physical component. When they did talk about the sex itself, it was heavily euphemistic and often referenced sensations of explosion, e.g., "He closed his eyes, body rigid, and felt the world crash around him," or "Static excitement wired her into an electric grid of frantic, sparking need," or "Frustration built up her back as she pushed toward release, until fireworks burst beneath her stomach." Which somehow made perfect sense in context, but now that she was lying here with her hands between her legs, none of that seemed even tangential to reality. Maybe she wasn't reading the right smut. She had to clear her search history.

Here was that mysterious component so often decorated to complete obscurity by pretty language. Her body. Rubbing at herself from experimental angles. Pushing her fingers along grooves of different-textured skin, like the inside of her lip. She tried to make herself think about people she knew she was attracted to. Half the cast of *The Rest*. Samuel, Sebastian. For a second, Felix, but that felt invasive and she stopped. Then Hannah, but that disturbed a wave of panic and doubt and she thought herself frantically elsewhere. She couldn't focus on people, in the end. She ended up thinking about dangerous performance art. Dogs shaking off rain. Greenhouse gases. She thought about how it might feel to write a sex scene, how secret warmth would alight in her and how her fingers would pass over the keyboard. She thought about soap. She thought about small circles, smaller circles, unexpected moisture. About anatomy diagrams—no, too medical, made her think of dissection. Of heat and comfort, instead. She strained against her own hand. Drew her palm experimentally upward, liked the warm pulse down her thighs that resulted, and did it again. Shivered. She felt, for a moment, galaxies distant from her body, and in the next moment, closer to herself than she had felt in her life. She thought about those videos from sixth grade, the red stain in her teacher's pale cheeks as the woman had stammered out the definition of an orgasm to a room full of kids who in that moment would have preferred death to eye contact. Laila thought about the girl in freshman biology who'd accidentally answered a question with *orgasm* instead of *organism*. She thought about the laughter. She thought, as she moved her hand in a sharp, urgent rhythm, about descriptions of explosion, tension, thirst, and hunger. Of joy. Of power. But the instant it happened—the sudden gridlock of her muscles, the hard press of an index knuckle, the pleasure that threw itself down her limbs and radiated back between her legs, where it buckled, throbbed, redoubled—she felt like it was nothing but a body-wide function of relief, having arrived somewhere that should always have been familiar.

The trip to the red planet's fifth colony always made Eden think about stitches. She still had the cord of scarring up her calf where Diara fit the arch of her foot. When they took the Bullet from Earth's surface out to Mars, colony five like a steel spider ahead, they always had the same discussion. Eden told Diara she would not go back to the drowning place, where she could look into the artificial river and still see her leg catching on the jutting strip of metal. Diara told her, "I'll hold you the whole way there. I'll hold you the whole way back."

Felix and Hannah joked often about how Leo was too good for them, about how there was no reason he should put up with them. The joke came from a place of deep collective insecurity, but Laila was pretty sure it was also true. She knew the second she sat down for lunch on Monday that Felix and Hannah were angry, and that Leo had already tried his best to arbitrate. She opened her mouth to help, but then Felix spoke, and she realized she'd misjudged the situation. For once, Hannah and Felix weren't angry at each other.

"So you go out with two of my best friends and one of my worst enemies?" Felix demanded, glaring at Laila.

Laila looked to Hannah, but Hannah was stabbing at a salad with vehemence that suggested she'd sworn a vow to eradicate all the world's croutons.

"Dude," Laila said, "I had a crush on Samuel before you hated each other."

"Well, now we hate each other. You know he's still trying to get with Imani, right? That wasn't a date, what you guys went on."

Laila's eyes stung. She was too quick to tears. They came at the same time as the sensation of hurt. "I know, Felix," she said, letting him hear her anger. "You don't have to throw it in my face that we can't all get dates with whoever we want."

Felix looked guilty for a moment, but rallied. "Yeah, but now Sebastian thinks you want to date him. Because, *you know*."

Laila felt a slow, creeping shame that had nothing to do with Sebastian and everything to do with what her friends thought. How much did they know? Had Sebastian told Felix they'd reached second base in the slick-walled stairwell of the Ave Maria?

Hannah had renewed her efforts to impale her food.

"Okay," Laila said. "So you're mad that I kissed one of your friends. This isn't actually about Samuel."

"Yeah, no shit," Felix said and looked to Hannah. "Because—"

"You let us hear about it through Sebastian," Hannah interrupted. "You couldn't, I don't know, throw a text out there? You couldn't have walked up the stairs and told me?" She tossed down her fork. "Also, I'm just going to say it, you deserve better."

"You're so impossible, Hannah," Felix shot back. "I mean, no wonder you can't hold down a girlfriend for thirty seconds when you have these fucking ridiculous standards."

Laila looked to Leo. He shook his head, hand poised over his physics problem set, drawing a right angle against a shallow incline. She could see his irritation drawing his narrow shoulders tight.

"Okay," Laila said, standing. "I'm letting you two cool off. Let me know if you figure out an actual, coherent reason to be mad at me. Leo, you want to work in the library?"

"Yes, please," Leo said. They left Felix and Hannah glaring at each other across the speckled plastic.

One of the school librarians, Ms. Jennings, was definitely a lesser demon from hell, but the other, Ms. Andrade, turned a blind eye to kids eating in the library as long as they kept a cap on the volume and cleaned up after themselves. Luckily, Ms. A. was in charge that period, so Laila and Leo holed up in the corner to eat where Laila could use a computer, too.

From: Laila Piedra <lpiedra2000@gmail.com>
To: Tim Madison <timothy.j.madison87@gmail.com>
Subject: stuff   12:08 PM

Hi Mr. Madison,

I really wish you were back at school right now. Hannah and Felix are having one of those lunch fights again, but this time they're mad at me. The reason is so hypocritical. Since freshman year, they've both been trying to get me to go out with them on weekends and cut loose, and now when I finally do—not even that much!—they're both angry. Just because of some guy I don't even like. And now Leo and I have to deal with them being dramatic, and it's not like we have spare time to have fights that don't matter and make up.

Maybe I'm the only one who thinks this, but in my opinion, if you make friends with somebody, you should be happy with what they are. If you get all these ideas about what needs improving, you didn't make a friend, you took on an art project. And oh my gosh, if you're so obsessed with fixing problems, fix your own problems!!! Like Felix and Hannah don't both have a million issues they could work through!!!!!

Sorry, this is so stupid that I'm telling you. I would tell my parents, but my dad would just be all "WELL THEN NO MORE DATES FOR YOU," and Mom would turn on psychologist mode and I would just want to leave.

In less completely obnoxious news, I wrote a new draft of the Eden story . . . and this one is set on Earth! Kind of. It's Earth in 2730, but still. So that's attached.

Also? Important. Ms. Bird brought a get-well card to Ms. Nazarenko's class yesterday for us to sign. She said she was going to deliver it to you when all your classes signed it. I bet she wanted to surprise you, but I knew you'd want to know beforehand so you can prepare yourself, so just act surprised? Anyway, I'm not saying this means anything, but you should probably buy a cage of doves and an engagement ring.

Laila

From: Tim Madison <timothy.j.madison87@gmail.com>
To: Laila Piedra <lpiedra2000@gmail.com>
Subject: stuff   12:39 PM

Dear Laila,

I'm not an expert on your friends, and I am very sorry to hear that you're fighting, but once you have a little distance, it might be helpful to ask yourself where they're coming from. I find that a lot of the time, students have these fights with each other because they're scared or nervous themselves, and end up lashing out to cover up that insecurity. From what you've told me about Hannah and Felix, I wouldn't be surprised if they thought acting angry toward you was easier than admitting they felt vulnerable in some way.

That's just a bit of conjecture. But nothing is better than talking openly. Being fully honest can fix so many frustrating communication problems.

As for Ms. Bird's card: thank you for telling me. You know me well . . . I find that sort of surprise very stressful . . . hehe

I am excited to read your next draft!

Sincerely,

Mr. Madison

13

55/100, SAID THE PAPER. A TERRIBLE GRADE, OBVIOUS-
ly, but also the first grade Laila or anyone had made that was closer to an A than a zero. Laila had been reconditioned, and she felt
a sweep of excitement that lasted the rest of the day, the need to
draw out her laptop and labor forward. Two more eighteen-point
leaps would put her on track for an A with a week to spare for
Bowdoin's deadline.

When she flipped through, she saw that Nazarenko had un-
derlined a phrase on page thirteen and left no notes beside the
red mark—implicit approval. The exhilarating thing was that Laila
had known, as she'd written that phrase, that it would make impact. She remembered the sense that this idea struggling for description was something so true that it would no longer belong to
her once she shook it loose. Upon rereading, she'd felt a satisfying
sting, like the removal of a splinter. She'd felt that her words were
valuable, even original.

Mostly Laila didn't buy into originality. Everything she loved
came into her life feeling familiar. Sometimes she was sure the
human race had only a handful of sentiments to express and had
spent three thousand years shuffling words around to express
those feelings in ways that could masquerade as new. And why did

it have to be a shortcoming to write about death or love like people had a thousand years ago, or wonder about pain and comfort like they had a thousand years before that? Old feelings strung rope bridges through history.

Still, there was nothing quite like the feeling of being unique. Even if she'd invented it. Even if she was wrong.

She arrived at Nazarenko's room after school, trying not to let her sense of triumph show, but discovered the door closed. Through the strip of wire-gridded window, she saw Samuel Marquez speaking with Nazarenko.

Laila leaned against a set of rust-spotted lockers, looking at the last texts between her, Felix, Hannah, and Leo. The four of them had been exclaiming over a YouTube video that had taken the most dramatic clips from season twelve, episode one, and replaced the score with audio of a miserable-sounding soprano saxophone. "That's good shit," Hannah said. "Revelatory," Leo said. "I cant breathe," Felix said.

That had been last Friday. Nobody was speaking in the group text now. Breaking silence took activation energy. Laila wanted to say something, but she couldn't find an appropriate catalyst.

She knew Mr. Madison was right. Hannah had all but admitted she was hurt because Laila hadn't prioritized them, and for all she knew, Felix was fighting with Imani about Samuel, and Laila's not-date had come at the wrong time. Still, she didn't know why they would feel better taking that out on her.

Laila peeked through the window again and went still as Nazarenko's eyes found her. She started to pull away, but Nazarenko beckoned with two fingers. Samuel looked over his shoulder, met her eyes, and half smiled. Laila felt a stupid lightness.

When she walked in, Nazarenko gestured for them both to sit. "Your pieces this week," she said, "had similar deficiencies." She pointed at Laila. "Your main character has a little chat about trauma with the one who loves her, and with a feeling of great relief, her psychological issues resolve." Then at Samuel. "Your main character makes a single alteration to his self-presentation, and suddenly, he becomes attractive to his muse. The question here is of risk. What has either character endangered in making their choice? Was there ever a chance they would fail? Neither of them experiences any discomfort throughout the narrative. You are being far too kind to these people."

Nazarenko rose from her stool, crooked a knuckle into a steel triangle at the top of the whiteboard, and pulled a world map down into multicolored life. "I was born here," she said, tapping Ukraine, pastel purple, at its center. "After the Soviet collapse, Ukraine was left in disrepair. In the mid-1990s, hyperinflation made worthless paper out of the currency we earned by the end of the day we'd earned it. During the worst months, a friend of mine would take his paycheck to a store the instant it was put into his hands; he would buy one loaf of white bread with a week's wages, cut it into seven slices, and eat a slice a day."

Laila had never sat so still.

"You know this still happens," said Nazarenko. "Especially now, when at your fingertips you have the nexus of all human information, you live in the shadow of the knowledge that no matter what happiness you take, someone in the world is in pain. If suffering is necessary to art, it's because the recognition of suffering is a necessary step toward full consciousness in the world. The likelihood of suffering, whether physical or emotional—that is risk; that's what frightens us; that makes a story. Go find some struggle. Go find some fear. Few things are more useful."

Nazarenko tugged on the world map to dismiss it. The matte plastic trailed out of sight sluggishly. Something in the hanging mechanism had rusted. "I will see you both tomorrow," she said, shouldered her bag, and left.

"Well," Laila said faintly. "That was dark."

"Yeah," Samuel said. "Does she want us to go play on the subway tracks or something?"

"Let's not do that," Laila said.

Samuel sighed, looking down at his story drafts jammed into a folder, which wore the same logo as his sneakers. "Okay, what, then?"

Laila wasn't sure why he thought she would have the answers, but she searched for something. They could take a risk together. She pictured climbing a mountainside with him, his hand pulling her up over the edge of a cliff, and the sensation of relief as they both tumbled back onto solid ground.

Before she could suggest anything, though, a voice at the back of the class said, "Marquez." Laila didn't recognize the boy, but he looked angry.

"One minute," Samuel said to Laila, and he jogged out into the hall. Laila looked at the whiteboard a long while. She tried to imagine Nazarenko wandering the streets of some documentary they'd watched in European history. Imagining her as a teenager was impossible. If she had ever been longer-haired, gangly or ungainly, or dirty, dressed in anything but the uniform she'd imposed on herself, the woman had lifted the image entirely away from the paper. If she'd been born once in Soviet Ukraine, she'd been born again in South Africa, again in France, again in New York City, her own deliverer at her own rebirth. Laila thought how liberating that must feel, to be something so carefully conceived and curated and brought to life.

Samuel and his friend were yelling outside. "I don't want her talking to him," Samuel was saying. Laila looked around for a distraction, but temptation presented itself instead. Samuel had left his folder open. A library of his stories was there.

As the voices in the hall piled over each other, she tugged one of the stories loose, dated to the previous week. With the pages came a scrap of paper Laila recognized at once: a page from Nazarenko's notebook, covered in her red script. Laila found herself morbidly curious. Maybe Nazarenko *had* given Samuel a reason he should befriend a stranger, a reason that had been too embarrassing for him to tell Laila, the same way she'd hidden from Hannah why she was really going to Felix's party.

I shouldn't read it, she thought, but the more she tried to ignore the questions, the further they multiplied. Was Nazarenko skewering Samuel's private life the same way she was skewering Laila's? Was she making him grapple with some deep, private shame?

Laila caved. She dropped his story and flattened the fragment to decipher Nazarenko's handwriting.

This draft is an improvement, but barely. The narrative hinges on the behavior of a "female character" cobbled together from the weariest clichés about what supposedly comprises female behavior, an exhausting and stunningly shallow parade of hysteria, jealousy, two-timing, and hypersexual allure. Perhaps something upsetting has happened in the student's personal life?

Either way, the piece suggests that the student sees women as paths to validation, receptacles for sexual frustration, or metaphors for the psychological state of men, but certainly not people in their own right. I cannot recommend strongly enough that the author spend time with a girl in whom he has no romantic interest, ideally a girl he finds unattractive. A hearty conversation with a female relative could do. Perhaps the experience will give him insight into expecting something of women besides sexual contact.

Laila looked blankly at the paper for a long time.

Finally she slipped the note back into his story, and the story into the folder. She left, walking right past Samuel Marquez, who was saying, "I'm done, I'm not kidding anymore." He didn't notice.

The next day, Laila slid into the lunch booth beside Hannah with the latest draft of her story folded open to the last page.

"This is why I wanted to go out," she said. "Okay?" She turned the paper to face between the three of them.

She felt like she'd stripped half-naked. Her friends all stared at the story. Leo gave his best effort not to look repulsed, but Laila could tell the sight of the 55/100 made him want to shield his eyes.

She explained how the entire class was failing, explained Nazarenko's assignments and how Samuel had received them, too. The only thing she omitted was his lie, "Make friends with a stranger." She had no idea how she'd believed that. As if Samuel Marquez, one of the crowd who went out every weekend, would ever need to expand his horizons by meeting somebody new at a bar.

"Look," she said, "I'm on your side, Felix. Not his. That was never even a question. Sorry if I didn't make that clear."

The only thing that made Felix more uncomfortable than giving apologies was accepting apologies. He muttered something that involved the word "sure," waved a hand, and took a long draw from his slushy, so that for a long moment, she saw a circle of wax-coated white paper instead of his face.

"Truth is," he mumbled, "Sebastian told me Imani was just going out with me because she thought I was cute and wanted to make Samuel jealous."

Felix looked so dejected that Laila almost reached across the table to squeeze his hand. Sometimes he acted so bulletproof that she forgot just how badly he wanted what Leo had. They all wanted what Leo had—until he and Angela went through a rough patch, anyway, and then they remembered why they were all varying shades of single.

"At least she thought you were cute?" Laila offered.

"Yeah, but I *knew* that," Felix said, his full bottom lip pushed out in a surly pout. Laila looked at Hannah, and for the first time in too long, Hannah was looking back with their usual barely concealed amusement. Laila felt a rush of relief.

Felix dropped the pout, seeming to remember something.

"Wait, you know why I was *actually* mad? Half the school hunts down every rumor trying to land at one of those Knight Gard shows, and you just waltz into one, first try. How?"

"She's magic," Hannah said. "We should bring her everywhere now that she's fun."

"*Now* that I'm fun?" Laila said, indignant.

"Idea," Leo cut in.

"Yeah, space cadet?" Hannah said.

Leo spun his phone so they could see a map of the world, half darkened by a loop of gray. "The lunar eclipse is two weeks from Saturday. What if we went up to your place in the Catskills, Hannah? I'll bring my telescope."

"Probably a bad time to tell you I turn into a rare breed of werewolf during lunar eclipses, but sure. I'll make sure Molly and her friends aren't trashing it that weekend." Hannah glanced to Felix and Laila. "You two in?"

"In," Felix said.

"In," Laila agreed, and then the four of them were exchanging irrepressible grins, looking away, throwing out plans for the weekend, joking furiously back and forth as if the lapse in their friendship had never happened. This, Laila remembered, was why she and Leo put up with all the fights. Because the sensation as they clicked back together, like the tumblers in a lock, was a sweeter relief than any other.

Hannah was halfway through listing which *The Rest* episodes they needed to rewatch in the mountains, a best-of reel, when a hand sank into Felix's hoodie, formed a fist at his collar, and yanked him to the side. Laila saw two vertebrae jutting out from his upper back as he twisted out of the booth, on his feet at once.

Felix twisted out of Samuel's grasp. "Don't *fucking* touch me."

"How about you don't touch my girlfriend?" Samuel said. "You don't touch my girlfriend, you don't look at her, you don't—"

"I don't want to touch your lying-ass girlfriend."

Now they were yelling over each other, leaning in, a dangerous inch separating them. A heavy weight had dropped at their table, and ripples of impact were spreading across the cafeteria. Tiny freshmen two booths down looked openly overjoyed, as if this were just the thing they'd needed to turn the week around.

"Stop," Laila said, sliding out of the booth. "Stop it!"

Felix met her eyes. She saw him the way they'd met in freshman year, when he was hardly bigger than Hannah, boasting with such enthusiasm he seemed to think the words could make him physically larger. Now he and Samuel almost looked like strangers, two guys she might see getting into a fight on a subway platform before shaking her head and pretending not to notice.

"Teacher," hissed one of Samuel's friends at his back. "Teacher's coming."

Samuel spared a look to the woman flouncing across the linoleum, her forehead crumpled up beneath flyaway gray hair. He gave Felix a hard shove before taking a step back. As Felix caught himself against the lunch table, Samuel said, "See you Saturday," and then to his friend, "Este hijueputa."

Felix snapped, "Yeah, you'd better bring a fucking doctor, asshole." By the time the teacher arrived at their booth, Felix was slumping back into his seat, and Samuel was gone.

14

THAT SATURDAY, LAILA WOKE UP AT 8 A.M. SHE couldn't sleep any later, genetically. Her parents and sister had already finished breakfast by the time she emerged.

She spent the morning brainstorming for her next draft. When her dad sent her out for groceries at noon, Laila walked out of the building to find the street was green, the dead winter trees having evolved overnight into living things. Spring always lifted a weight from her, with the freedom of summer vacation as bright as water immediately ahead. The neighborhood rose from its long hibernation, too. Barbecues had already smoked into life down every block, the hazy smell of marijuana mixing with the juicy, full-to-bursting scent of sausages newly sleeved. At the bodega two blocks toward Bushwick Ave., Mr. Cabrera, the grumpiest man for a mile in any direction, had propped the door wide open and was humming—*humming!*—as he stacked single toilet paper rolls on the top shelf. That said, his cat, the grumpiest bodega cat for a mile in any direction, looked just as pissed-off as usual, prowling past the canned foods like an assassination of Chef Boyardee was in the works.

As Laila walked back home, somebody called to her from a simmering grill. "Laila, chica, how have you been?"

"I've been good, Mr. Reyes," she called back over the half-fence into his concrete front yard, scanning the dozen people perched on steps and in yard chairs. Mostly she was just looking for the dominoes. Mr. Reyes's friends played dominoes like some people played slot machines: incessant, high-stakes, dead serious.

"How about you?" she asked.

"Never been better," he said, waving a browning ear of corn. A drop of hot butter flew off its tip and landed on his wife's neck. She let out a little shriek and swatted the spot like she'd been stung by a wasp. Mr. Reyes started laughing, and she rounded on him with eyes blazing.

Mr. Reyes was one of her father's best friends, a big Afro-Dominican guy, six-two at least, who still looked tiny next to her dad. His daughter, Clara, went to the high school a half-mile away. She and Laila had been close in elementary school but started to drift apart in middle, and now Laila hardly saw her around the neighborhood without her squad of three other gorgeous Domini-can girls. The most Laila could do when they passed was wave and feel self-conscious. And try not to notice their curves.

Laila wondered if, in some parallel universe, she had a squad like that. She wouldn't have traded Felix, Leo, and Hannah for any-thing, obviously, but sometimes she felt like her choice of friends was some weird signifier that she wasn't Latin enough. When her dad took her and Camille to the Ecuadorian Day Parade in Queens every fall—a small affair compared to the massive Puerto Rican Day parade in the spring, but still enough to overwhelm—she felt adrift. Or worse, like an impostor. Even there, her family was an anomaly, her father half a head taller than anybody else, her sister conspicuously pale, all their extended family absent. All around were clusters of cousins and siblings, half-hunched grandmothers laughing along with great-aunts, matched sets of brothers cracking Pilseners. And here were the three of them, an island.

The sight of so much family made Laila sneak glances at her father, wondering if he missed home. He was the only one of five siblings to leave Ecuador, and he'd left young, too, barely nineteen when he flew halfway up the globe. Laila knew he'd originally intended to go back someday, but then he'd gone and landed himself a life here. There seemed to be something wistful to the way he guided her and Camille through the parade, calling out to the friends he'd made since then.

But Laila never wanted to miss it. That day was always highs and lows. There were those rushes of pride every time she understood a snatch of Spanish, even if more often there was incomprehension. There was the relief of knowing nobody would assume she was Mexican or Indian, that everybody else there would look at her and see an Ecuadorian girl, no explanation needed, no justification. But just as often, there was the feeling that they shouldn't see her that way. Laila couldn't shake the suspicion that she didn't count in some fundamental way, that her looks were enough to distance her from her white half but not nearly enough to make her belong with her Latin half. If anybody were to ask her how it felt, being mixed, she knew how she would answer. It was the feeling that even in the quietest and most personal place, a score had been assigned to her, a mark calculated to gauge authenticity or ownership, and just as in every other coldly numerical analysis, 50 percent would never be a passing mark. But who was going to ask?

She sometimes wondered how blonde, white Camille felt. Her little sister's friends were mostly white. Laila wasn't sure whether this was because of subconscious racial behavior or because Camille's ballet studio was the whitest place in the world besides Iceland.

She wished they had thousands of dollars to spend on a family trip to Ecuador. Maybe there was some answer down there. Maybe when she touched that soil, she'd feel some clicking mechanism underneath her skin, and she'd realize how to engage with who she was in a way that was all natural, no performance, pure instinct. Sometimes she dreamed about it. Not rhetorical dreams. Vivid, 3-D, Prismacolor dreams that dragged rainbow contrails into the morning hours after she woke up. She and Camille gave her father crap for all his reminiscence of Ecuador, but they loved it, he knew they loved it. Her father talked poetry about mountain air. He bragged about the Galápagos and described the monumental carvings of Quito's cathedrals, their gold-brushed insides. Home makes you believe in God, he'd told her once. But she knew that first she had to believe in home.

Laila passed another barbecue on the way down her cross-street, but this time, people were sucking their teeth, glancing up at the quickly gathering clouds. All week, the air had been choked with charge, as if the city were holding its breath for Felix's fight just like Laila.

The thunderstorm came during midafternoon, and Camille, cooped up inside, took on the energy of a golden retriever. Malak skittering anxiously at her heels, she paced the hall with her hair glued inside a flatiron. The instrument looked like it needed reinforcements to finish the job. Camille's hair was even more uncooperative than Camille.

In the afternoon, Hannah showed up at Laila's apartment wearing combat boots and work gloves, her hair soaked.

"How's the construction site?" Laila asked as she let Hannah in.

"Rife with code violations."

"Seriously, what's with the outfit?"

Hannah shouldered into Laila's room. "I found out where Samuel and Felix are planning on fighting."

"Okay," Laila said, shutting the door. "So how do we stop him from going through with this, because he's going to get the crap kicked out of him."

Hannah kicked off her boots and leapt onto Laila's bed, a movement so familiar that Laila leaned forward knowingly to compensate for the well Hannah stamped into the center of her comforter. "Yeah," Hannah said. "All of the crap, kicked right out. By the way, do people cuss in your stories, or do they all talk like you?"

"It's a mix," Laila said. "Some of them cuss. Some of them care about being linguistically creative."

"Objection! God. Three-plus years of being friends with me, and you still don't think cussing can be linguistically creative."

Laila grinned and lay on the other side of the bed, looking over at Hannah, who was scowling at the ceiling. Laila remembered, suddenly, a fragment from a story she and Hannah had written together, such a filthy, detailed bit of profanity that Laila had ripped up the note and flushed it down the toilet out of an irrational fear that some teacher would fish it out of a recycling bin. They'd done this sophomore and junior years: They would write stories back and forth in ten-word segments, leaving them stashed around the school in places only they knew to look. Tucked beneath the bathroom sink on the third floor. Wedged into the broken locker near the biology room. Mostly they ended horribly; Hannah had a penchant for cutting a story off with a sudden explosion:

So the girl walked to the top of the building
And discovered that Dr. Doom had been planning for this
The entire time, and she quickly took out her blaster
But then unfortunately his Doom weapon decimated the whole city.

"So," Laila said, "the gloves."

Hannah's scowl melted, replaced by her usual bored skepticism. "Okay, yes, let me explain. Felix and Samuel have decided that the best place to fight is this busted-up warehouse by the Ridgewood border, because they apparently want to get tetanus as well as indulge in unnecessary masculine posturing."

"So you're skirting the tetanus with those."

"This is the plan," Hannah said, tugging the work gloves off. "They smell like ass, though."

"That's probably just your hands."

Hannah shoved the gloves toward Laila's face, and Laila yelped, swatting them away. Hannah laughed and chucked the gloves onto her boots, taking the ridged neck of her sweatshirt into her mouth, chewing contemplatively. "So?" she said, mouth full. She looked shy, as if it embarrassed her even to ask Laila along. "You in, or what?"

"Is Leo coming?"

"We're going to meet up there."

Laila hesitated, but the doubts had hardly crept in when Hannah said, "I know it's kind of risky, so I get it if you want to stay home."

She couldn't have convinced Laila faster if she'd tried. "I'm in," Laila said, already planning how she would graft this shudder of adrenaline onto a page.

When Laila was nine, her father had still been clinging to his first car, a Toyota from the late eighties that he worked on during weekends. Not work toward any discernible end, to fix the perpetually blinking "Check Engine" light or to keep the tubes beneath the car from drooling flammable-looking fluid every time it clanked to a halt at stop signs—just work to keep his hands busy, and to have an excuse to blast Julio Jaramillo's boleros so loud that the whole block could hear. Laila had walked past the car once as he threw open the hood and had been met with an acrid scent of metal that seemed somehow to have gone rancid, like it had been infected by some mechanical version of gangrene. This warehouse smelled the same way.

Hannah vaulted through a broken window, having pushed an ancient metal frame halfway up and swatted aside corners of glass that spiked from the bottom. Laila crawled in after Leo, feeling ungainly, and staggered when she hit the concrete floor. Outside, the dusk was a burnt periwinkle, so clear in the aftermath of the rain that the promise of stars pressed in at the light pollution, but the warehouse's interior was a soup of storm light. Greenish scum had clouded into the windows and dyed the whole place the ominous color of coming lightning.

"Nice-looking place," Leo said mildly. With his sneaker, he nudged an iron bar that passed over half an old advertisement. BUY ONE GET, it said.

Laila checked her phone. They were half an hour early. "You think Felix is going to be late to this, too?"

"I hope not," Leo murmured.

"Okay, but if he is," Laila said, "how are we going to ward him off?"

"Did you bring the chloroform?" Hannah asked.

"Shut up," Laila said.

Hannah grinned. "They said by the stairwell. We'll just, I don't know, lie in wait."

"Should someone stay here?" Laila said. "Keep an eye on the door?"

"I got it," Leo said, slipping between a column and the wall so the shadow swallowed him. "I'll text you if he shows. Go, move."

Laila followed Hannah through columns that rose from the floor with no apparent planning. Deep blue paint peeled from the I-beams that spanned the ceiling, and every so often, a whisper of nimble feet made Laila picture a rat the length of her forearm. In a back corner, Hannah yanked a rusting chain through a pair of door handles, revealing a pitch-black threshold. Laila's phone flashlight betrayed it as a stairwell, clouded with cellophane and rotten candy and, depressingly, condom wrappers.

"God," Hannah said, kicking an entire condom box away. "Find a nice alley somewhere. This shit is desperate."

The dark gave Laila a temporary, anonymous hit of boldness, and she said, "You mean you don't only do it in warehouse stair-wells?"

Hannah glanced back at her. The LED flashlight turned her face into an exercise in artistic values. Her left eye was a dark pit; her cheek was a blinding curve. "I never reveal my secrets," she said, and winked.

"Dweeb," Laila said. Her face had filled with heat, but she let herself hold Hannah's eyes, because she knew that—for once—Hannah wouldn't be able to see her cheeks darkening.

Hannah paused on the landing to the second floor, still regarding Laila with impish amusement. Laila waited for a gentle insult volleyed back, but Hannah just shook her head, grinning, and pushed through the door.

The warehouse's second floor had twelve-foot ceilings, crown molding, and decaying walls with significant holes, like a demolition crew had gone to lunch and forgotten to return. "The old offices," Hannah said knowingly. She tended to speak about things she'd never encountered as if they'd been known to her since childhood.

"Did they mean here?" Laila whispered. "Which floor? How are we supposed to know?"

"Keep that light away from the window."

"Yeah. Sorry."

"No, it's fine. Let's check the next floor."

They did. This was storage, ancient cardboard towers stacked against plaster columns, corners of boxes pried out and their contents raided.

They'd barely entered the fourth floor when a beam of light swung through a threshold ahead. They sucked in a unified breath and dodged back into the stairwell. Hannah caught Laila's shoulder in a viselike grip, keeping her from the edge of the steps.

"Found it, I guess," Hannah breathed. "You think that was him?"

"I don't know," Laila said. They were motionless for a second, studying the door. Hannah seemed to realize she was still gripping Laila's shoulder, and she drew her hand away as if Laila's jacket had grown uncomfortably hot.

"Um, I'll just," Laila said quickly and hurried forward. Before putting her ear against the door, she passed her gloved hand over the metal, knowing it would probably clear away approximately none of the germs, but at least the gesture was reassuring. The voices behind were deeper than Felix's.

"Not him," Laila whispered. "Let's go wait with Leo."

They retreated, but on the second floor, Hannah's phone buzzed. "Leo says he heard a door open down there," she whispered. "He thinks maybe there's a back entrance or something."

"So we should watch the stairs," Laila said.

"Yeah. I'll tell him to stay put. Let's just—" They slipped into the second-floor offices but left the door cracked enough to monitor the stairs, and they watched as a procession of unfamiliar bodies trickled upward. Fifteen minutes until the fight, then ten. All but two of the arrivals were boys, and they were all talking at earsplitting volume, which ruined the tense, breathless feeling that had given Laila the ability to hear her heart knocking gently behind her eardrums since they'd crawled through the windows. "People come here a lot?" she asked Hannah.

"I'm sure, to smoke," Hannah said. "I've smoked on the roof of the warehouse a few doors down a half dozen times. It's really nice, there's a skyline view and everything."

"What's smoking like?" Laila asked.

"Why, is this next on your gotta-try-it-to-impress-a-teacher list? Because if she says anything about meth, please give that shit a hard pass."

"I'm not trying to *impress* her, I'm . . . I don't know."

"Hey, you don't need to explain." Hannah was looking at her with something unusually like fondness. "I get it."

"Do you?" Laila said. Her eyes were adjusting to the streetlight bleeding in from the windows in the next room over. It made Hannah's hair look colorless and soft.

"Yeah," Hannah said, folding her legs, "I do, I get it." That cross-legged position made Laila remember sleeping over at Hannah's for the first time, in freshman year. Laila's mother had been thrilled. Camille had slept over at her friends' houses since she'd been seven years old, staying after ballet class with their tiny feet red and suffused with blood, getting up early to slurp cereal from matching bowls. Laila had never been anything but alone, and the sleepovers came late, at a time when Hannah was still ferocious and loudmouthed and hardly even admitted to enjoying Laila's company—utterly unsocialized, like a girl raised by mountain lions who'd loped in from the wild.

"I don't want people to think this is some rebellious phase or whatever," Laila said. "She's making me better at the only thing I care about. I feel like I'm waking up."

"So this isn't a bucket list," Hannah said.

"Nah, it's just—it's insurance," Laila said. In case she never got the chance to do these things again, here, with people she loved. In case she was going to leave, and Felix and Hannah and Leo would never have seen her become something or anything else, never seen her slip into any chrysalis and emerge evolved, and then they would think of her as a crystallized artifact of their previous lives, and they would leave her behind. In case she stepped out onto a street and a truck took a corner too fast. In case she put her fingers to the keyboard and nothing came out, and suddenly she was dry of experience or thought.

Then Hannah's hand was on her wrist. Her fingers were warm. The touch sent a rush of strange white heat up to Laila's shoulder, and her eyes landed on the chewed neck of Hannah's sweatshirt, which was high couture and therefore looked as if somebody had assembled it with iron-on prints at an eighth-grade birthday party.

But Hannah wasn't looking at her. She had her phone out again. "Leo says the cops are here," Hannah whispered.

"*What?*"

"Get up, we have to go. Hurry."

They stumbled to the next room, peered down through its row of windows at the street. Two police cars sat at the bottom of the road, empty. Four officers crawling around this place.

Laila knew that Hannah was thinking the same thing: They had to find Felix before he got caught. Then they had to run from the cops. This wasn't what she'd planned for. Laila wondered if every questionable decision was destined to snowball, if that was just how risk always played out, with particular attention to gravity.

She and Hannah hesitated at the door to the stairwell but hadn't taken a breath before two bodies, bulky with items at their belts, jogged upward. They flinched back, waited, and hardly a minute later, Felix's long body twitched up the steps before them. They barreled through the door, grabbed him, and yanked him back. He was halfway to punching them before he realized.

"What are you guys doing here?" he said. "I didn't tell—"

"The police are here," Laila hissed.

"I—they *what*?"

"Two of them are upstairs," Hannah said. "Let's go. Come on."

"No. I need to get this over with."

Laila snapped her fingers in his face. "Are you listening? The cops! Do you want to go to jail? You want me and Hannah to be the ones to tell your mom about that? Because—"

Yelling ricocheted from the fourth floor of the stairwell. Hannah shoved the door open and shouldered them both through. *"Fucking go."*

They fucking went. Laila leapt down two steps at a time, dodging the silvery snatches of chip bags. Each time her toes missed one, she pictured turning her ankle, hurtling headfirst down the poorly lit steps, arms outstretched, two snapped forearms, skull meeting wall. She reached the bottom of the first stairwell and grabbed the rail, which felt like pure slime, a fulcrum to send her rocketing down the next set of steps. Beside her, Felix was going three at a time, until—suddenly—his feet became misplaced, his arms overreached, his body betrayed him. His right foot hit the ground floor at an angle that Laila could see was wrong, even in the vibrating light from Hannah's phone. He didn't let out a sound, but his jaw fell, lashes drawn up from widened eyes as if electrified. Laila staggered to place herself beneath him, to catch his fall. Her arms closed around his waist, and she stumbled back with his momentum until her head knocked into the cinder block. Showers of light rained into the stairwell. Hannah was stringing together curses in new and spectacular formations, her hands seizing both of their forearms, because footsteps were so close above now that Laila could hear the details around their corners, the specific scrape of grit.

Felix drooped. Laila's back pulled with the weight of him. Hannah rotated them—Laila had a faceful of Felix's hair, could see only slivers of barely lit concrete—and then Hannah killed her phone light, and they were beneath the bottom stairwell, hunched into a triangle of black space so thick with cobwebs that Laila couldn't breathe without feeling them tremble around her lips. Felix had slumped back against her. She hadn't thought of him so physically before. He smelled like afternoon rain and fabric softener, and he quivered in her grip, tiny breaths tripping from his mouth as his hands thrashed the air in desperate pursuit of his ankle.

Laila remembered season six, episode nine, of *The Rest*, the most controversial episode of the most controversial season, which took place entirely in a blackout, with fragmented objects in negative space the only thing visible. "The experimental cinematography doesn't guide the eye," a scathing review had said, "so much as suggest that the episode's director considered that somebody might be watching and decided, deliberately, fuck your need for guidance." Which, to Laila, had sounded strangely like praise amid the rest of the sentences in the review, which had been filled with phrases like "overwhelming incompetence" and "this backbreaking disappointment of what used to be so enjoyable."

Light broke the nest of invisible sensation, and a clank rang out from the door's long-rusted opening mechanism. Somebody barreled out of the stairwell door and directly into the two other police officers, who were waiting calmly on the first floor for the kids they'd known would run, terrified. That could so easily have been them if Felix hadn't twisted his ankle. This seemed unfair— the police's advantage of experience and training, a totally unbalanced situation, although that was of course how law enforcement was supposed to work. Laila closed her eyes, her hand finding Hannah's and squeezing so hard that Hannah's grip gave out beneath her fingers. "It's okay," she heard Hannah whisper, barely loud enough to hear, but so close that she could feel Hannah's mouth moving a millimeter from her earlobe. "Just wait. It's okay."

Felix had sagged too far. Laila pulled Hannah's hand to the front of his hoodie, and they maneuvered him silently to the filthy floor. Laila tried not to picture vermin or insects ground into dirt by the years. She squatted by Felix's twitching body, still in shock, and stroked his hair back from his face, which was a labyrinth of sweat trails, and they waited in the shadows until the first police officers, the ones who had run up the stairs to flush out all the miscreants, had returned down the stairs, saying to a trio of strangers with slumped shoulders, "Go. Go. Watch your step."

"You can tell the truth," Leo said. "You just did this to get out of going to the Catskills."

"You got me," Felix said. His twisted ankle was propped ostentatiously on a mound of cushions, an ice-filled Ziploc sagging over the joint. "I hate nature and I hate you."

"Hmm," Leo said, unbothered. "Doesn't matter, I guess. Hannah can give you a piggyback up the mountain if this isn't better in two weeks."

"Are you trying to kill me, Leo?" Hannah said. "Come on, let the guy rest." She set a bottle of ibuprofen and a glass of water by Felix's bedside. "Get some sleep, Wrestlemania. Or else."

"Remind me on Monday," Felix said. "I gotta add doctor to the list of jobs you should never have."

Leo ushered Hannah out into Felix's living room before she could retort. In the threshold, Laila looked back at Felix and smiled. "Rest up?"

"Yeah," he said. "Thanks, by the way. I owe you guys."

"Of course you don't," Laila said. "See you Monday."

Five minutes later, Laila and Hannah were outside Felix's building, silent, watching Leo's cab edge down the one-way street. After he disappeared, Hannah said, "You okay?" She'd absorbed her parents' rushed, reluctant pronunciation of these words. *Y'kay?*

"Yeah," Laila said. "You?"

"Fine."

"Weird night, right?"

"There have been more normal nights," Hannah said. "Want to get some ice cream or something else packed with sugar?"

"Yes. Please."

"Thought so. I already found a place." Hannah zoomed in on a cluster of red pins on her screen. She turned once, then in the other direction. "This way. I think. No, this way."

This was the first warm evening of spring. They were close enough to a street full of clubs to hear the distant syncopated thuds and to hear bands of people laughing their way from block to block, their voices blending into a lively cluster of midtones. Hannah and Laila were quiet, walking. Hannah pulled at the shred of a scarf tucked into her weathered army jacket. There was a spot of something dark and sticky from the warehouse on the thigh of her charcoal jeans, which formed drainpipes into her most severely decomposed vintage sneakers.

They exited the northwest corner of Crown Heights, heading through Fort Greene, then passed between the waist-high iron grilles that bounded a tiny park. In this neighborhood, the pursuit of green space had become a ferocious battle between housing commissioners and wealthy residents. This was a malnourished alleyway more than a park, a ten-foot-wide strip of gravel bounded by a dozen skinny willow trees, but it had been the subject of meetings and petitions and counter-petitions and protests since 2011. In the wake of the rain, the park smelled as soft and damp as moss.

They'd been walking in contented silence, but suddenly Laila was speaking. "You didn't mean what you said on Thursday, did you?" she asked. She hadn't even realized she'd been thinking about it.

"Which part?" Hannah said.

"About me being boring," Laila said. "You—I don't know, you said I wasn't fun."

"I don't mean anything I say. Ever."

"Right . . . but—"

"No," Hannah said. "Being serious: I thought you'd know I didn't mean that. Sorry."

"Yeah. I know you were kidding," Laila said. "Sorry, I don't know why I brought it up."

But she did know, as Hannah went quiet and looked back over the strings of chains, scrutinizing the willow bark. Laila wanted Hannah to tell her all the ways she was exciting and fun. Hannah never did that, though. Laila would lead her to the precipice of some obvious compliment and Hannah would stop every time, yanking, obstinate, refusing to say the words. In the early stages, Laila had used to think this was a tactic Hannah used to keep people interested. Like playing hard-to-get. Now she knew Hannah had no language to express things like appreciation or affection; they were too difficult, and had to be talked around for years in phrases like "I already found a place."

As Hannah perched on a bench near the park exit to lace up her sneakers, she said, "So, was tonight useful? Going to write it into something?"

"Yeah. Nazarenko told me to take a risk." Laila sat down beside her. "I guess I pictured risk being fun, but I'm kind of freaked out. Those guys could get time for that. Could've been us."

Hannah sighed. "Yeah, well, that's what happens after the adrenaline rush. Consequences."

"The likelihood of suffering."

"What?"

"Nazarenko told Samuel and me that risk is the likelihood of suffering."

"God, she sounds emo."

Laila laughed and looked up at the street of sky overhead. After a quiet moment, her smile faded. "You know, one of his assignments," she began, and hesitated.

"Samuel's?" Hannah said.

"Yeah, his last assignment. I found this note Nazarenko wrote. She told him his female characters seemed like glorified sex dolls."

"I retract my derision, I love her."

"So, she said he should spend some time with a girl he thought was unattractive."

Hannah waited a second for her to continue. Then it seemed to sink in. She straightened up. "Laila."

"I've always tried so hard not to think about what I look like," Laila said, rushing through the words. "Or, I mean, what strangers think of me, generally. It seems like such a waste of time. But now that I'm trying to put myself out there and get out in the world, I feel like—I don't know, I'm losing all this control I had when there was only us four, and Mr. Madison, and my family." She swallowed hard. "This would never have happened before. Suddenly wondering whether I'm *attractive*. I miss when I could just send you guys a biweekly picture of me with Malak, and I knew you guys loved me, and I didn't have to care that this is what people see when they look at me."

Hannah was quiet for long enough that Laila managed to blink away the hot itch of tears.

"Look," Hannah said. "I had a lot of those same thoughts freshman year. I had no friends in middle school. I mean, none. So getting close with you three, and then with Ethan and the others, and then dating—all of it felt so invasive, like I had to give up this power I used to have, back when I could call all the shots and be distant and not give a shit."

"Caring sucks," Laila said.

"For real," Hannah said. "But . . . I don't know, the payoff is such a rush. One day I spend with you guys is better than my entire middle school life. Even when we're fighting. So, yeah, you give up control and you take your risks and there's the likelihood of suffering."

Laila half-smiled. "Yeah." She rubbed one of her eyebrows over and over, the soft hair rising and flattening beneath the pad of her index finger. "I just felt hollow when I read that note. Not even hurt so much as totally taken aback. I mean, I guess I'm realizing I don't even know my own face. Know what I mean? I look in a mirror and see what changes. If I get a spot or a bruise. Otherwise, I have no concept of the way I look."

"Do you care what Samuel Marquez thinks?" Hannah asked.

"No. Yes." Laila leaned back. One of the rivets on the bench knuckled against her spine. "I thought so. I wanted him so bad for three years, and he lied to me, and he was using me, and all that sucks, but mostly I think I'm disappointed that he was nothing like I imagined he would be. I need to stop doing that. Making people up."

"Do you care what I think?" said Hannah.

Laila examined the uneven paint on the bench planks, so many coats of so many colors that beneath the chips, she could see hair-thin layers of white, pink, dark green, gray. "Yes," Laila said, and she felt like she'd never made a bigger understatement.

"Okay," Hannah said. "I'm glad it didn't work out. You and him."

They were looking at each other now. There was a smudge of something grayish and mineral against Hannah's temple, a touch of grime from the warehouse. She had a split in her lower lip; they were always chapped.

"Because I'm selfish," Hannah said. Laila couldn't remember ever hearing Hannah's voice so careful, so strained.

There was a person's width between them. Laila remembered the footsteps in the warehouse stairwell, and her pulse drummed along with the erratic rhythm. This, here, sitting in silence, was the risk. They could stand, finish the gravel path, emerge back into the city, joke over ice cream until Laila's curfew. Or they could stay.

"How was kissing Sebastian?" Hannah asked, and Laila experienced the uncomfortable jolt of knowing, definitively, that they were thinking the same thing.

"It was okay," Laila managed.

"Weird. I've heard guys are supposed to be gross and nervous. Lots of tongue, so say the rumors, and by 'the rumors,' I mean Bridget."

"He was—no tongue excess. He was fine. But I also have zero reference points."

"Fair."

They weren't far from the park's exit. One of the gates had come free of its stanchion, and it was half-closed and creaking. A net of ivy that hadn't let its spears peek through yet wrapped around two brick columns. The noise of the bars seemed isolated to the streets beyond, where whoops and bass rang as if inside a fishbowl.

"Do you want one?" Hannah said.

"Do I . . ."

"A reference point."

The night contracted, suddenly darker and closer. Laila's focus couldn't settle. Hannah's wrist peeked out from her army jacket, wrapped in a golden watch. Her hair had been bleached so many times that sometimes chalky threads would flake off and stick, as they did now, to her earlobes and neck. Laila heard more than felt the wind shift and suddenly caught the scent of something burning: Hannah's perfume, or maybe cologne. Hannah didn't hug, only ever put up with hugs from Leo, but Laila knew that scent anyway. Laila thought of the crown of Hannah's head against her thigh as the halo of afterglow simmered around a recently extinguished television, Hannah's hand bound around her forearm at the bottom of the warehouse steps, Hannah's foot against her calf upon her bed.

Laila waited for her to break, anticipating the grin that always followed Hannah's fake flirtations with Felix and Leo, wondering how she would laugh this one off. She didn't.

"Yeah," Laila said.

Hannah slid over haltingly until they were side by side. She leaned up and hesitated, her lips so close that Laila could feel a slow, careful breath loosed against her skin, as warm as the evening. The tip of Hannah's nose grazed Laila's cheek. The tiny, gentle piece of sensation sliced in like a razor. Laila closed her eyes. She had to focus on the dark, the stillness—her systems were going so fast, neurons in overload, heart in breakneck pursuit of something.

Hannah's lips pressed to Laila's jaw. Her mouth was rough and warm, and Laila's eyes drew open, her gaze fixed on a willow tree on the opposite side of the path. Hannah's fingertips shook over the shell of Laila's ear, sank into the thick frizz of her hair, and Hannah slid a leg over Laila's lap until her knees met bench on either side, and Laila couldn't see the trees anymore, because Hannah's nose and eyes and the miniature channel pressed into her upper lip were suddenly the center of the known universe, the point around which Laila had been orbiting for longer than she'd realized.

—

The apartment is one-eighth mine. The infrastructure greets me when I walk in. "Hello, Eden," the voice in the ceiling tells me, as the curtains open and I am shown the brown of the Hudson River, exposed to one million points of sun glare that ricochet off Chrysler roofs and aviator sunglasses and windows of lesser skyscrapers.

My months are December and one half of January. Bad, cheap months. Not so bad or so cheap as the second half of January plus February, which belong to Ali. I have never met Ali, but the landlord has told me that he's considering revoking her bloc of tenancy because he has recently learned that she is artificially intelligent. When the Dismantling bill comes through Congress, he says happily, he wants to be shot of all that.

Then, on January 6, the Epiphany, she arrives one week early.

From: Laila Piedra <lpiedra2000@gmail.com>
To: Tim Madison <timothy.j.madison87@gmail.com>
Subject: stuff   3:11 PM

Hi Mr. Madison,

I have a new draft for you. Here it is.

Also, have you ever had a day that felt like it changed the trajectory of your entire life?

Laila

From: Tim Madison <timothy.j.madison87@gmail.com>

To: Laila Piedra <lpiedra2000@gmail.com>

Subject: stuff   3:18 PM

Dear Laila,

That sounds like a stressful sort of day. Excepting days that I have been hit by cars, not that I can think of; why?

I loved your last draft, and I can't wait to see how this one tops it!

Sincerely,

Mr. Madison

From: Laila Piedra <lpiedra2000@gmail.com>

To: Tim Madison <timothy.j.madison87@gmail.com>

Subject: stuff   3:26 PM

Hi Mr. Madison,

It was a stressful day, even though I'm also ecstatic. Not getting hit by a car stressful, but still. To be honest, I'm scared to tell anyone else, but: I think Hannah and I are going to be together.

I'm probably not thinking straight right now (lol get it), but I feel like going up to the top of my building and screaming, "Take that chance you're scared to take," and I *know* it's freaking live-laugh-love cheesy, but I also feel like I just jumped off a mountain and started flying.

What I'm saying is, DO IT, ASK HER OUT! haha

Laila

From: Tim Madison <timothy.j.madison87@gmail.com>
To: Laila Piedra <lpiedra2000@gmail.com>
Subject: stuff   3:34 PM

Dear Laila,

I'm so very happy for both of you. From the way you speak about Hannah, it's always been obvious you have something special.

Significant events unearth those greeting-card emotions, don't they? I'll admit, in the moment of disorientation after the accident, when I wasn't sure what had happened, the words that came to my mind weren't Shakespeare or Plath or Milton—and I wrote my thesis on Milton! I actually thought about an insurance ad I used to see playing before every other video I watched online. (I must have been their perfect target demographic.) There was a scene of a house burning and a family watching. I think they added cheerful music to make the image less sordid—they turned it into a joke somehow. At the end of the video, a banner scrolls across the screen that says, "We know what all this means to you." That was what I was thinking after I was hit! Somebody's tagline.

I will *very tentatively* consider asking Ms. Bird to coffee. Fear historically gets the better of me. We'll see.

Sincerely,

Mr. Madison

p.s. This story is my new favorite.

15

THEY WERE THE FIRST TO THEIR BOOTH ON MONDAY, and they sat on their usual side, spending inordinate amounts of time "preparing" their lunches. Laila couldn't speak. They hadn't spoken since Saturday, hadn't texted, nothing. Did that mean Hannah wasn't interested after all? But then again, Laila hadn't said anything, either, and she wasn't trying to avoid Hannah. It was just that everything they normally talked about—even the deeper, larger things, like Laila's family frictions or the way that looking college freedom in the face felt like looking over the edge of a precipice—seemed miniature and temporary. Now they were something new to each other, and that defined everything else they cared about.

To add to the disorientation, Laila's memories of Saturday kept expanding and contracting. In yesterday afternoon's vivid reimagining, they were kissing for an hour; this morning in physics, barely a minute. Last night, Laila had a dream about lying beneath a willow tree with Hannah—not the anemic willow trees in the park but a lush one the size of a forest, miniature trees blooming and cascading out from its thick umbrella—somewhere by a murmuring river, while Hannah drew patterns over Laila's bare thigh, up between them, and she woke blazing with heat and shame, pushing the heel of her hand desperately between her legs.

The cafeteria's reverberant noise only made their agonizing silence feel more obvious. Laila wondered wildly if they'd ruined this forever. Maybe this was the time to ruin things, if they were going to be ruined, because they only had four months left, anyway.

Four months ago, Laila had been dusting up the last of her college applications, Mr. Madison had been encouraging her through a story about interdimensional travel—a thinly veiled riff on *In the After Path*—and she'd still never done anything without checking it against her parents' sensibilities. How could that time move so quickly, and how could her life before that barrier shrink so dramatically into a vacuum-sealed packet of memories? Where would she be sitting in four more months: Bowdoin or Brooklyn College, alongside Felix? Would she be remembering this weekend as the one that had taken away her best friend forever and replaced her with unnavigable territory?

Hannah said quietly, "You look nice today."

Laila met her eyes. Hannah was wearing a rare dash of eyeliner. Laila's first instinct was to reply, wide-eyed, *Wait, we do compliments now?*

Hannah's pinky finger was tapping the table in moth-quick beats, though. She was nervous, Laila realized. Nervous in a way Laila hadn't seen her since sophomore year, when she'd accidentally broken one of her parents' sculptures during one of their watch parties (throwing a pillow at Felix, of course).

"Thanks, Han," Laila said.

Hannah's cheeks suffused with a brilliant rose color that Laila had never seen.

—

Hannah (1:06 a.m.): you up?

Laila (1:06 a.m.): Sorry! I'm not conscious at the moment! Please leave a text at the beep!

Hannah (1:07 a.m.): VERY CLEVER but I SEE THROUGH UR RUSE

Hannah (1:07 a.m.): so. how are you feeling

Laila (1:07 a.m.): You mean like in general?

Hannah (1:07 a.m.): nope

Laila (1:07 a.m.): Didn't think so.

Laila (1:07 a.m.): Um, I've been thinking a lot about it and I feel really good. Do you?

Hannah (1:08 a.m.): yes. very, very good. the best actually.

Laila (1:10 a.m.): It's just. I've never done this before. So I don't really know what we do next? What do we do next

Hannah (1:13 a.m.): oh in my experience we either 1) dive into things so quickly we crack our metaphorical skulls open on the metaphorical pool floor or 2) have a confusing text conversation about taking things slowly and then make out in the gym supply closet

Hannah (1:14 a.m.): there's about 8 million excruciating shades of gray in between those though

Hannah (1:15 a.m.): take your pick

Laila (1:15 a.m.): How did you date five girls and learn nothing?

Hannah (1:16 a.m.): look. none of them were you. this is a fickle business

Laila (1:16 a.m.): A fickle, yet highly profitable Fortune 500 business

Hannah (1:17 a.m.): fuck yeah, i'll get informatics to loop me in on the updated projections so we can explore actionable options

Laila (1:18 a.m.): Screenshot that text to Harvard Business School and you'll have grad school locked in before you even get next year's roommate placement

Hannah (1:19 a.m.): EXCUSE you, business schools will take one look at a photograph of me and throw my resume ON THE FIRE or I have NOT DONE MY AESTHETIC CORRECTLY

Laila (1:19 a.m.): No, okay, that's way more likely.

Hannah (1:20 a.m.): lmao

Hannah (1:20 a.m.): listen, I didn't tell the guys anything. do you want to?

Laila (1:20 a.m.): Maybe we should wait.

Hannah (1:21 a.m.): sounds good, we are very good at waiting for things apparently

Laila (1:21 a.m.): hehe

Hannah (1:21 a.m.): hoho

Laila (1:21 a.m.): Hey, I need to go to sleep. Talk more about this tomorrow? I guess?

Hannah (1:22 a.m.): yeah. definitely. have a monster-free dream sequence

Laila (1:22 a.m.): :)

Hannah (1:22 a.m.): :D

The note said, "See me." The score was a 68. A passing grade.

Throughout Nazarenko's lesson on—of course!—manufacturing methods in late-1800s China, Laila pushed so much energy into repressing a smile that the corners of her mouth ached. After seventh period, she returned to room 431, but before she could ask for advice, Nazarenko beckoned her to the front of the class and offered her a brown paper bag with twisted crêpe paper handles. Inside were two books: a copy of Nazarenko's *A Flight of Roses* and a tiny leather-bound journal. Laila drew out the journal, which was identical to Nazarenko's and whose pages were blank.

"Th-thank you," Laila said, startled. Nadiya Nazarenko had given her a present. She felt as if she should inspect the paper for anthrax.

"Use this to write," said Nazarenko. "Wherever you work in this book, do not bring your cellphone. Do not bring your computer. Write down what you see, smell, hear, feel. Write down the associations you make between those sensory points and your own memories."

"Okay," Laila said.

"Your piece suffers from a nebulous sense of place. You could exaggerate this effect and create the illusion of an everyplace setting, or you could narrow down on a world that your reader can feel, but be decisive. Practice existing in your present physical space."

Laila nodded.

"This is a workable draft," said Nazarenko, and Laila's lungs seemed to fill with helium. She held her breath and expected herself to float.

That night, at dinner, Laila left the books stacked at her right hand, and her mother didn't resist the bait. "Lolly, what are those?"

"Mr. Madison's substitute gave them to me. She wrote that book."

Her father hefted the hardcover, brushing his rough palm over the canvas-textured jacket, *hiss, hiss*. "Hija," he said, "this is great. You have a real author helping you with your stories?"

"Yeah. She's giving me special assignments. I think she actually likes my writing. I mean, she's scary, so I can't really tell, but she gave me that notebook to write in. She isn't doing this for the other kids."

"Laila," said her mother, "I'm so proud of you."

Laila felt giddy. Pride had swelled within her like a paint bubble, so bright and big that its curvature tinted the world. So this was the feeling Mr. Madison had been trying to give her. Even alongside the knowledge she could still do better, this was bliss.

"That's actually really cool," said Camille, and she only sounded a little begrudging.

Laila nearly did it then. She nearly told them about Hannah. She came so close that she could see Hannah's blush clashing with her red hair. But this was a perfect night, full of triumph, and she didn't want to introduce that uncertainty. Not yet. Not when her family was regarding her with not just affection, but with respect, with admiration. For the first time, Laila looked back at her parents, those tall, imposing figures, and she felt grown-up, too.

Before first period the next day, Laila tucked the journal into her desk, pinning the covers open with the textbooks that occupied most of the metal slot. She would jot notes on the history classroom, the smell of pencil shavings and dry-erase marker, the whirr of air-conditioning. In any other class, Laila would have felt bad about being inattentive, but in general, nobody seemed less interested in Mrs. Stanton's lectures than Mrs. Stanton.

When the Pledge of Allegiance was recited and the shuffling had settled, Mrs. Stanton said, "Good morning, class."

The class mumbled an unenthusiastic good morning back at her. Rather than giving them her usual disappointed sigh, though, Mrs. Stanton hesitated and tilted her face up toward the white squares of ceiling busy with black dashes. She looked at the ceiling so long that a few of the kids glanced up, too.

"Excuse me," Mrs. Stanton said, looking back at them. "I am so sorry."

Laila realized with a strange, hot jolt that Mrs. Stanton's dark eyes were full, shining with two thick bands of water. The sight was as bizarre as if she had lifted her face to reveal a stranger underneath.

"We heard some awful news this morning," Mrs. Stanton said hoarsely. "Our creative writing teacher, Mr. Madison, passed away suddenly last night from complications after his car accident."

There was an instant filled with recoil, the moment that trails the punch of the hammer into the bullet.

Something alien happened to Laila's body. She was sinking into the ground. She was hovering in zero gravity, somersaulting underwater, feeling the nauseating effects of slow revolution. Mrs. Stanton was taking what couldn't have been more than a second's breath, but a year's worth of space accordioned out within that pause, fold after heavy fold, creating a gross excess of time that seemed to unbalance the axis of reality, so that by the time the woman's voice stirred back to life, Laila had already slipped from her world as it had existed.

What was Mrs. Stanton even saying? Talking about counseling

services, about the school body? How did any of that matter? What mattered was Mr. Madison getting the card they'd all signed. Ms. Bird had to bring that to him, with all their initials and flippant little notes, and he had to ask her, in some faltering, nervous way, if she wanted to get coffee sometime. He had to go home from the rehab center and catch up on season twelve of *The Rest*, no spoilers, please. He had to read the last *Moondowners* book when it came out this September. He'd been anticipating the last installment for five years with everybody else, worked into a frenzy of theories, and he and Laila had to tear through the thirteen-hundred-page finale in a breathless twenty-four hours, and Laila had to send him an email the instant she closed the cover—*What did you think? Can you believe it? Can you believe what happened?* And by then, September, he had to be back here at school, shaky but healed, waiting at Open House to welcome a new class of freshmen who needed somebody to show them a little faith.

Laila couldn't breathe. Her hands felt cold, tingling in an absence of oxygen. She wished he had been wearing his glasses when she'd visited the hospital. She wished his last sight of her had been clear, and that she'd seen him clearly, but she'd been crying, and she remembered a blur. She had no idea, now, what she'd been crying about. He had been alive. He'd been right there, right in front of her.

16

"LAILA?" THREE TENTATIVE TAPS ON HER DOOR. "YOU have visitors."

As her mother drew the door wide, Felix, Leo, and Hannah crowded into the threshold.

"Hey," she said.

They closed the door at their backs. "You weren't answering our texts," Hannah said.

"Which is fine," Leo added.

Laila knew Hannah didn't think it was fine. Hannah had been stressed. Laila had watched a torrent of Hannah's messages come in for eighteen hours before her phone died.

"You think you'll miss school tomorrow, too?" Felix asked.

"I don't think so."

"If you do come," Leo said, "they brought a half-dozen counselors in. They're on call in the office."

"My mom's a psychologist," Laila said. "If I needed one. I don't need one."

Nobody had to reply. The words gained an absurd edge as Laila sat there behind them, wearing yesterday's clothes, smelling like herself in a way that wild animals probably did to create a unique scent identity, having slept for maybe three hours because last night her dreams had been determined to wake her up. Room 431 had appeared in every dream, but not as a classroom. First it was a transitional chamber where a flickering python chased her through a window into an eternal drop. Next came a sanitized-white version of the room lined with surgical carts, onto which Laila crawled and lay spread-eagle, the ceiling spiraling up above her, her skin tingling as she waited for a scalpel. Once she saw him. Mr. Madison was sitting at his desk, but his face was different, unrecognizable, and when she woke up, she wondered how she'd even known it was him, that bizarre imitation with thick dark hair, a face she might have stitched together from advertisements on the subway or faces in the school halls.

Hannah muttered something under her breath to the boys. Leo rummaged around in his backpack. Felix moved to her desk, and Hannah crouched to collect clothes from the floor.

"What are you doing?" Laila said.

"Making sure you don't rot in squalor," Hannah said, hanging towels from hooks on the back of the door.

Laila considered protesting, but that would take energy. And as her floor revealed itself, as Felix stowed binders and loose-leaf and old assignments inside drawers, she felt a small stressor smooth away.

Leo approached her bed with a short stack of books he'd fished from his backpack, which he placed on her dresser. Laila took one of the books, *Halla's Promise*, which she knew was Leo's favorite, but she didn't open it.

"What's wrong?" Leo asked.

"I haven't been reading much of this stuff lately," Laila said.

After leaving school yesterday morning, she'd tried for the first time in a while to dive back into her favorites of these worlds, hungry for escape. But she couldn't read *Moondowners*, with the immortal Darsinnians questioning the meaning of life. She couldn't read *In the After Path* without picturing Mr. Madison listening to a CD player in her sunny, peaceful concept of a rehab center. Besides, that series centered on a family of aliens who lived along the rim of a black hole and knit alternate realities into existence, and the jealousy she felt at the idea of alternate realities was so intense it nauseated her.

"Why not?" Hannah asked.

"I don't know," Laila said. "Maybe I'm growing out of it." She scanned the posters on her walls, weary. The *Season IX* mural seemed cartoonish. She looked at it and all she could see was Mr. Madison's classroom. Brutal reality.

For the next hour, Hannah and Felix sprawled on Laila's ragged deep-pile rug and did homework. Leo took the desk. Occasionally they spoke. Felix read out tidbits from the section he was reading on the Cold War. Leo explained that the density of a dwarf star was so high that a tablespoon's volume scooped out of such a star would weigh several tons. Laila huddled under her covers and made a few small comments in reply, which the others treated as normal.

By the time Leo and Felix left, she was sitting upright on her bed, feeling as if a balm had been spread over a burn.

Hannah had lingered afterward. She approached Laila, stopped a pace away. She hadn't slept either, Laila saw. Without eight hours' sleep a night, the circles beneath Hannah's eyes darkened as quickly as paper over flame.

It felt strange for her to be so close. With a sort of desperation, Laila had been turning the memory of last Saturday over and over, a memory that felt louder and more destructive than a demolition, utterly destabilizing. If she didn't have anything else that felt real, she had this. She had them. She remembered Hannah's tongue brushing her upper lip. The darkness of a bench shielded from a streetlight by rustling leaves. Hannah's fingers forming roots up the back of her neck: hard, fixed, necessary.

Laila touched Hannah's forearm, let her fingers brush down to the knob of her wrist. She could see points of gooseflesh lift in response, but Hannah moved her arm away.

"Listen," Hannah said quietly. "I'm thinking we should hold off."

Laila's hand faltered. *No*, she thought. *Don't make an idiot out of me. Don't decide this was a mistake and walk it back. Not now.*

"I want this to start right," Hannah said. "You need to be taking care of yourself right now, not some new thing."

"You came to tell me you don't want to be with me?" Laila said blankly. Her thoughts were leaden and wouldn't transfer correctly from neuron to neuron. She couldn't believe how alone the idea made her feel, run through with a potent mixture of panic and fear, as cold and strong as the drink she'd sipped at the Ave Maria.

"Laila, no—I do," Hannah said. "I do, so badly, but this isn't the right time."

Laila's voice rose, shaking. "We don't have any other time. You're moving across the country in four months."

"I know. But if we start now, the dynamic will be this shitty imbalance. Me trying to hold you up, probably getting in the way. And you not having space to heal."

The pieces began to work together. Laila could see with perfect, sober clarity. Hannah didn't want to invest a fortune of emotional energy into propping her up. Hannah needed to slip out from beneath the promise she'd made when they'd kissed. Hannah was going to leave her apartment, and then, soon, this city, and she wanted a clean cut.

"I get it," Laila said.

"Laila—"

"I get it. You can go."

"But—"

"Go."

Hannah stood there a moment, her mouth a tight line. Finally, she moved for the door. She kept hesitating, kept inviting Laila to ask her to stay. But then the door was closed. She was gone.

Laila showered, changed, brushed her teeth, and sat down to dinner. Her parents matched today. Her father had swung by her mother's yoga studio to try out her class that afternoon. They were wearing neon, a yellow so pure it verged on green. She couldn't look at them.

"How are you feeling today, sweetheart?" asked her mother. Camille and her father seemed to have surrendered all talking duties to her mother. Laila felt like a patient.

"Hungry," Laila said.

"That's good," said her mother. "An appetite is good news. So is being out of bed. Here." She offered a basket of rolls. Laila practically breathed one in, the first thing she'd eaten all day.

"You have wonderful friends," her mother went on. "They're so thoughtful to come over and help out."

Laila couldn't watch the veins trailing from her mother's mouth to her soft jawline. She eyed the checkmark logos of her parents' workout clothes, those matching marks, making them a unit positioned against her.

"I think getting back to school will be good for you, Lolly. Getting back into a routine."

Laila ate another roll and didn't reply. Didn't meet Camille's wary eyes or her father's concerned gaze. All three of them were a Battleship cohort, like they'd used to play when she was younger, sending over missiles at her invisible playing field, hoping to make impact. From here any attempt at contact felt like an attempt at brutality.

"Laila?"

She'd eaten too quickly. A cavity had ballooned open somewhere between her stomach and her heart, contorting both inward. Its reach stretched up to her head to yank her thoughts downward, affecting her vision, so the kitchen seemed to turn slowly until she was corkscrewed too deeply inside this apartment, she was stuck in the tightest, smallest space, she had to get out.

"Sorry," she said. "I feel sick."

She dashed back to her room, locked the door, and gagged twice over her trash can. Nothing came out. She collapsed onto her bed and hid herself beneath the covers, squeezing handfuls of comforter in a death grip, but the air grew so hot, so close. She needed breath. She needed *out*.

She slid her window wide and climbed down the fire escape into the chirping spring night.

—

Laila lived a fifteen-minute walk from a club called Turntable. Hannah went there on a monthly basis. At 10:30, Laila stopped wandering around Bushwick and joined the line outside the club almost without realizing it. The queue was filled with people who stood, spoke, and dressed exactly like Hannah. Laila felt as if she'd fallen into some ancient hipster primordial soup from which Hannah had emerged at age fourteen, fully formed. Kiss a girl once and suddenly the world seems built to support her existence.

Have you ever had a day that felt like it changed the trajectory of your entire life?

She shouldn't have spent so many of her last words to Mr. Madison on something doomed to fail. She should have seen the expiration date printed against the memory of herself and Hannah together.

Laila cycled through the line that snaked up the sidewalk. A woman beyond the ropes yelled over the crowd to have their IDs out. The bouncer, in the roaring warmth just behind the door, was a tall man with a tattoo of a snake coiled around his throat. He hardly glanced at Laila's ID before waving her through. As she hunted through the front room's wall-to-wall crowds for anything that might indicate a coat check, Sebastian's story about sneaking his friend into Turntable returned to mind. Laila could understand the joke in everything he'd said, now. Just think about this place, with its golden railings and opulent cloth ceilings, getting fooled by a kid and a hand truck wheeling some garbage into a side door. Wasn't it funny?

Two drinks and twenty-six dollars later, because apparently

drinking was an exercise in bankruptcy, Laila had managed to stop seeing Hannah in every short girl with dyed hair. Another drink in, she forgot to care about the price of what she was pouring down her throat, and she launched herself up the purple-carpeted steps, where a spinoff current of clubbers was lured toward a beat that staggered behind the rhythm of the main dance hall. A pair of tall walnut doors cracked wide and admitted her into a room that alternated between electric pink and pitch black, swimming soporifically from light to dark in thirty-second alternation. Laila looked up. The light oozed across the ceiling like lava, migrating toward a distant stack of speakers. For a moment, she thought Knight Gard was performing, had shown up to urge her along again, but it was some skinny pale kid who looked hardly older than Laila, cutting some of Knight Gard's most avant-garde tracks into a repetitive synth hook from an eighties disco song. Circular booths spanned the nearest wall, pressing into one another's oblong sides like soap bubbles, and Laila trailed down the line. She would settle for half a booth. A quarter of a booth. Any empty space.

When a hand grabbed her wrist, she looked down, thinking for a wild second that it was Hannah's hand, thinking that in the place she'd banished herself for distraction's sake, she'd sent herself right back into Hannah's palms, but of course Hannah wasn't there. Instead she saw four girls in a booth, one wearing a sweatshirt with cutoff sleeves that advertised *The Rest: Season IV*. With nauseating clarity, Laila remembered the *Season IV* poster Mr. Madison had pinned beside his desk, all those beautiful faces gazing sternly down on them as they debated the boy prophet's motives. She remembered the noon light drawing gridded squares on the linoleum in his classroom, toeing those lines with her sneaker sophomore year, during one of Hannah and Felix's worst fights. He'd talked her down every day for a week. She remembered when Mr. Madison had the flu in junior year, and he'd missed eight days of class, and Laila had nearly punched Peter Goldman for snidely suggesting they should just replace him. Every day, every conversation, these faces had looked out from the poster on the wall, the sleeping people suspended in their Resting fluid, just waiting to wake up.

"Your patch," sweatshirt girl said. "I looked for that patch for like seven seasons."

Laila didn't know what she was talking about for a moment. Then she looked down at herself. "Oh," she said. "I found it in a thrift shop." The patch on her denim jacket's left pocket was a silhouette of the USR *Washington*, with the motto of Earth's former postapocalyptic dictator stitched in red lettering. LEAVE NOTHING BEHIND.

"You should sit down," said the girl, and Laila didn't argue.

By 2 A.M., delirious with lack of sleep and too-strong whiskey gingers, Laila felt like she'd known the girls at the table since birth. They'd told her they were seniors at NYU and had spent more time introducing their majors than their names (economics, French, chemical engineering, art history). Laila had told them she was a senior, too, but at a small school in Brooklyn. She'd also said she was here with a couple of friends who had ditched her. Amazing that they'd believed her. Everything she said sounded like bullshit; she could hardly sit up straight anymore.

They were still talking. The one with the rimless glasses, Ella or maybe Etta or Anna, it was hard to hear, was from Brooklyn, too. The others were all planning to move to Brooklyn after graduation and live with each other, and were trying to convince Ella/Etta/Anna to go in on a four-bedroom with them, despite the fact that she could live at home for free. This was a tough sell, Ella/Etta/Anna told Laila confidingly, and everyone else told her to shut up because she was an economics major and already had a job offer from Goldman that was set to pay her—according to Aditi, art history major—"like practically six figures, which, what? You're not even twenty-two yet." Aditi, art history major, said *twenty-two* as if it were impossibly young, instead of the way the number felt to Laila, which was like an impossibly distant and ancient future. These girls were so nice, even if they were old in that undecided way—jobless and kidless but so distinct from Laila and her friends that she could have circled the giveaways in one of those spot-the-differences images. The tattoo on the wrist, the wallet thick with cards, the way they spoke without any evident fear of being cut off or taken like a joke. The way they were obviously comfortable with being alone, the offhand way they referenced it. They were being so welcoming to her.

She felt an urge to tell them that the thought of her college decision made her feel ill. It would give her away, but who cared? How could consequences intrude into a space like this?

No—she cared. She did. She had to stay discreet. Normal. Sit up. Drink a little more water, wake the hell up.

"Also, wow," said Jen with the cutoff sweatshirt, "sorry, but your friends suck. They haven't texted you?"

"My phone's dead," Laila said. "We should have figured out a place to meet."

Jen, Aditi, Ella/Etta/Anna, and the other one (Chloe? Carly?) were exchanging looks. Laila had overstayed her welcome. She was angling her torso to slide out of the booth when Jen said, "Okay, well, you should stick with us."

"What?"

"Like, if you need to put down your drink . . . I don't know, this place is usually fine, but there are always creeps hanging around when it's this busy."

"Oh." Laila hadn't thought of that. She got the sudden sense of existing inside a PSA, as if somebody with a camera were going to squat down beside their booth and pan around the table and add text in postproduction that read "Real New Yorkers keep each other safe!" "Thanks," she said. "Yeah, you're right."

"But also," said Ella/Etta/Anna, lifting a baggie out of her pocket for a moment, "we were going to do some molly. I don't know if you're into that, but we tested it earlier and everything and I promise it's not cut with cyanide." She popped one as proof. The others laughed—mirror laughter, the same raspy, back-of-the-hand-to-the-lips laughter. Laila laughed too. The noise sounded manufactured to her own ears, but they didn't seem to notice.

Hannah had done ecstasy every few weekends for the greater part of junior year, and in a protracted instant of decision-making, this seemed like a sufficient reason for Laila to say, *Yeah, okay, I'll take one.* Because she could do anything Hannah could do. Because whatever happened, she could use it later, pour it out on paper, lavishly described. Because Laila needed to understand everything Hannah understood, so that Hannah no longer had the home-court advantage in reality, the ability to look at everything with a knowing, jaded eye and pretend she'd seen it a thousand times before. If Laila could call her bluff, maybe Hannah would never do this again, kiss her so hard she saw stars and walk off as if she were some footnote on a list of conquests. If Laila took this, maybe she would stop fucking thinking about Hannah, as if having Hannah would fix the horrible empty pit drilled down the center of her body—how delusional did she have to be to believe that? So Laila took the pill and swallowed it with half a mouthful of whiskey. She waited to stop thinking at all, thinking about any of this. She didn't want anything of the world outside the marbled walnut doors. She wanted this circular table and these welcoming strangers and the feeling that some people in the world were doing okay. She wanted this night to open its mouth and swallow the rest of her life. As the ecstasy warmed her body, made her skin an electric field and her hands happy to touch anything alive, Laila journeyed from hall to hall in this thousand-person complex and saw herself in every single one, bent on escape and still trying to find something.

17

LAILA AWOKE TO THE SOUND OF A COLOSSAL MOUTH hushing. The sound surged and receded. The breeze at the hollow of her neck crept up to her jaw. She reached for it, but her hand became tangled in whatever covered her, waist to collarbones. It was soft and inside out. A coat, but not hers. A felt coat. The section that faced outward was glossed in silk.

Laila forced her eyelids up, replacing velvet black with dirty gray. The night sky had unrolled and seemed to flutter as she shook her head, which was a horribly misguided move. She felt each individual muscle pulling and tensing, compromising, to move the impossible weight of her skull. The thing perched atop her spinal column weighed a thousand pounds. During the night, somebody had apparently split her head open, packed her cranium with a leaden reproduction of a brain, and stitched her scalp back together with all the precision of a pigeon stabbing its beak at the ground. Nothing else could explain this.

She licked her lips and spat out what crept into her mouth. The grit of sand and salt. It occurred to her, then, that she shouldn't be able to see the sky when she woke up; the sound of waves kept repeating—she was on a beach.

"Laila," said a voice beside her.

"*Ahh*," she said, scrambling a foot to the right.

There was a girl. Not one of the NYU girls. Somebody else, pale, tall. She had sleepy eyes and her hair blended in with the dunes. Her prominent ears looked like handles to the vase of her head. "It's okay. It's just me," the girl said, which might have been calming if Laila had known who she was.

"Okay," Laila said. She must have met this person last night, at some point after her final memories sputtered out. (Holding to the smooth metal of the spiral staircase, feeling its cohesiveness, admiring its warmth, as around her the bodies blended into pink.)

She didn't have the energy for panic. What time was it? No. No time. Her phone was dead. She jammed her thumb harder into the *On* button. This time it had to work. This time.

"Check mine," said the stranger. "It's in my pocket."

Laila peeled the coat away from her own coat—the girl was lucky she hadn't frozen to death—and shook out the girl's phone. The dead battery signal glared out at them.

"Well, great," the girl said. "Ha, ha. Yeah." She was standing now, looking around. She wore black jeans, and in the moonlight, Laila could see that her shirt said *NO, NO, NEVER*.

Laila stood. Her head flopped, a bowling ball balanced on a dandelion stem. Her hand clutched her stomach, but the sick feeling resided elsewhere in her body, too. It had traveled freely and set up satellite colonies. She'd never felt nausea in her hips and tonsils and forearms and ribs before. If she'd known this was possible, she would have felt more sympathy and less amusement when Hannah texted her in agony on Sunday mornings.

Hannah.

This other girl had given Laila her coat, a romantic gesture. They were alone together in the middle of the night. Had they kissed? Done more than kissed? Laila scrabbled at the void in her memory, trying to pull something out of it, anything—

"Where are we?" Laila said. Her voice broke. She needed to go home. She'd only wanted a bit of distance. She had to get home before her parents finished breakfast and knocked at her door.

"Not sure." The girl didn't seem to care much about this. "Awesome night," she said. "So blue."

Laila walked toward a bridge at the top of the beach, moving as quickly as her head would allow. The stranger followed.

"How long was I asleep?" Laila asked.

"Maybe an hour."

They crossed the bridge, and Laila felt a flicker of familiarity. "This road looks . . . I think we're at the Rockaways."

"Oh, yeah, that's it. You mentioned that. For sure."

Dislike coursed through Laila's body. She walked faster.

"Hey," said the girl, as they shifted footfuls of white sand. "I wanted to say thanks."

"What?" Laila heard the panicked edge to her voice and tried to dull it. "Thanks for what?"

"For talking last night. I was thinking before you woke up, and you know what? You're right. I'm going to get the tickets, just *get* them, and start planning. What am I saving up for if I'm letting this go? Right?" The stranger nodded, convincing herself into something. "I can decide for myself how to spend my own money. I bet my parents are just trying to hang on to controlling me because I don't live there anymore."

Laila wanted to stick her head in the dunes. Earlier that night, she must have felt enough of a bond with this person to have some soul-baring conversation, to take some blacked-out adventure to the beach. Two people high and drunk out of their minds and looking for connection—they'd had everything in common. But now the world was real again. She'd run. Her life had caught up. The last seventy-two hours were snapping at her heels, and the girl had become a burden she needed to discard.

The disinterest was draining. Laila wanted to *want* to connect, to have the energy to care about other people. But she didn't—couldn't—care. Not sober.

Laila seriously considered the possibility that she was an asshole. Maybe Hannah had rubbed off on her. Hannah, who tasted like lime. Hannah, who smelled like wood smoke. The sense memory was so sharp and palpable that it displaced reality. Laila was there again, her hip pressed into the bench, with willow leaves batting at her hair. Hannah was holding her hands up in claws, negotiating the wind with newly painted nails, looking as if she were cradling a fantasy flame. Laila felt as if she were staring into a manipulated photograph. The angle of Hannah's face as she leaned down.

Laila could never tell Hannah she'd done this. Going to a club alone was pathetic rebound behavior. Twice as pathetic, since they'd never even dated in the first place.

Laila and the stranger walked to the subway stop. They sat on the A train side by side. For a moment, she considered asking the girl some leading questions. If she cracked this door back open and peeked through again, maybe she would feel everything she'd felt two or four hours ago. Had they staggered in unison through the streets of Bushwick and torn into wisps of music that trailed out from row houses, put clumsy hands at each other's backs and shoulders? Had Laila told her about Hannah? About Mr. Madison? Had she been hunting for consolation from this person, forgetting that a stranger's drunken reassurances would seem shallow and meaningless once the unforgiving daylight arrived?

Had she been looking for consolation some other way?

Laila wanted to stand in a hot shower, scrub away the stickiness, and fall beneath her covers. She'd probably broken eight different laws last night, and she couldn't even remember what she'd felt as a result. She should have stuck to imagining reality.

The girl's face looked flat and distant in the train lighting. She was sorting through her wallet, now, counting cards and dollar bills.

"Hey," Laila said. Her voice sounded younger than Camille's.

"Yeah?"

"We didn't hook up last night, did we?"

The girl's motions slowed. She pressed her wallet closed and looked at Laila, and Laila felt a sharper dread than she'd ever felt in her life.

"I don't hook up with drunk girls," said the girl. "Especially not when I'm drunk."

Laila took a slow, cold breath. Her body felt like a taut rubber band being let loose by degrees. "Okay," she said, tears prickling at her numb eyes. She blinked them away. She decided, then: She had seen enough, done enough. The reservoir of experience was full, and now she would lock herself away to empty it. If she'd become somebody who blacked out and woke up somewhere unrecognizable, she was unrecognizable.

Laila switched to the J train at Broadway Junction, and the girl boarded the C. Laila wondered if she would ever see the girl's face again, hovering at the edges of a crowd. Of the millions of people in this city, the same handful seemed to make recurring appearances. But maybe that was the last glimpse she'd get, a flash of white-blond hair behind closing doors. Maybe they would see each other but not notice each other, see but not recognize, see but not remember. She was already forgetting the way that face had looked.

Eden had begun leaving video cameras around the house. Motion-activated. They saw her at one in the morning, walking and mumbling, and captured her six nights in a row. She liked seeing herself like this. "Creepy," her brother had said when she told him about the tapes, but the sight of her rounds relaxed her.

"Why?" he asked.

"Because I always end up safe," she said.

The one

"Laila?"

Laila looked up midsentence.

The world was an obstacle course for Jaime Piedra's skull. He ducked beneath her lintel, dodged the Ecuadorian flag that hung over her door, and poked his head into her bedroom.

"Have you been writing all day?" he asked.

"Yeah."

"¿Cómo va?"

"Not bad."

She'd snuck back in at six that morning, her parents already bustling around outside her bedroom door, obviously trying to speak quietly in order not to wake her. They hadn't knocked until

7:45 and had decided to let her stay home from school for a second day. So she had to put the time to use.

Getting back to work felt right. Her hangover had half-receded and left the world looking sharp and dehydrated, like oil paint left in the sun. She prayed her father couldn't tell. He seemed to have an uncanny knack for identifying hangovers, occasionally calling cousins at ungodly hours of the morning, listening for a few sentences, and mouthing "chuchaqui" over the counter at Laila. Hungover. This used to make her laugh. Now she understood her cousins' anguish.

She wanted to tell her father to leave. Words were coiled like springs inside her fingertips. She had to scribble them out before they uncurled and receded.

"Is this homework," he asked, "or your own stories?"

"Both. Ms. Nazarenko wanted us to rewrite our last assignment."

"I thought she liked it."

"I don't know. She's obsessed with editing."

"You going to let me read this one?" he asked.

Laila heard the careful humor in his voice but didn't smile. She was looking at Nazarenko's notebook again, scanning her last paragraph. Something off about that sentence. If he would leave, she could murmur it to herself and pinpoint the stutter in the rhythm. "Sure," she said with no conviction.

"Hey, I'll hold you to that," he said. "When do I get to see it?"

The unexpected pleasure in his voice caught her, and she looked up. "I don't know," she told him. The answer she'd given Hannah for years. But this time it wasn't true. She knew her finish line now, a rippling red ribbon for herself to break through: *100/100*.

She rewound, revised. "When it's perfect."

—

The funeral was on Sunday. Laila looked up the church on an on-line map and magnified the image until she could see the roof. She placed herself in street view and looked at the bland white walls of the building, the wrought-iron cages over the windows, and she knew she couldn't go. She knew Felix, Leo, or Hannah would have gone with her if she'd asked, but she couldn't ask them to sit there for an hour while she cried.

Besides, the service was for any of his family who could travel to the city. His grown-up friends. What had she meant to his life, compared to them? How could she watch them grieve and pretend her hurt matched up?

Instead, she locked herself in her room and reread all Mr. Madison's emails. The whole backlog, from the first assignment she'd submitted freshman year to the last words—"p.s. This story is my new favorite."

She looked up the insurance ad he'd mentioned, the one he'd remembered the moment after the accident. The video was thirty-six seconds, and cheerful strings played over a house fire. Two little kids asked about a stream of absurdly specific things trapped in the house. "What about my one-armed action figure that Buddy chewed in half while we were out at a baseball game?" "What about the dollhouse I painted with violet nail polish until I got a headache from the fumes?" "What about the Christmas tree I broke two crystal ornaments from this year?" "Mom, what about— what about . . . ?" The company motto unrolled eventually. "We know what all this means to you." She wondered if he'd thought of this again, one more time, in the last seconds.

She turned off her computer, stowed it beneath her bed, and went back to her notebook. The internet was her enemy. She'd used to love the stream of pictures that made her snort and those twenty-second videos into other people's worlds, but all that felt, suddenly, like both a waste of time and an unbearable responsibility. Hannah had been texting and messaging her, and she hadn't replied. The edited videos Felix emailed her, the short stories Leo sent—she'd been ignoring all of it. Real life was what she needed. Reality.

Laila was back at school on Monday. She felt her friends' concern at lunch over the way she looked, eyes bloodshot and downcast, hair an unbrushed blur, but otherwise, everything seemed too normal. The sight of people laughing in the lunch line seemed obscene and made her avert her eyes. Even her friends seemed too willing to accept that life was zipping along at a merciless pace. "Are any of you having a graduation party?" Felix asked over lunch.

Hannah scoffed lightly. "I think my parents would be more likely to ritually burn my graduation cap."

Laila couldn't laugh. Sitting at this booth felt masochistic, especially beside Hannah, whose forced nonchalance was palpable. Laila's eyes felt too open, although maybe that discomfort was from looking at Hannah in strained sideways glances. Hannah wore a white T-shirt so delicate that, through it, Laila could see the three moles that dotted her back, a small isosceles triangle at the center of her spine. The clasp of her bra ridged like a prominent Band-Aid beneath it, a tan a shade darker than her skin.

"The only celebration I need is this weekend," Leo said, and Laila remembered. The Catskills. The eclipse. How had they only decided on this trip ten days ago? How had her life rattled around so many roller-coaster loops between then and now? Maybe she could fake an illness to stay home. Leo and Felix would understand, especially if she explained the Hannah situation.

Maybe not, though. "It's just Hannah," Felix would say. "You mean you two hadn't made out by now?" And Leo—no, he would take the kiss too seriously, more seriously than Hannah ever would, maybe more seriously than Laila. His overanalysis could be disastrous to her perspective.

Laila flipped through another few excuses but then felt a surge of anger at herself. She'd been so excited about this trip. She'd already done enough she regretted because of Hannah—she wouldn't let herself miss this, too. She would spend as much time as possible with Leo and Felix, and she would take walks, reinvigorate herself, bring her notebook everywhere.

"I'm going to need to work while we're up there," Laila said. "Our last revisions are due next Monday."

"How's it going?" Hannah asked.

Laila shrugged and didn't answer.

She caught Leo and Felix trading an instant's glance. Laila wondered at once if Hannah had told them something. They could have guessed on their own. Maybe Laila should have been more subtle about her avoidance.

"You'll probably be twice as inspired up there, right?" Felix said, a little too loudly. "Don't writers go into the woods and get all romantic about nature?"

"If you need any help with the space bits," Leo said, and pointed to himself.

"Not much space in there anymore," Laila said. "But thanks."

Maybe, she dared hope, she would make an A this time around. Then she might even be able to relax a little.

Sixth period arrived, and with it, another checkerboard of papers splayed across the front desk. She was aiming for an 84, halfway between her previous 68 and a 100. With an 84, an A grade would be an achievable goal.

The number on her last page was 62. A backslide. No longer a passing grade.

Laila walked into Nazarenko's classroom after school and didn't bother saying hello. "Why did you mark this down?"

Nazarenko was drawing something in her notebook. She didn't look up, didn't sound surprised. "Because it's less compelling than your last story."

"How? Tell me how."

"Now that you've abandoned the genre constraints, something feels missing from your main characters."

"What's missing?"

"If I could tell you, I wouldn't describe the element as missing." Nazarenko gave her head a curious tilt. "Piedra, is my opinion on the piece the thing that matters most to you?"

"No."

"So why the interrogation?"

"Because I want this *perfect*. And you're the only other person who wants it perfect, and I—I can't *do* any more."

Nazarenko surveyed her a moment. She appeared to be deciding something, a little hollow puckered in her cheek where she was teasing the inside.

Finally, Nazarenko said, "I recommend you take this week away from the piece."

"I can't," Laila said. "Next week is the deadline for my second application update. Bowdoin can't see an F on my transcript."

"Second application updates are optional."

"They *say* that, but how interested are they going to think I am if I skip something? I have to."

"You don't have to; you want to. Take the week. You have half a dozen more opportunities to revise before class ends."

Laila stared into her calm gray eyes. Was this a test? The same woman who'd kept a four-year vow of silence—she couldn't mean that. Or was this about Mr. Madison? Putting her writing on hold would only make her feel like she was letting him down. She wasn't going to quit. Nothing could make her quit.

"No," she said and went for the door. "I'm going to get this right."

Spring exploded out of adolescence into summer over the next forty-eight hours. Laila reacquainted herself with the million types of heat that marked the transition: the damp heat between backpack and T-shirt and sticky lower back; the frictional warmth rubbed into life between her chafing thighs; the heat interspersed with wisps of cool, earthy dryness when she passed the mouths of cavernous garages; the scented roar radiating from the sides of empanada trucks that made her irrationally angry at the existence of food; the reasonable heat in shade punctuated by crosstown bluster; the unreasonable heat at crosswalks in relentless, beating sun; and her own attempted avoidance by standing in the squat shadows of streetlamps. There was nowhere to escape. Even inside, when she stationed herself in front of her family's living room air conditioner, the sweat that caught between her wrists and her laptop gave the season away. Summer, like dust, had settled into every crack, and it made irritation twice as easy. Waiting in grocery store lines, sweat itching at the roots of her hair, and standing on the J platform as sunbeams prickled dangerously at the exposed skin around her flip-flops' straps, Laila found it depressingly easy to hate other people just for being thickets of heat generation.

"Hey," Camille said on Thursday afternoon, peeking into Laila's room, "I finished the first *Moondowners*."

Laila waved a hand toward her bookcase and didn't turn around. "Help yourself," she mumbled, vaguely aware that several weeks ago, she would have asked Camille everything she thought about the series. No—several weeks ago, she would have had the *time* to ask Camille everything. With five days until her last deadline, there was no more time now. Not for anything except this. Her life felt utterly irrelevant, something to be abandoned as she threw herself instead into a place that didn't exist: the mansion on the seaside of an unnamed country, home to her new main characters during their week together, torn between the crash of the ocean and the quiet whisper of a meadow.

These people she meant to build were proving problematic. She'd never had an issue finding Eden's voice, but twice now, she'd tried to write Eden's dialogue and she'd recognized Hannah's voice before writing a full sentence. Not acceptable.

Hannah had tried to text her three times that week. On Tuesday:

Hannah (12:32 p.m.): hey, you ready for the trip? i'm trying to decide what sour movie concession snacks to bring

Then, Wednesday:

Hannah (4:03 p.m.): how's the story going?

Hannah (6:23 p.m.): so not great?

Then, in the tiny hours of Thursday morning, when Laila was still sitting at her desk, a smear of graphite down the side of her hand, scribbling and erasing fourteen variations of an opening paragraph:

Hannah (1:14 a.m.): this weekend is going to be really awkward if you don't talk to me.

Hannah (1:14 a.m.): not that i don't want you to be there. i do.

Hannah (1:18 a.m.): laila, can we please talk about this

No. They couldn't talk about this. Laila couldn't even think about the kiss; it was a distraction, nothing had come of it, it meant nothing. She had discovered a preternatural talent for directing her mind away from topics that might drain or disturb her. Of course, happiness felt distant. Instead she felt a single median emotion, the epicenter of a spoked dartboard of anger, sadness, cheerfulness, mirth, partitioned from them by an impenetrable metal ring. There were drawbacks. Trying to write when she couldn't access emotional variation felt like trying to walk on feet that didn't exist.

Laila didn't quite trust herself anymore. Was that twisted little jolt what happiness usually felt like? Or that dull, hazy satisfaction? She didn't remember feeling that way in happy memories.

What if the description wasn't accurate? Over the course of the week, she'd started collecting other people's words on the sidewalk or behind the register, to build voices and worlds out of snippets like "Three fifty, there you go, sweetheart" or "That's the thing, bro, you don't even know what he thinking," or "She told me—no, she deadass said, 'Frankly, you're not cut out for'—like, blah blah *blah*, Kristen." All these people had seemed more real than she felt, in possession of full and well-rounded lives, whereas hers was a two-dimensional blue-print. She'd tried to assemble a life for herself and had instead let the whole thing collapse. Fine. This was what she had on the other end. She needed a final shot of inspiration, that was all.

But the more she watched and listened and mined for information, the hollower her interior felt. She was trying to fill a bottomless pit. She started to think that had to be part of the process. Wouldn't she have to be a chameleon, no natural color of her own, to adopt everybody else's? But it made everything so slow, imagining how everyone else went about feeling, and she had no time. She was starting to rely on the idea of the Catskills as the place she would have to shake that last inspiration loose, but she couldn't trust the trip would give her that last shot of inspiration.

So on Thursday afternoon, desperate, Laila flipped the loose caps on a pair of overflowing mailboxes near her subway stop and drew out a pair of postcards, crumpled them into her pockets, and unfolded them later in her bedroom. One said, in minuscule lettering that formed a word search of text in cheap blue pen,

Sammy—

Wonderful to receive your letter. Thank you for thinking of us. Yes, Otto is okay, he has been moved. He would like to hear from you if you can find time to give him a call. Jean and I are preparing to take a trip to Salt Lake City to meet Jean's niece for the first time, so it appears that our travels will overlap, inconvenient, but the bird must fly! Do feel free to email me if that is faster and if you would like to. Jean has started to hate her email because the office sends her requests at ten-thirty! Miss you greatly!

Yours,
Ron

The other read,

Hey dork you asked for a postcard so heres that postcard you asked for.
Rome is awesome, you suck, see you in 2 weeks,

Your Worst Nightmare,
David

Laila returned the postcards to their mailboxes just before dinner and finished her final character sketches: Otto, the sickly sixty-five-year-old in and out of hospitals for decades, and David, the basketball player in love with his younger brother's best friend. Loose adaptations, but she'd needed these seeds. She wondered if she should feel guilty; she didn't. She would never meet any of those people. They would never meet her. Maybe these letters had felt like intimate confessions to the senders, but without context of them as people, the words felt anesthetized and general.

She had to imagine the rest into place: a crooked joint that made Ron's writing that shaky, the way David's looping letters probably got him teased mercilessly in middle school.

The lack of guilt wasn't because she thought her story was more important than their privacy. Privacy hadn't even occurred to her. Being hideously sad creates a type of myopic self-regard that is truly spectacular, and you can perceive this shift even from the inside. You can feel your perspective changing, but that doesn't lessen the effect. The world's population becomes a monolith of people you are letting down, an indistinguishable other, a force of stress and expectation, which makes them strangely into an object for your consumption. They're all bound to hate you in the end, so why not snap at them, withdraw from them, borrow their mail and rifle through their personal lives, stare numbly at them as if they were speaking to you in Russian. Why even attempt positive engagement. What the fuck is the point.

Really, since last week, the only thing that had really made Laila smile was her need to demonstrate to her parents that she was coping, her best act over dinner every night. They never mentioned Mr. Madison, but she'd never been able to hear an unspoken topic so clearly.

"Feeling okay today?" her mother always asked, or some detail about the Catskills trip, which she and Laila's father seemed to be clinging to as evidence that Laila was doing all right, that she was functional.

"A little better today," Laila always said, injecting as much energy as she could into the lie. Nothing stressed her out more physically than those dinners.

Tonight was particularly bad. "How are you getting up to the mountains tomorrow?" "Are you excited for the eclipse?" "Is Leo bringing his equipment?" (Car, yes, yes.)

The moment Laila's plate was clean, she retreated to her room. For the first time in a while, she cracked open her laptop instead of her notebook. Maybe watching *The Rest* might relax her, she thought. She'd never finished the new season, after all. So she signed up for a free Yahoo! trial and made a little event out of the occasion, doused a bowl of popcorn in powdered Parmesan cheese like her father always did.

She turned off the lights in her room, settled in, and couldn't last through one episode. She kept thinking of Mr. Madison. How he'd gushed over the show's surreal visuals, how they'd debated back and forth about the fate of the boy prophet, and how he would never know how that story ended. She remembered how he'd swooned over Grayson's character, and in junior year, she'd let herself start agreeing, silently coming out to him in a way he'd never pushed or questioned. If he'd been there, maybe she would have been able to talk about Hannah, or even think about Hannah without feeling like a hand was clasping her throat. Maybe all this emptiness in her life would have been fixed if he'd been there, if he'd still lived in his apartment in Harlem that he used to joke about because of his awful upstairs neighbors and the heat that gave out every few weeks. If he'd still come into class anxious and humming and still talked to her over lunch about Camille and her parents and her friends even though he'd never known any of them. If she'd still been able to confide things to him that she'd barely admitted to herself yet. If he'd still been there for her. As the characters of *The Rest* fought off their own dreams, she thought of that unreal non-person she'd dreamed up behind Mr. Madison's desk, and by the time she closed the computer, unable to take any more nightmare than she'd been prescribed, she was wondering if anyone else would ever look at her the way he had, with such transparent acceptance that they could arrive wearing someone else's skin and she would still know, *It's you.*

19

HANNAH'S CABIN GAZED OUT FROM COOPER'S HAWK Mountain, a small but defined peak in the Catskills known for the beak of gray stone at its summit. The trail up the mountainside was complex and exhausting, much like Hannah's family. Generally the hike took two hours. Hannah's mother believed everything worthwhile required grueling work, including, apparently, relaxation.

When they began their hike on Friday, the evening light was still crisp and clean, whittling narrow shafts to fit between evergreen needles. Plastic circles tacked to trees, bright yellow, lit the way up like little suns. As the group ascended, the smell of the air took on a subterranean coolness, as if it had just been exhumed from the heart of the mountain. Nothing in the city smelled like this, so recognizably like the life cycle, the pure emissions of oxygen from the breathing trees and the organic materials breaking down underfoot.

They had to stop half a dozen times to hand off Leo's telescope bag, which nobody could carry for longer than twenty minutes without falling behind, but eventually they reached the summit. On the outside, the cabin looked slick and greenish, as if there had just been rain. Its interior was modern, open-plan, minimalist. Leo vanished up the steps with his telescope, preparing to set up on the roof, and Felix loped after him, calling, "Yo, careful, the roof's slippery."

Laila set her backpack beside the downstairs sofa, which she knew was more comfortable than any of the beds. *This could still be a good weekend*, she told herself as she followed them upstairs. A productive weekend.

She perched in the seat by the bay windows upstairs, flipped her notebook open, and looked out at the mountains. She heard the others. Hannah was setting up pots and pans downstairs, moving too carelessly; they banged vocally against one another. Leo's and Felix's voices were muffled through the skylight in the next room, where they'd climbed up into the open air.

Laila couldn't focus. She slipped into a spare room and shut the door, put pen to paper, and tried to draw Eden out into the world again.

Eden's cousins had always described the mansion in colors. Pink for the twee columns their grandparents had wanted to remove and green for the marsh that stretched out behind its patio. The murk of the water was coming closer every day. She'd imagined a building bright as candy luring her out from the drive.

But the light was cloudy that day, and the colorlessness of it was infectious. When she exited her car, the mansion looked threadbare and thin. Time had rubbed out the flesh and left bone.

"Hey! You in there, Hemingway?" Felix swung the door open. "Dinner."

Laila wanted to protest. Finally, she'd gotten past the first paragraph.

But Felix had a warning look in his eye that reminded her of his mother. Ms. Martinez was roughly as compromising as a brick wall.

Laila took a deep breath, stowed her journal, and followed him downstairs.

"Wait," Hannah was saying, flipping a golden flapjack onto Leo's plate, "Angela's parents won't let her take a trip with you after five years?"

"Are you kidding?" Leo asked. "It's a miracle they're even letting her go to the same school as me."

"It's Northwestern," Hannah said.

"Yeah. That's why."

Laila sat at the table and waited quietly for the others to join her. Dinner passed in the same weird, anthropological silence she'd held the whole week, with the others bantering comfortably and her watching them, feeling like a ghost figure from a movie, unable to interact with anyone made from flesh and blood. The pen in her pocket was warm, heavy, waiting for her to return to that quiet upstairs room.

After dinner, Hannah insisted on getting the dishes, Leo and Felix returned upstairs, and Laila set up her pillow and blanket on the downstairs sofa.

Then Hannah sank onto the couch next to her. "Did Bowdoin ever get back to you?"

It was the first time they'd been alone since arriving. Laila wanted to stay quiet. Hannah couldn't *make* her talk.

But apparently Laila couldn't make herself stay silent, either. "I still need to turn in my updated grades from this semester," she muttered.

"They're dumbasses for wait-listing you in the first place," Hannah said. "Didn't Mr. Madison write your recommendation?"

Laila didn't answer. She stared down at Hannah's coffee table, a slab of white stone. The picture of him that printed itself onto the stone was painfully vivid, bottom rims of his glasses pressing into his fleshy cheeks, as if reserves of unsummoned memory had built up and combined.

"He had to have told them you were a genius," Hannah said.

Stop, Laila wanted to say. *Leave it.* She wasn't going to bare her heart to Hannah anymore. Maybe she should have been clearer when she told Hannah to get out of her room. *Things can't be the same*, she should have said. *They can't just go back to the way they were.*

"Doesn't matter," Laila said stiffly. "I didn't turn in my best writing with my application. My best writing wouldn't exist if Nazarenko hadn't taken over."

"Maybe. Didn't Madison love your old stuff?"

"Yeah. I don't know. He loved a lot of things."

"So . . . that makes his opinion invalid?"

Finally Laila looked Hannah in the eye. She didn't want to answer that. Actually, she wanted to leave, bolt up the steps to meet Leo and Felix on the roof, help them with the tripod, listen to Leo talking about the moon and Earth and sun aligned in perfect syzygy. She wanted to be anywhere but here.

"His opinion wasn't invalid," Laila said. "His opinion meant the world to me. And you know that. So don't—" She swallowed twice, once to remove the lump and once to clear out whatever she'd been about to say. She stood. Enough of this. "Nazarenko's pushing me to do better, is all I'm saying," she said and headed for the steps.

"She's pushing you, for sure," Hannah said.

At the threshold to the stairs, Laila rounded on her. "Can you stop that? Half saying something?"

"Okay. Fine. I'm—I'm fucking *worried* about you, okay?"

"What?"

"Getting so obsessed with this story has been terrible for you. You've been so—"

"My mom's a psychologist, I don't need it from you, too."

"Jesus Christ, Laila, I'm not psychoanalyzing you." Hannah stood. "I'm talking the absolute simplest facts. You used to be so excited about what you used to write, and now it seems like it's sucking the life out of you. You're not sleeping, you're not smiling. You're not *you*. And I know you, even if you want to pretend I don't."

Laila felt like somebody had shoved a hand through her torso and grasped some bundle of nerves at her center, squeezing until erratic pulses rang in her extremities. She swallowed panic. She didn't have time for this. She could walk away, singe the strings off this bullshit conversation and come back to Hannah after graduation when the electric charge had faded from the air.

"The writing isn't *making* me miserable," she said. "I'm already miserable, okay? I'm trying to use it."

"So, what, you're okay with staying like this, not getting any help, if you get some good material out of it?"

Laila snapped. "I'm trying to wring one good thing out of all this, Hannah!" she yelled. "Do you want to take that away, too? How much do you need to take?"

Then a messy clutter of footsteps echoed down the wooden stairs, and Leo and Felix emerged.

"—than season nine," Felix finished, but Leo went still. Felix looked over at Laila and Hannah and froze, too, uncertain.

Nobody moved. Then Hannah spoke. "We just want you to be okay," she said quietly. "Leo and Felix both agree with me. We always used to joke about you working too hard, and it's not a joke anymore. Every day, you look like you walked out of a tornado. We can't talk to you about anything. You don't text, you don't talk—you're impossible to get in touch with even when you're right in front of us."

It took everything not to say, *Why are you acting like we have nothing to do with this? You and me?* But Laila couldn't make the words come out. Instead, she rounded on Leo and Felix.

"You guys have been talking about this?" she demanded.

"Yes, obviously," Hannah said, before they could answer. "And it's this teacher—"

"She's *helping* me. She's making me better."

"Really? What's with her getting you to stop reading the books you loved? Stop watching our show? Everything that used to make you happy?"

"That's not everything that used to make me happy. What I read and watched wasn't my whole personality. And *she* didn't do that, I did."

"Then what are you trying to do here? It's freaking me out. What are you trying to turn yourself into? What's next on the chopping block, huh? Felix or Leo? Me?"

"You know what, maybe," Laila said, and felt a shot of vindictive glee when hurt flashed across Hannah's face. "Because I'm not worth the effort right now, I guess."

Hannah froze. Her eyes were the only thing that moved, fixing over Laila's shoulder on Felix and Leo.

She hadn't told them, then. Fine. Laila didn't care if it was out in the open.

"I never said that," Hannah said.

"Yet here we are," Laila said. "You know what, I'm fine. I know what I'm doing, I know where I'm going, and I don't need you trying to hold me back because you think I finally care about something more than I care about you."

Hannah was never speechless. Now she just looked at Laila with a crack of darkness hanging between her lips. The clock on the end table clicked and whirred, hushing into the gearshift before the strike of eight. Hannah said, "I don't even know why you're friends with me, if that's who you think I am."

Laila considered for a moment and realized she didn't know, either. Laila was suddenly sure of it: She'd never been anything to Hannah but a dim reflection of her own cleverness. For four years, Laila must have seen something different in Hannah, or she wouldn't have been so reliant. So excited to see her every lunch period and so eager to organize their watch parties, so willing to quip back and forth with a sharpness that nobody else seemed to be able to manage. But now her tired eyes were itching with openness. Not just in Hannah, but in every person in her life, she saw nothing but curated selections they'd opted to show her, and she didn't have the patience anymore for their bluffs and hesitancies and filters. Finally, she was free of that, no longer a moon to reflect other people's light. Mr. Madison was the only one who'd really seen her, who'd never tried to push or change her, who'd understood her to her core. But that was gone. All the simple, innocent, effortless things were gone. And she was done with pretending anybody else could measure up. With Felix, Leo, and Hannah watching as if she were a wild animal, she grabbed her backpack off the sofa and backed over the threshold.

"Laila," said Leo, but she was already zipping her backpack shut.

"I'm going for a walk," she said. "Don't wait up." She let the door slam behind her, grabbed a flashlight from the porch, and practically ran into the woods.

What they'd said didn't matter. She had no intention of going back. Buses ran at the bottom of the mountain, and the last was scheduled to leave at 10:15. She could still catch it if she hurried.

Laila forged down the mountainside, hot and numb with anger. She kept replaying Hannah's words, and her own, and she didn't know whose she detested more. She hiked until she was sore, until her eyes felt hard with strain.

She had to be most of the way there, although her phone was still lying dead in her desk at home, so she didn't have the time. She stopped. How long had it been since she saw a trail marker?

Laila turned, aiming the flashlight up the slope, and retraced her steps as far as she could remember. Beyond a crosshatch of fallen logs, the trees blended into one another, soldiers identically uniformed in lichen and moss. That patch of brambles looked familiar, but so did that lace of wildflowers to the left.

She needed the trail markers. Cooper's Hawk ended against the road on one side, but on the other, the slope melted into the valleys below. If she wound up in the valleys, she was lost.

She heard shuffling ahead. She clambered forward over a shelf of rock to call her friends' names. She let out a spark of sound—"Han—" before the sight ahead slammed a glottal stop over Hannah's name. A dark, massive figure was crawling out from behind a tree, a glistening hulk of fur that didn't even look like an animal until it turned its great head and fixed its eyes on her.

Bears are somewhat romanticized by the media, like mental illness and adolescence and other things that look questionable on pedestals. This thing was unrecognizable as the source material of anything Disney. Laila had heard somewhere, or maybe seen in a video somewhere, that black bears were small, but this bear stood a foot taller than her at the shoulder, hundreds of pounds of glossy black coat and muscle. When it came to a standstill half a dozen trees uphill, Laila looked into the blank gleam of its eyes and saw her future stretch between them, as fragile and disposable as tissue paper. The bear's eyes were primal and unrecognizable, more alien than anything she'd ever read.

It shrank. Ducked shyly back into the forest. Disappeared.

Laila sank against the nearest tree, suddenly so drained that she thought she might collapse. She looked up at the dusk. Tangles of her hair caught against the bark. The evening's last color had leached from the sky.

She walked and walked. She thought herself in figure eights, coming back to the same defining points. The fury in Hannah's voice. "I know you." The way Felix and Leo had looked at her as if she were a stranger. She climbed back toward the mountaintop, the only certain destination, detoured again and again by trees and bramble patches and stone gulfs.

She imagined the air was thinning, but really everything was getting colder, and her body was tiring. The sound of water brushed the air. She followed it, and when the hiss had turned to a hush and then to an energetic gargle, she emerged from a line of trees onto a cliffside that overlooked a thick cataract pouring through the dark, releasing clouds of mist that she could smell and taste, practically gather up into her mouth.

Laila knew this place. She remembered perching here in the summer after sophomore year, listening to some softly reverberating EDM track through Hannah's speakers, talking about how they would be happy to stay here forever.

Something glinted nearby. Tacked to a tree not a dozen steps away was a yellow circle of matte plastic.

Laila's legs gave out. She collapsed feet from the edge of the cliff and crept into a nearby cubbyhole of stone, which shielded her from the wind that skated over the mountain's east face. She looked a thousand feet below her, down at the carpet of the forest.

Orange light began to pour onto the stone at her feet and hands. Chips of mineral glowed like LEDs. She looked up as a red blot crept across the moon, widening, and everything seemed to coalesce, all the pieces that had broken apart in the cavern of the woods. Earth was casting a distant shadow across its most faithful satellite. Leo would be watching from Hannah's roof, eye pressed to spotless glass, twiddling fine mechanisms with careful fingertips. Hannah would target the sky with her phone, cradle an elbow in her soft palm to stabilize the shot, and add six seconds of red moon to the choppy film reel of her video story, watched by fifty people the next morning who would regret, instantly, that they'd slept through this. Laila could almost see her friends balanced on the shingles, Felix peering into the telescope, Leo's hand guiding the focus, could almost feel Hannah's breathing. She remembered the feeling she'd had in her last conscious instants on the floor of Turntable, everyone hunting for the same fragile thing. She imagined she could hear the crackle of celestial noise three solar systems away. She was swallowed with wonder—it was like nothing she'd seen before, this ripening stamp in the sky—but mostly, she wanted something instant and filled with circuits. She wanted to capture this second in high-definition forever and fire it out, limitless, self-reproducing, like love or regret.

20

THE NEXT MORNING, LAILA CAME DOWN THE MOUN-
tain, out of the trees, tufts of hair escaping her braid, and hitched
a ride to the bus station. At 11:15 she climbed into the belly of
her bus back to the city, and the instant she sat, she dropped into
a deep sleep. When she closed her eyes, the sky was all around.
When she opened them, it had disappeared, replaced with a throng
of people at the bus terminal talking and turning and fumbling
with their tickets and checking their work email on their iPads
and struggling with the zippers on their suitcases.

Laila arrived home shivering. Her parents asked questions
about the trip. She satisfied them with a false smile and some
platitudes about relaxation and retreated to her room, where the
smile sagged away into nothing and she crawled under her covers
to shield herself from the tapestry of other worlds she'd taped
across her bedroom. Nazarenko's exercises had worked. She'd wo-
ken up, come out into the real world, and found so much life that
she didn't want those worlds on the walls anymore. They seemed
small and too-bright and childish.

Laila sat at her desk all day as a skull-spinning fever took her.
Every time she lifted her pen to write, though, she found herself
remembering instead how she'd once felt when she sat down to

work. This had been happening in other aspects of her life too. Last week, every morning, when she'd taken the train to school, she remembered how she'd felt standing on the platform months ago, focused and energetic, when she'd had lunchtime brainstorms to anticipate. The mismatch from the present to the past made her feel as if she were an actor assigned to the part of herself, and she kept forgetting her lines, unable to inject this character's movements with convincing inner life. Her parents, she knew, were beginning to notice, because her smiles at dinner that night looked as if she'd been told to show her teeth, and she'd run out of even enough energy to feign interest in conversation. Let them notice. Let them realize. Later she heard them arguing intently about something and couldn't even give enough of a shit to eavesdrop.

She spiraled through Saturday like a corkscrew, and by Sunday, the last day before her deadline, she was racked with coughs that belted up lengths of horribly polychromatic phlegm. "I left herbal tea for you on the counter, okay, Lolly?" her mother called from the door as she left for her morning run. "Anita from Tuesdays told me how to make it."

"Thanks, Mom," Laila croaked from the kitchen table. The tea was a radioactive yellow and would look beautiful when she poured it down the sink. Anita from Tuesdays was a Los Angeles expat who trafficked in homeopathic herbal remedies, or, as Laila knew them, poisons.

She wrote, erased, wrote, erased. At 4 a.m. on Monday, she had sixteen pages of scraps, nowhere near coherent. She couldn't see the words clearly anymore. What she could see was herself, as if in the third person, the distant point of view sometimes brought on by dreams. She had been convinced that something deep and spectacular could be wrung out of something as small and petty as misery, even though she was too old to believe in alchemy. She was one more person out of billions terrified of being forgotten, scrambling at the thing that seemed the most permanent, because a blood clot the size of a baby tooth could crush an entire life into nothing without an ounce of warning, overnight, to be announced in deadened tones the following morning. She was a romantic reject, a Bowdoin tryhard, a 62 out of 100 person who should give up, stop *trying*—was there anything sadder than somebody who gave a metric ton of effort and would never, the rest of the world knew, see results?

How could Mr. Madison have looked at her and seen anything else? If he'd lived, how long would it have taken for him to have realized he was wrong?

At sunrise, she sat sleepless at her desk, eyes ringed darkly, hair heavy with grease, in front of something she hated. She wondered how she could have made something she hated. Why would she keep going if sentence by sentence she could feel how malformed the piece would eventually be? Shouldn't she have been able to feel, like running through something that hurt, the difference between the soreness of growth versus the stab of muscular damage?

She stood up at 7 A.M., hours before she was supposed to palm gold into Nazarenko's waiting hands, and collapsed onto her bed. Sleep came too easily, a default setting waiting to reclaim her, to switch off the circuit board and let her go dark.

From: Bowdoin Admissions Office <admissions@bowdoin.edu>

To: Laila Piedra <lpiedra2000@gmail.com>

Subject: Waiting List   4:15 PM

May 27

Dear Laila,

We regret to inform you that Bowdoin College's incoming class has been filled to capacity. As such, the College is unable to extend offers of admission to any applicants on the waiting list. However, we wish you success in your future endeavors.

Sincerely,

Paulina Dearborn

Director of Admissions

21

LAILA HAD BEEN EATING LUNCH IN CLASSROOM 344 for a month. Classroom 344 was a biology classroom, and it occasionally smelled of formaldehyde, but the impact on the taste of her food was negligible if she held her breath.

Leo joined Laila here sometimes. They rarely spoke. He sat beside her. The grips of his chair squeaked against the tile as he shrugged his backpack off. Then he spent the period inking perfect answers to problem sets in beautiful cursive. That was his level of confidence: He answered his problem sets in ink. Sometimes his presence made Laila want to embrace him. Sometimes his presence made her want to cry instead, but that was rare.

The past month had been gray. After she'd recovered from her mountain fever, she'd gone through several nights where she could only cry instead of sleep, although she'd forgotten the actual feeling of sadness; the crying was a reflex associated with night, like exhaustion. Staying that sad for so long had started to feel selfish. *Look at me*, her lack of recovery had said. *Look, I'm a sad teenager.* Laila couldn't think of anything more boring. But that awareness didn't help at all with the omnipresent sadness, just gave it a superficial layer of irony. *Look, I'm a sad teenager, but at least I* know *that's a cliché thing to be. Now can I stop breaking down a minimum four times a day? No? Fine.*

So now the crying was gone, and that was better. A deadening quiet had lowered over her head. The days felt pointless and overlong and identical, like an infinite ream of those syndicated comics that never have punch lines, and that was also better.

Hannah had tried to call, twice. Hannah hated phone calls. They made her anxious, disrupting the unflappable exterior she'd fashioned for herself, so she avoided them at all costs. But she'd called twice. Before the second, she'd sent a text: "pick up this time?"

Laila hadn't picked up. There had been no more texts.

Felix seemed to have chosen Hannah in the realignment, but he and Laila had both committed to Brooklyn College. Felix wasn't in the honors program, but sometimes, in little spurts of hope, Laila imagined them reconciling. Mostly she tried not to think about him, or about Hannah.

She completed her homework. She was pleasant at home. She hadn't spoken to Nazarenko in a month and had reverted to a previous draft of her story, the one that had earned her a 68/100. She'd submitted the same draft for four consecutive weeks and hadn't bothered trying to change a word.

Peter Goldman had finally gotten his wish, bringing forth a campaign of outraged parents to rail against the class's 30-percent quarter averages. With three weeks left in the school year, Nazarenko had announced, looking slightly bored, that they would be changing the format of the class to adapt to the school's unnecessary curricular standards. With that, she began assigning them entire books to read in three days. Five-page essays to write overnight. Laila didn't mind. Work filled the space.

Nazarenko's notebook was stashed in her desk's bottom drawer at home. She occasionally reread Mr. Madison's last email to her, because the words made something turn over in her chest, and otherwise, she felt very little.

The auditorium at Impact Future Leaders Charter School had recently been discovered to have a type of poisonous mildew growing in the folds of its curtains, so as a result of the toxic fumigation process, Laila's graduation took place in the cafeteria. A coalition of school moms from the immediate area had done their best to beautify the most soulless-looking room in a building full of soulless-looking rooms. Along the walls, they'd planted long-necked lamps topped with globes of light in deep golds and moody blues. They'd strung heavy cloth in billows at the corners of the low ceiling and constructed an elegant fake stage in front of the kitchen doors, which extended from the place the trash cans began to where the refrigerators made vengeful sounds, like hordes of wasps. Even moms could only do so much.

When Laila walked the stage and received her diploma, the drooping back end of her graduation cap bobby-pinned deep into her hair, she gauged the amount of cheering for her name, the metric by which she'd been subconsciously measuring everybody else's success as human beings for the last forty-five minutes. She couldn't hear anything at all, a fishbowl effect from the echo of her shoes against the resonant fake stage. She was also distracted by the sight of Principal Greene's teeth. How could she have watched him make so many speeches and missed the gap between his teeth, between which she could easily have passed a pair of quarters? And now she would likely never look him in the face again, for the rest of her life. Strange.

None of her extended family had the means to travel from Quebec or Quito for her graduation. A blessing in disguise, so that her mom and dad could afford to take her and Camille to a ridiculously overpriced tapas-fusion restaurant that night. They sat out in the fresh-smelling heat of the garden and sopped up thin, strong gravy with crisp French bread. They pierced rosemary chorizo on delicate-tined silver forks. "Summer," her mother said.

Her father agreed: "Summertime. Heaven."

Laila was watching the people at the table beside them, who were flailing their arms in an aerobic disagreement over the wine list. She looked back at her plate. She could see herself slipping into summer as if feetfirst into the deep end, letting it close over her head. Maybe she shouldn't have committed to Brooklyn College, she thought, folding her wine-red napkin between her fingers in a soft accordion. She didn't think she could live at home any longer. Maybe she should return to the woods, crawl into a thicket, and let it turn her to mulch.

Her dad splurged even more on a cab back home, a luxurious forty-dollar procession of horns and furious exclamations. At home, two presents were waiting, one of which was relative silence, and the other of which was a box wrapped in gold paper, sitting on the counter.

"What is that?" Laila asked.

"Open it," said her mother.

Laila cut the flaps and peeled them back. Her parents had given her a spaceship.

Only five hundred of these models had been manufactured, elegant titanium bullets that clicked and unfurled, revealing a to-scale model of the interior shielded from damage by sapphire glass. The showrunners of *The Rest* had released them in anticipation of season eight. Laila lifted the ship from the box, pressed the white button, and watched one of the worlds she'd loved open itself up to her. There was the Resting room, with those carefully preserved people for her to gaze at, static, unmoving. The same way she could rewind and watch them live out their joys and losses again and again.

Her eyes watered. From the skew of her tears, electric-white stalactites grew down from the spaceship's escape vents.

"Laila?" said her father.

"What's—is something wrong? Lolly?" said her mother, at her side instantly as Laila bowed her head over the counter.

She could almost hear herself telling them that, in fact, everything was wrong. She fought it back. God, so melodramatic, who did she think she was? She could hear herself saying she was so grateful, this was so thoughtful, everything was fine and thank you so much. She pressed that down, too, with more effort.

"M-m-mom," was all she could say. She turned until her head fit against her mother's long, wrinkling neck. "I w—I—" She gasped for air and let too much in, her fingertips curling and icy with an excess of oxygen. "I w-want to wa-a-wake up."

"Jaime," her mother was saying. She heard the rattling of the icebox as her father poured her a glass of water, the thing he knew to do best when faced with strain. When Laila closed her eyes against her mother's dress, she felt as if she were pressing her face into layers of heated blankets, that her mother could keep her safe from everything cold and huge, everything from the vacuum of space to the unforgiving infinity of the future. With all her stories, she'd tried again and again to probe that question with her imagination—what's next?—and found nothing but fear and her own smallness. She bowed under the heaviness of the hours she hadn't lived yet.

22

"NECESITAN SER SUAVES," HER FATHER SAID, POKING the potato with a knife. "Let's give them a few more minutes."

In the week since her breakdown, Laila had hardly left the house. Since then, her parents had been purposefully involving her in their everyday activities. She'd cleaned the apartment with her mother, a strangely relaxing activity once her mother turned on some folk music and started warbling along. They'd dropped Camille off at ballet together, and on the way back, stopped for ice cream. Now her father was cooking with her every night, teaching her recipes and generally treating her like a chef's assistant. It was like being nine years old again, the inability to be alone, the reminders to shower, eat, and go to bed on time. The rhythm soothed rather than angered her, like the swaying of a cradle.

"How about those onions?" her father asked. "We need them soon."

"Almost," Laila said, looking up to the ceiling as she blinked back onion burn. "I told Camille to get the gum out of my room like half an hour ago, I knew this would happen."

"Gum?"

"Chewing strong gum stops you from crying."

"An onion shield?" her father said. "Why didn't you tell me about this ten years ago?"

"Because I was eight and not yet sentient?"

"You make a decent case. Want me to go get it?"

"It's all right; I'll do it." Laila rinsed shreds of onion skin from her fingertips and slid down the hall in threadbare socks.

Hand stabilized against the lintel to her room, she stopped. Camille sat at her desk, back to Laila, with a pack of gum and an orange folder at her elbow. Pages lay in an uneven stack before her.

"Naña?" Laila said.

Camille whirled around. "Oh," she said, her hands already shuffling pages back together. "The gum was in your top drawer, and this fell out when I opened—I didn't mean to—" She wheeled onto the offensive, suddenly indignant at an attack Laila hadn't made yet. "If you didn't want me to read it you shouldn't have—"

"Camille. It's fine."

"It is?" Camille said, deflating. "Right. Yeah. I just know how weird you get about this stuff."

Laila looked at the mess of printouts in her sister's hands and felt a weird longing. She hadn't read a word of that story in months. Had it held her sister's notoriously difficult-to-keep attention for a full half hour?

"What did you think?" Laila asked, when she was sure she wanted to know the answer.

"What?"

"Of the story. What did you think?"

Camille shrugged, not meeting Laila's eyes.

"Seriously. You can say."

"Okay. What's with the bit where she *dies*?"

"You read to the end?"

"Yeah, obviously." Camille dropped the stack on the desk. "It's kind of awesome, Laila."

Laila's mouth was dry. "You think so?"

"Yeah. I liked it better than *Moondowners*."

Laila felt a wave of disbelief so strong it felt like revulsion. That had to be a lie, she thought—there was no way—except that Camille had never lied to her. Laila could have listed two dozen of Camille's personality flaws in under a minute, but her sister never lied. And she especially never lied in service of being generous.

Camille sighed. "Except the bit where she *dies*. Were you just trying to get out of giving her a better ending? Because that seriously seems like a huge cop-out."

"I thought it would be less predictable."

"Um, no," Camille said. "Everybody dies in these epic whatever stories these days. I'm not even surprised anymore. It's like okay, guys, we get it, life is futile, existing is a tragedy. Smile for once, oh my God." She made a face at the outline page, dropped the orange folder on the desk, and brushed past Laila, palming her the gum. "Harriet was reading this trilogy," she said, already bouncing down the hall, "where literally the narrator dies at the end of every book and it switches perspective for the next one. I don't even know *why* they . . ."

Laila gave a last look to the folder before following her sister back into the kitchen. Her father had diced the last of the onions and begun to fry them. The room was filled with steam, her mother had arrived home from grocery shopping, and the rustle of a plastic bag against itself as she unloaded peanut butter onto the counter, the sight of her mother kissing her father on the cheek, two larger-than-life figures wreathed in white billows of condensation, the reluctant thunk as her mother yanked the sticky window up to reveal the evening, waving out the steam—this was what her life had always been. She remembered, now, or was beginning to.

Later that evening, there was a soft knock on Laila's door, and her mother slipped in.

"Can we talk?" she said.

"Yeah."

She settled at Laila's desk, her long back curved in a slight hunch. "We need you to tell us what's happening."

"I know."

"Not necessarily all at once, and not necessarily everything. You deserve your privacy, but—"

"I miss my friends," Laila said, her voice tiny.

"Oh, sweetie." Her mother sighed. "Are you four not speaking?"

"We haven't been in the same room together in six weeks. And it's hard to convince myself that I didn't ruin everything forever. Everything feels really permanent right now. Like I'm always going to—" Her eyes prickled. "—be kind of numb and feel like it's best that nobody spends time with me, because who wants to spend time with someone who doesn't want to be here anymore, you know?"

"Here in New York, or . . . ?"

"Anywhere, I don't want to be anywhere." Laila scratched at a crusted spot on her jeans. "I don't know. I keep feeling like everything would be easier if I . . . not even if I died, like, I don't want to jump in front of a train. I don't want to hurt myself. I just want to stop *being*. If we all get hurt for no reason and good people wind up in morgues when they're thirty-one, overnight, when everything seemed like it was going to be okay, then what's the point? And I feel like everyone's thinking this all the time. Every second they get alone with themselves, really alone. When you're awake too late or you just said something stupid and impulsive to somebody you really love, like the moment you stop resisting, it all floods in, this big nothing, and you start thinking what's the *point*, and I guess I just forgot how to stop asking that question."

Laila could feel her heartbeat everywhere, in the tip of her tongue, in her straining throat. She couldn't stop looking at her mother's sandals, at her toes painted in cheerful stripes. "And if I do get better," she said, "I don't want to be somebody who—you see people coming out of these horrible places emotionally, and they always say, like, I'm grateful for this awful time I had because I came out stronger on the other side. But how much of that is actually real, and how much of it is them telling themselves there was something worthwhile in it because otherwise they went through hell for nothing?" Hell wasn't the right word. Laila rewound. "I mean, I'm not hurting anymore. That freaks me out maybe more than anything else, because, I don't know, will I ever be able to feel something that strongly again, even if it was misery? Was that the most human I'm ever going to get? And why am I not grateful that I don't hurt anymore? Why do I just feel like I'm in this purgatory?"

Her mother waited a long minute, maybe to see if the questions were hypothetical. Eventually she said, "The absence of hurt doesn't always feel like relief. Draw your hand from an ice bucket and your skin smarts, then adjusts, and you forget how the ache felt. It's natural, after you feel something so strongly, to worry that neutrality is a symptom, but most of the time, existing should feel like nothing, in the way that breathing feels like nothing."

Her mother's voice was low and frank and lovely, and Laila wondered why it had ever made her want to hide.

"And no, sweetie," her mother said. "Humanness is not unhappiness. Don't worry. The world isn't nearly as dramatic as that."

Laila looked over her desk, still mostly clean from when Felix had reorganized it for her. A photo of Malak in a jeweled frame brushed her laptop, and beside that, a rainbow of folders and a jar of candied pecans wrapped in gingham ribbon. Her mother's nail tugged at the wired edge of the ribbon. Outside the window, the sky was such an elegant blue that wisps of cirrus cloud looked like iridescence. She heard an imagined voice saying, *We know what all this means to you.*

23

LAILA AND HER PARENTS WENT INTO MANHATTAN SO she could meet with a psychiatrist. While they were waiting for the train, Laila tugged at the edges of her shorts and sat on the lip of the bench, positioning herself so that none of her skin touched the wood. Hannah used to joke that the wood had rabies, or possibly scabies, which she would turn into a limerick with the other rhyme being babies, an inevitable disaster. Her father was standing farther down the platform, drinking up the afternoon light, holding out his corded arms to admire the way the sun glanced off his wrists.

Laila looked down at her crossed legs. She remembered Hannah sitting at the end of this bench as they waited for a train. In sophomore year, they'd passed one particular ten-word-story note by leaving it in a deep crevice in this blocky wooden bench at the Gates Ave. stop, the dark gash that began next to Laila's thigh. They'd used tweezers to plant and extract that one, because God knew what lived in that deep hole besides their fake spy messages. Laila wished she had kept a copy.

For a moment, looking at that crevice, she wondered.

Laila's tongue seemed to have grown a size too large for her mouth, making it difficult to swallow. Quickly, so she wouldn't think too much, she pulled a Pilot pen from her purse, clicked its nib out, and jabbed the end into the bench. It punctured something. Laila carefully drew the pen back until a corner of paper crept into the light.

As she spread the note across her knees, she recognized the tea stain in the upper-left-hand corner, and her heart began to flutter. She recognized her own handwriting, but rounder, younger. And Hannah's, but looser, freer. Laila hadn't made a copy, but Hannah had kept the original.

Once there was a girl who lived at the edge
of a cliff in France also she was a robot
Who had been discriminated against by France's strict antirobot
laws
So she lived in her cliff house in complete isolation
Waiting for the day another robot would come along and
tell her, "We must overthrow France's government—get your musket"
One day there came the fated robot who was a
giant, eight feet tall. And she could shoot lasers out
of her fingertips. The first robot emerged from her cliff
house and said, "Hello, my friend. Is it time, then?"
So they began to walk toward Paris holding their muskets
And hoping not to short-circuit out in the rain before
they arrived side by side at the silver electric gates

Below was a single line of crisp new writing.

Let's short-circuit in the rain. I loved you then, too.

"What is that?" said Laila's mother, looking over her shoulder.

Laila folded the note quickly. "Hannah."

Her mother was quiet, waiting. Laila knew then that her mother already knew.

Laila let the paper flower in her hands, tugged by the wind. "Me and Hannah."

Her mother settled onto the bench beside her. "We wondered." She laid an arm around Laila's shoulders and gave her a small, bracing squeeze. "We love you."

"I'm sorry I didn't . . ."

"You have nothing to be sorry for, sweetheart."

"I just felt like I couldn't say it."

"Why not?"

"Because it doesn't feel like anybody's business. Hardly even feels like *my* business."

Her mother let a flicker of confusion show. Laila looked away. Hannah had understood that night on the bench, without Laila needing to tell her, that when Laila felt something—really *felt*—it became too huge and too personal for description. Of course Hannah had known. Hannah knew everything, knew Laila's favorite shape of snowflake, and her preference for centered camera angles, and her love for the left eyebrow of *The Rest*'s Jason Kendo, and her affinity for swirl soft-serve out of those clunking ice cream trucks that sat screaming "Do Your Ears Hang Low?" on her block in July, and she even had a couple of spare jumbo-size tampons buried in her backpack in case Laila needed them, for God's sake. She knew everything in the same way Laila knew that Hannah's biggest shames weren't her parents' victim complexes or her older sister's compulsive spending, but the tiny vanities Hannah let herself nurse every so often: making sure that the right side of eyeliner, which she drew on second, didn't come out jagged. Laila knew why

Hannah tracked marriages of people she hated, the tabloid darlings, when she stood in lines to buy waxed mint floss and toilet paper ("Isn't it kind of refreshing to see people lying about each other's lives out in the open?"). Laila knew the gushing liquid synth that poured from the headphones Hannah pushed deep into her ear canals— careful, Laila's mother had told her once, you'll lose your hearing by the time you're fifty, but what the hell did Hannah care about fifty? Laila knew what Hannah expected for herself beyond the threshold of adulthood. Laila looked forward to age and knowledge like a sort of preemptive nostalgia, her future dyed sepia, but Hannah looked ahead at middle age like a curse waiting to be cast, sure she would be crisp and dry and flavorless and unsurprising at fifty, packed too full of prior experience and preexisting memory, and if it ever became more interesting for Hannah to dissect what she'd already lived than for her to look down the eye of the telescope into the next hour, she would just drop dead then and there. Laila knew so much about Hannah that she wondered whether, like the number of microbial cells in the human body can outnumber human cells, her knowledge of Hannah could be compared to her knowledge of herself at a two-to-one ratio. She knew so much that maybe the knowledge of Hannah's fingertips over her waist had been too much. Maybe that had been the final tipping point, the heat of Hannah's tongue at the sensitive juncture of her neck and jawline, her own body pushing back, saying, *No, I can't let any more of this in or I'll lose myself in her.*

Laila's mother didn't push her to speak. She couldn't have if she'd tried. Laila just looked blankly at the train tracks as she realized she was in love with Hannah. So in love she could have recognized the back curve of her jaw in a Times Square crowd. So in love she'd had to stamp it down a mile to call it anything else, that diminishing term, "complicated." Right now this was so simple as to be insulting. The tracks rattled with the approaching train. Here came the rush of wind, and the bone-deep scream of motion.

24

HANNAH'S FATHER ANSWERED THE DOOR THAT EVE-
ning with a frown. "Oh," he said, sounding disgusted. Laila had
forgotten how effortlessly rude and self-centered Hannah's family
was. And so efficient in displaying it. The type of people who made
a waiter's life hell for forty minutes and then tipped 6 percent.

Mr. Park smoothed the sides of his hair as he offered his sharp
profile into the house. "Hannah," he yelled. "Did you invite somebody over? I told you the Lewises were visiting for drinks." Back
to Laila: "We have guests due in an hour." He strode away and up
the stairs, leaving the door hanging open.

Hannah's footsteps echoed down the hall. Laila considered
backing down the steps. She squeezed her hands into fists and
looked up at the brass numbers above Hannah's door.

Then Hannah was eighteen inches away, and it became impossible to look at anything else. Laila always forgot how good
summer looked when Hannah wore it. Black skirt, white tank top,
suede sandals, a pristine light tan. Laila had spent so long examining herself in the mirror before leaving, going so far as to smooth
mascara over her eyelashes, to pluck a few stray threads from
her thick eyebrows. Had that mattered? Hannah knew how she
looked. Hannah had never expected anything from her, had never

pushed her, never tried to insinuate anything. "Let's short-circuit in the rain. I loved you then, too." Had everyone seen it except her? Had Felix always seemed so close to Hannah, despite their fights, because she'd told him she loved Laila and sworn him to secrecy?

"Your hair," Laila said. The red dye had been stripped out of Hannah's hair, replaced with a glossy black that didn't quite match her hair's natural luster.

"Yeah," Hannah said, "they said they'd had enough of looking at it." Which Laila thought was obviously melodrama, as Hannah's parents saw her for—optimistically—ninety minutes a day.

"I got the note," Laila said quietly.

"I figured." For once, Hannah's unflappable act wasn't working. She didn't seem to know what to do with her hands—which grasped her elbows—or her eyes—which fixed over Laila's shoulder. "Come in."

They slipped into Hannah's bedroom on the second floor. Hannah dropped onto her sofa. Laila settled onto the other end, a safe buffer of three feet between them.

"So," Laila said.

"Yeah."

Laila swallowed, looking at the five-foot scroll of Hannah's mirror, where her own terrified face looked back. She shouldn't have been the scared one. She wasn't the one with her soul laid bare on an 8.5 x 11 sheet of paper.

"You still writing?" Hannah asked.

"Not for now."

She could tell Hannah had to battle not to say, *Thank God.*

"Listen," Laila said. "About our fight thing."

"Yeah, I'm—"

"No, listen," Laila said. "I'm sorry. And thanks for being worried about me. You were right to be worried."

"Got it. Are you, you know. Okay?"

"I'm better than I was at graduation. Like, I'm here instead of lying in bed not having showered for four days, so there's that."

"That seems better."

"I'm trying therapy for real," Laila added. "And I've got this Lexapro prescription, so I guess we'll see if that helps."

For a second Laila wondered if Hannah would laugh, curl her lip at the idea of therapy. Sometimes the bits of Hannah's parents that seeped out from her edges could still surprise.

But Hannah just nodded.

Laila ran her hand over the smooth velveteen cushion, remembering the last time she'd been in this house, downstairs, all four of them tangled up in one another.

"I got lost in the Catskills," Laila said. "On my way back down."

"Dude, what?"

"Yeah, I almost got killed by a bear."

"A *bear*?" Hannah raised her eyebrows. "And you did not even bring the pelt as tribute, puny mortal?"

Laila loosed an exasperated sigh. "As I *clearly stated* in the Prophecy of Old, I shall only relinquish the pelt to you for the antlers of the Immortal Stag."

Hannah smiled, and she couldn't seem to stop smiling. The chandelier was dim overhead. Hannah looked built out of gold. Laila's throat was tight.

"God, we're weird," Hannah said. "I miss being weird. You know how normal my family is? It's so incredibly boring."

"I don't know if 'normal' is the word I'd use."

"You know what I mean."

"Yeah. I do."

Hannah was fiddling with the grimy pewter rings on her pinky fingers now. Although Hannah's face was downturned, Laila saw her swallow and close her eyes hard for a moment before looking back up.

"Hey," Laila said.

Hannah nodded.

"You know I love you, too," Laila said.

She was quiet a second. Laila imagined a million words coming from Hannah's lips. Words in configurations that would feel familiar, as they always did, but surprise her with every turn, take her aback with their shine. As they always did. Something clever or confessional. But when Hannah opened her mouth, all she said was, hoarsely, "Come here."

Laila didn't know how she arrived at Hannah's side so quickly, some trick of magnetism, some gap in space-time that blinked them together, but suddenly her fingers were touching Hannah's cheek, and Hannah's fingers were touching hers. A summer formed between them, instant sun-bright heat. Laila's heart felt twisted, overrun by brambles or strapped together by elastic, full of discomfort. Erratic beats tapped in her neck, in her stomach, in the tips of her ears. Hannah's eyes were dark as oak, her eyebrows straight wisps, like feathers. Soft to the touch when Laila brushed one.

"Where are we?" Laila asked.

"We'll figure it out," Hannah said as she leaned in. The last hint of a word brushed Laila's mouth before Hannah's lips met hers.

They'd been slow and questioning on the bench. A drifting kiss, an exploration, that felt like a mirage in retrospect, something unreal. This was different. Laila felt the timeline wrapped around them, pulling them in opposite directions, and if they didn't hold on tightly enough they would be torn apart. She curled her hand into Hannah's hair and tightened her grip until a groan echoed low in Hannah's throat, buzzing through her lips against Laila's mouth. She wouldn't let go. Hannah's tongue pressed against hers, still an unfamiliar sensation, but one Hannah was so clearly used to, a neat swipe of slippery texture along Laila's tongue. Laila pushed forward until Hannah reclined onto her back, shoulders pressing against the velvet, until her hair formed a splatter of black paint around her head, and the light gleamed like oil against her irises.

Laila's forearms sank deep into the sofa, and her chin knocked into Hannah's cheekbone. "Oops," she muttered, and Hannah grinned, pulled her back in and drew lines up and down her spine with one nail. They kissed until Laila's mouth itched, almost sore from the roughness of Hannah's bitten lips, and strands of Laila's hair were coming loose, corkscrewing down into her vision. As she broke back to smooth them into place, Hannah sat up and drew her tank top over her head. Laila stared, considered going still, considered panic. Hannah was wearing a gray slip of a bra, and Laila had seen her in swimsuits before, every summer, but she'd never looked this way, shadowy and close.

Laila wanted nothing more than to look, but then Hannah's mouth was on her neck, and she let her head fall back against the cushion, let Hannah lift her shirt over her head and squeeze her breasts, pass her thumbs experimentally into her bra cups and across her nipples. Laila went rigid, feeling like she might burst, like she might just tear apart at the seams. Her palms on Hannah's naked back, she felt too much. She needed too much, one hand grasping Hannah's knee and pressing up against the smoothness of her thigh, under her skirt. Hannah's motions slowed for a moment, but then she moved forward into Laila's hand, reached down to take Laila's wrist and urge her hand between her legs until her fingers met rough lace, heat, damp. Laila drew two fingers up, pressing hard into the softness there, and Hannah drew two sharp breaths. Suddenly they were still. Just for an instant, eyes locked, Laila wondering how this could be real, feeling—terrified—like she might wake up. "You have no idea," Hannah said, "how bad I've wanted this."

"Yeah, I do," Laila said, and leaned forward, and said against Hannah's lips, "I know." Hannah's arm slipped around her waist, and they pressed so tightly there was nothing between them, no dividing line, no thought or event or future that could exist in any potential universe. Only this, only here.

25

"MY DAD'S DIVORCING MY STEPMOM," FELIX TOLD them as they hiked up Cooper's Hawk.

"Wow," Leo said. "That's big."

"He's building a great track record," Hannah said.

Felix didn't reply, and Laila wondered if that had been too much for Hannah to say. There was a particular grade of insult that Felix enjoyed toward his dad, but at a point, that hatred belonged exclusively to him.

"I think this is around where I got lost," Laila said, spinning one of the yellow trail markers against the bark. "We're not leaving the trail, though, forget that. I'm not getting lost again."

"What happened to Adventurous Laila?" Felix said.

"She split off from me like a starfish arm and now leads her own life down in Ecuador."

"Nice," Felix said.

"Let's go up to the lookout point instead," Hannah called, already darting ahead.

All four of their T-shirts were soaked through with sweat by the time they reached the cliffside. White light slicked across their foreheads. Laila knew something was different, but didn't pinpoint the absence of the thundering sound of thousands of gallons of water until they emerged from the trees. The waterfall had been choked by drought. A finger of water reached from the source and fractured the instant it left the mountain. Darts of refracted light shot out as the thin spray disappeared soundlessly.

Laila knelt in the spot she'd slept before. "Looks nicer when I'm not delirious," she said, flicking a bug off her thigh. The Catskills rolled away from their perch, a mass of green felt humped smoothly over hidden objects.

"Yep, this is what I needed," Felix said, spreading himself out on his back. Leo and Laila lay back, too, and examined the clouds splayed around the sun, whose fringes occasionally cast flickers of shadow.

"It's so quiet," Laila said, as Hannah's fingers wound into hers.

"I know," Leo said. "I can hear you guys breathing."

"Stop listening to me breathing, weirdo," Hannah said, and Leo laughed.

After a moment, Laila said, "Guys?"

"Yeah?" Leo said.

"We'll keep in touch next year, right?"

"Yeah," Felix said.

"Of course we will," Leo said.

They didn't hesitate, and sounded honest, but somehow Laila knew that they were just as uncertain as she was. She couldn't make herself say more about it. They were quiet a while.

"You know," Leo said, "if we just lie here until the sun sets, we'll see an extra star."

"What?" Laila said.

"A little over a thousand years ago there was this explosion," he said dreamily. "Ages away, two stars collided and exploded, I mean, so far away that the light is just now reaching the earth, even at lightspeed. From last week through the next few months, there's going to be an extra star in the middle of Sagittarius. What you're seeing is two suns crashing into each other a thousand years ago."

Laila's eyes were beginning to water. She shielded them from the sun, but that didn't help. She thought of those bolts of light ricocheting through the universe, ripping through the dark, sending echoes to the farthest corners of space. The hugeness of the idea overwhelmed her, and she felt as if she were sitting in the far reaches of the atmosphere, observing the smallness of the four of them against the face of the mountain. She wondered if she would remember this day after college, this and the taste of Hannah's lip balm and the sound of her breath catching, this and Felix's mom's tiny apartment packed to the walls with people she'd never gotten to know, this and Leo leaping onto Hannah back-first, this and the day they'd all first met, Hannah having pulled them together in the nonchalant way she'd always changed Laila's life. Would she remember this when she was Mr. Madison's age? Her mom's age? When she was about to die, would she keep hold of this mountainside? She imagined the nightfall, and imagined that star, burning through time to meet her eyes. *It's a miracle*, Laila thought. A miracle that in the year 1006 this collision happened, and the light created in the aftermath is still pouring our way. A miracle that anything temporary could reach so far.

NAZARENKO ANNOUNCES NEW BOOK FOR FALL 2019 RELEASE
by Eliot Sandberg,
senior correspondent

for *Letters*

Representatives for Pulitzer Prize-winning author Nadiya Nazarenko (*Catalina's Mothers*, 2003; *A Flight of Roses*, 2017; et al.) have announced a fall release next year of her latest novel, to be titled *May I*. The publisher has described *May I* as "an audacious, kaleidoscopic romp spanning continents, generations, and realities."

This story will be updated as details emerge.

26

THE SCHOOL DURING SUMMER WAS A BIZARRE, free-feeling place, empty of social pressures or noise or signs of life. Two weeks after graduation, the teachers had nearly completed the great end-of-year purge. The walls were bare, the cubbies empty, the lockers agleam with antiseptic. Just teachers cleaning out their hobbit holes, all disproportionately pleased-looking not to be saddled with students.

"Piedra," said Nazarenko, as Laila pushed the door open. She was still writing in that notebook of hers.

"Hi," Laila said.

Nazarenko beckoned. "Yes?"

Laila walked up to the front of the room. The desks had been cleared away, leaving a linoleum plain. "The new book. I saw the announcement."

"Yes. A project I've been tinkering with since I finished *A Flight of Roses*. It's about young people in New York City. Your age."

"That's why you took this job?"

"That's why I took the job, yes."

"Were we useful?" Laila asked.

"Yes," said Nazarenko.

"Am I in there?"

"In traces, but most things are." Nazarenko closed her book.

Laila was quiet for a moment but didn't feel the need to speak. She remembered how Mr. Madison would wait for her, and for a moment, she saw a flash of him in the woman on the stool.

"You're still working on your story, I assume," Nazarenko said.

"Yeah, in a way."

"I'd be open to reading its next iteration, if you're interested."

Laila hesitated. She nearly frowned. There were no telltale symptoms of excitement, no leap of the heart, no instinct to blurt out immediate agreement. What had she come for, if not that?

After a moment, a question came loose, one she hadn't realized she'd wanted to ask:

"Did you ever meet Mr. Madison?"

"No," Nazarenko said. "You two were close, I assume."

"Yeah. He loved your books, you know."

Nazarenko idly brushed something off the cover of her notebook. For a moment, Laila thought she had no answer, that Nazarenko considered his enjoyment too beneath her even to merit a response. But when Nazarenko spoke, she sounded different: thoughtful, tired, almost gentle.

"That opinion never gets less surprising to me," she said. "But he was kind to say so."

"No," said Laila. "Not kind. Honest."

Nazarenko considered her. She seemed skeptical but didn't answer.

A smile found Laila's lips as she backed away.

"Thank you for everything," she said, turning, gaining momentum. Ahead, through the door, was a rectangle of sky, an undecided color that she could call gray or blue or heather. She fixed her eyes to that patch and imagined an unidentified object—oblong, maybe, with a silver bracing mechanism wrapped around its middle—that shone as it descended into that crevice of dusk, bringing first contact. Maybe, against all odds, the others would say, *Take me to your leader.* Maybe a multitude of voices had repeated the words this many times because they had something true in them. Or maybe the creatures aboard that ship would be silent, or all-knowing, or malevolent. Maybe they'd be a cloud of microscopic life too complex to understand even if a thousand people each spent a thousand years writing a thousand stories about them.

Maybe the ship would never arrive. Maybe Earth was alone in its buzz, in its blue-green bloom of oxygen and exhalation and time measured out burst by burst, and there was no galaxy on the opposite side of the universe where anybody dreamed in the same looping, illogical, impossible way that human beings could. No Darsinnians with dreams of love, no Watchers with secret dreams of power and redemption. No Resters who dreamed of sherbet-orange sky. She had seen these things so vividly, though, that she wondered if it mattered whether they could ever, in any conceivable universe, be true.

"Piedra," Nazarenko called, but her voice was as distant as the murmur of a jet plane at a stratospheric height. When Laila arrived home, she would rewrite the section with Eden crashing her ship into the enemy station. She could never see that clearly, anyway, the way her heroine would look on impact, and if she couldn't explain to Camille why it had to happen, it didn't have to happen. There would be some way for Eden to bounce back under the ricocheting sounds of laser fire, to return home and kiss her friends on their beautiful weird foreheads, greet them in their own language.

"Laila."

She crossed the threshold and strode down the hall. She felt happiness in concentrate, a dwarf star roaring at her center. Part of her wondered if Nazarenko would chase her; mostly she knew there was no chance. She walked until the voice faded and all she heard was the sound of her own footsteps, deliberate. New silver shoes squeaking against new wax, lit up white as starlight.

The End

Acknowledgments

MOST PEOPLE HAVE HEARD THE FAMOUS PROVERB: IT takes a village to prevent a writer from spiraling into paralyzing self-doubt, and even then, sometimes the village privately thinks to itself, *Jesus Christ, she's a lost cause.*

So I'd like to thank every person who, astoundingly, didn't voice the latter sentiment. For their friendship and humor, I'm so indebted to Noelle Wells, Li An, Nate Winer, Ben Jacoby, Liam Horsman, Nick Foster, Kate Markey, Amy Young, Sophia Babai, Lauren Michael, Lauren Melville, Bailey Luke, and especially Eamon Levesque: Thank you for—either advertently or inadvertently—helping me get through this one.

I'm so fortunate to have on my team Caryn Wiseman, dream literary agent, whose insight and advocacy can't be over-praised, and my editor at Abrams, Anne Heltzel, who shed her clarifying light through the formless chasms of this book's truly demoralizing first draft. As a rigorous agnostic, I thank the likely concept of God for both of y'all every day.

To Siofra, thank you for always giving me somebody to admire.

To my parents, thank you for absolutely everything else.